THE WIZARD'S TOUCH

Memory Guild Book 5

WARD PARKER

Mad Mangrove Media

CONTENTS

AUTHOR'S NOTE

The city of San Marcos, the setting of this tale, was inspired by St. Augustine, Florida, a truly unique and magical place. However, I wanted lots of *supernatural* magic! And monsters, too! So I created the alternate world of San Marcos. While some details and historical references may seem familiar, San Marcos is entirely fictional, as are all the characters, names, and places described herein.

CHAPTER 1

POOR MRS. OGGLETHWARP

J ust outside of the stone ruins that mark the original city
gate of San Marcos, Florida, stands a giant Southern live
oak tree. The tree is approximately sixty feet tall, with long,
meandering limbs that extend as far as a hundred feet from its
trunk. Wispy beards of gray Spanish moss hang from it like
tinsel on a Christmas tree. I read somewhere the tree was over
300 years old. Growing at the edge of a small park, it's beloved
by locals and used as a backdrop for photos by tourists. It even
has a name, Old Courage.

It was at the base of Old Courage that Mabel Ogglethwarp,
of Cassadaga, Florida, became my latest guest to die. I was
beginning to show a disturbing pattern of guests checking out
from earthly existence before checking out of my inn.

Mrs. Ogglethwarp was staying at my bed-and-breakfast, The
Esperanza Inn, as a spirit tourist (yes, that is a thing). San
Marcos has plenty of hauntings, as any centuries-old town
would, and she was here partly to attend ghost tours and

research some of the famed haunted houses. My inn, of course, was one of them.

She was staying in Room 303, haunted by a Victorian-era bride who was pushed from the window by her jealous spouse. Mrs. Ogglethwarp had hoped to commune with the ghost. I don't know if she had made any progress by the time her stay was unexpectedly cut short.

Mrs. Ogglethwarp was not a mere ghost tourist. She was a spiritualist, as were many residents of Cassadaga, a town born as a nineteenth-century spiritualist camp. The main objective of her visit to San Marcos was to communicate with the spirit of her Great-Aunt Bessie. But Bessie did not haunt my inn or any other structure in town. No, Bessie resided in a tree. Namely, Old Courage.

Pagans aren't the only folks who believe trees have spirits, apparently. Mrs. Ogglethwarp believed her great-aunt was in the giant live oak along with the tree's own spirit, whatever his or her name was.

Mrs. Ogglethwarp invited me to accompany her on her visit tonight to Old Courage. And I accepted, because I wanted to see how one communicated with a spirit in a tree. Not that I needed to learn how to do it. Summer, a fellow member of the Memory Guild, was a wood-speaker and could chat with a tree as easily as with a cashier at a grocery store.

To be honest, I was curious if Mrs. Ogglethwarp was a kook or if she truly had a gift.

"Oh, no, you wouldn't be intruding at all," she told me as I refilled her coffee at breakfast that morning. "Your energy will probably help me break through the veil to the other side."

I didn't need to ask her what she meant. Ever since I discovered my paranormal abilities, I'd gotten a taste of the other side. I preferred to stay on this side, to be honest.

"So, do you want to ask your Great-Aunt Bessie something specific, or just say hi?"

"Oh, I want to say hello, of course, but I'm also curious why she is living in the tree."

"Yeah, of all the places to haunt, why would you want to be in there, hammered by woodpeckers and having squirrels run around your bedroom? How did you know she's in this tree, of all places?"

"Someone told me," she said, draining the last of her coffee and dabbing her mouth with a napkin. She smelled strongly of patchouli. "A fellow spiritualist and friend. Jonathon was communicating with the tree, when Bessie introduced herself and asked him to tell me she said hi."

"How did Bessie know Jonathon knew you?"

"She's a spirit. She knows everything."

"Ah, I see. Can she tell you winning lottery numbers in advance?"

Mrs. Ogglethwarp frowned. "They don't concern themselves with trivial human matters."

"Of course not."

"Now, do you still want to go along with me tonight?" she asked.

"Sure. It should be enlightening."

"I'm having dinner with an associate in town first. I'll meet you at the tree at eight-thirty."

"Sounds good," I said. Actually, it sounded like it would be amusing, which was the only reason I would give up my preferred option of staying at home with a good book.

COMMUNICATING WITH A SPIRIT RESIDING IN OLD COURAGE was about as far from spooky as you could get. The tree's canopy was illuminated by lights mounted in the ground around it. Plus, the little park where it grew was in the main tourist zone of the city, so there was activity nearby. In fact, with cars passing along an adjacent street, it was hard to concentrate. But I didn't need to, since I wasn't a medium, as Mrs. Ogglethwarp claimed to be.

We sat in folding chairs she had brought along, the kind you'd bring to an outdoor concert. But instead of listening to an Eagles tribute band, I was listening to an old woman chanting while we held hands and stared at a tree.

"Aunt Bessie, can you hear me?" Mrs. Ogglethwarp asked in a voice loud enough that a passing couple glanced our way.

Bessie didn't respond. At least, not to me.

"I think she's stirring," Mrs. Ogglethwarp whispered.

"I come with love, Aunt Bessie," she intoned. "Please speak to me and tell me what it's like on the other side."

Silence. Except for the sputter of a motorcycle in the distance.

This went on for a while, with begging and pleading for Bessie to acknowledge us. I was losing interest. I had a craving to check my social media, but it would be rude to pull my phone out at this moment.

Mrs. Ogglethwarp was losing patience, too.

"Aunt Bessie, I implore you. Show me a sign."

Nothing.

"Do you think she's put off because I'm here?" I asked.

She shushed me. "Bessie, show me something, anything, to let me know you hear me."

Finally, Bessie showed a sign. It was a bit over the top.

A deafening cracking sound came from the tree. Both of us gasped.

4

"I think—"

Those were the last words Mrs. Ogglethwarp ever uttered.

Because a giant limb of the tree broke off and landed squarely on top of her.

Somehow, I was spared, with only a few cuts from a smaller branch that raked my neck and arm. Mrs. Ogglethwarp, though, was given a one-way express ticket to the other side.

SOMEONE WAS SCREAMING. IT TOOK A MOMENT TO REALIZE IT was me.

I tried in vain to lift the massive oak limb off Mrs. Ogglethwarp, and now I was on my knees looking for a path in between the branches to help her breathe or whatever I could do. People were already gathering around, and several had called 911. Fire-Rescue really needed to get here *now*.

I snaked a hand through the dense smaller branches and reached Mrs. Ogglethwarp's neck. There was no pulse. Moving my fingers to different parts of her neck, I kept hoping I'd feel a sign of life, but no such luck.

Two brawny men attempted to lift the oak limb. I helped them. A young woman joined in and then her friend. Finally, the limb rose a couple of feet.

"Be careful," I said.

"Move it to the left," the larger man said.

His slightly smaller friend, who was facing him, asked, "My left or yours?"

"Mine."

"No, move it the other way," the young woman said. "Or else that branch there will hit her head."

"Make up your minds, guys," her friend said. "This is too heavy."

"Come on, heave ho!" the larger man ordered.

"Wait, you said to heave to *your* left, not *my* left."

"My hands are slipping!"

"Careful!" I shouted.

CRUNCH!

The limb fell for a second time on poor Mrs. Ogglethwarp. For her sake, maybe it was best I hadn't felt a pulse.

A fire engine and an ambulance pulled up, followed by a police car. Amateur hour was over.

I overheard a paramedic say the victim was deceased, and I stepped aside while they used a hydraulic jack to lift the limb and carefully slide Mrs. Ogglethwarp from under it.

A Latina police officer took notes as I recounted what had happened.

"I'm sorry for the loss of your friend," she said.

"Actually, I don't know her very well. She's a guest at my inn. But she seemed like a very nice lady."

"You own an inn? Which one?"

"The Esperanza Inn."

"Ah," the cop said. "That's the one where all the guests end up dying."

"No," I said angrily. "Not *all* the guests. We've had a bit of bad luck lately. This city is filled with tourists and other visitors. It stands to reason that some visitors will die, and they will be guests in hotels and inns."

"I responded to two incidents at your inn before. Both involved victims dead at the scene."

"A married couple. That was a fluke."

"And there was that developer who was murdered. He was a guest, murdered by another guest."

6

"But not murdered *at* my inn."

"And another guest before that disappeared without a trace."

"Am I on trial here?" I demanded.

"I'm just saying."

"Is there any way at all that my inn could be responsible for the bough breaking on a three-hundred-year-old tree?"

"I didn't say you murdered this victim."

"No one murdered her. Except, maybe, Old Courage."

The officer shook her head. As she walked away, she muttered, "They say she's batty."

I wear my battiness as a badge of honor. But I was hoping for some sympathy. I was nearly killed by the same bough that crushed Mrs. Ogglethwarp. And now, I have to deal with the aftermath. Unfortunately, I've gained a fair amount of experience with handling bookings cut short by unexpected circumstances.

Specifically, death.

I milled about at the scene, unsure what to do. I wasn't Mrs. Ogglethwarp's family, but I was the closest thing at the moment. As an innkeeper, I had her home address, but not her next of kin. The police would find out who that was and inform them. Trust me, I know from experience.

Now that my adrenaline was fading after my close brush with death, as was the anger at the police officer, sadness crept in.

Mabel Ogglethwarp seemed like a nice enough lady. A small amount of imperiousness, perhaps. A heck of a lot of kookiness. I felt horrible she had to die this way. At least it seemed like she didn't suffer. She showed no sign she was conscious after the limb landed on her. And definitely no signs when it fell on her the second time. It was a blessedly quick way to depart, compared to suffering from a horrible illness.

Still, it didn't make me feel any better. Tomorrow, I would ask Bella to pack Mrs. Ogglethwarp's belongings, so I could ship them to her home address or wherever I was instructed to by the next of kin.

THE NEXT MORNING, I PREPARED AND SERVED BREAKFAST FOR my meager guest contingent of seven (things were always slow midweek, especially given my lack of marketing ability). The chimes rang at the main entrance, and Detective Michael Samson strolled in. He looked ruggedly handsome as always, although today he sported a blue blazer and a tie.

"You dressed up just to see me?" I joked.

He smiled. "A meeting this morning at City Hall, briefing the deputy mayor."

Our previous mayor no longer existed. I won't say she was killed, since she was already dead, being a vampire, as I found out. She was staked by my vampire friend, Diego, but that's another story for another time.

"And to what do I owe the honor of your presence?" I asked.

"Your deceased guest, Mabel Ogglethwarp."

"I thought you were a homicide detective."

"I am. There is reason to believe someone assisted her in becoming deceased."

"What are you talking about? Are you going to charge the oak tree?"

"We have surveillance footage of that park. On a prior evening, someone was doing something to the tree. It's difficult to make out just what he was doing, but the city's arborist believes the subject cut a notch, a V-cut, beneath the limb where it joined the trunk. This would have weakened the limb enough to allow it to break under its own weight. Whoever did this could be liable for the victim's death."

"I'm impressed," I said. "Very clever to check the surveillance footage."

"I can't take credit for the idea. There's more to the story. The arborist was checking out the tree this morning."

"I know. You said that."

"He was evaluating the health of the tree before he pruned around the wound."

"I never heard it described as a wound."

"It's what the arborist said. Anyway, he discovered a recess within the trunk. It might have been a hollow in the tree when it was younger, and as the tree grew, the trunk swallowed up the hollow."

"And?" I was impatient. I had a lot of work to do.

"I'm getting there. Inside the hollow, he found a colossal gem that could be worth hundreds of thousands, or even millions, of dollars. He said it was a giant pearl."

"Wow. Do you think the pearl has anything to do with Mrs. Ogglethwarp?"

"No. It was probably just a coincidence that it was revealed by the fallen bough. Although, I would like to find out if the person who was filmed messing with the tree was looking for the gem. Or sabotaging the tree so the bough would fall."

"Why would someone want the bough to fall? Was it just vandalism, or did they want it to land on someone?"

"I think they wanted it to land on someone. Someone, as in a random tourist walking by. Or, Mabel Ogglethwarp, in particular."

"I don't understand. How could this person be sure it would land on her?"

"I don't know. Maybe a small explosive charge triggered the break. Did you hear anything like that?"

"There was a loud noise when the bough broke," I said. "Not

9

really a bang or boom. More like a *crack*. Maybe magic caused the break."

"I hope not. I can't tell a prosecutor magic caused this."

Samson pursed his lips and furrowed his brow as he concentrated. The furrow kind of looked good on him. He should furrow his brow more often.

I realized I wouldn't be able to clean up breakfast just yet.

"Have a seat, Mike. Want some coffee?"

He nodded. I served him a cup from the urn.

"Why did the victim come to San Marcos?" he asked.

"She was a spirit tourist."

I explained her tour of the haunted places and her desire to communicate with her great-aunt who allegedly lived in the tree. Maybe her great-aunt caused her death. I never asked if they had gotten along.

When I told him Mrs. Ogglethwarp came from Cassadaga, Samson nodded, as if that explained everything. The town's reputation was well known.

"Do you know if she met with anyone while she was in town?" he asked.

"She had dinner with someone just before she was killed. She didn't say with whom, or where."

Samson wrote something on his notepad.

"She mentioned a spiritualist named Jonathon told her that Great-Aunt Bessie was inhabiting the tree," I said. "I don't know if that's whom she had dinner with."

"Did anyone else, besides you and possibly Jonathon, know she was visiting the tree last night?"

"Maybe the person she had dinner with. But who knows who else she told?"

The implication that Mrs. Ogglethwarp's death was intentional, rather than accidental, was difficult to get my head around.

"Are you telling me that someone knew she was going to visit the tree and sabotaged the limb so that it would fall on her?" I asked.

"If this someone could visually confirm she was there and was sitting in the right location. The thing about that piece of land and where the tree stands, there's only one side where you can comfortably view the tree up close. So, once her perp saw her sitting there, he set off the detonation, or whatever, to trigger the limb breaking."

"That seems rather far-fetched."

Samson shrugged. "A lot of murders seem far-fetched at first. Humans have devious minds, though."

"Are things slow at work, and you're trying really hard to find a murder to investigate?" I asked with a grin so he wouldn't take my comment as mockery.

"It's my job to make sure no one gets away with murder just because the murder seems unlikely."

"True."

"Also, to be perfectly honest, the City of San Marcos is legally liable for her death, since the tree is on public property. So, if there's even the slightest chance that this was intentional, I need to look into it."

"Ah, I see. It's the attorneys who are trying to keep busy."

Shortly, another possibility crept into my mind. A horrifying one.

"What if the target was actually me?" I asked. "I was sitting next to her. The limb was huge, and the branches spread wide. I'm very lucky I only got some scratches. How can you be sure this plan was so precise that it would take out her and not me? Or that I wasn't the target, and she got squashed by accident?"

"The thought did cross my mind," he said, with pain in his eyes. I appreciated seeing that pain. "Either one of you could have been the intended target, and he probably didn't care if the other was killed as well. Since she's the one who was killed, I'm beginning by investigating her. Is there any reason I should believe you were the intended target?"

"Um, I don't think so. I hope not. And I don't believe anyone knew I was going to be there with Mrs. Ogglethwarp except for her."

"Have you received any threats?"

"Nope."

"Any resentful guests or employees?"

"Not that I know of."

"Well, keep your ears open, and let me know if something concerns you. Meanwhile, I'm going to proceed as I intended. Forensics is examining the tree to confirm that it was tampered with to the point of limb failure. And I'd like access to the victim's room to look for an appointment book."

"Follow me," I said. Summer, the Memory Guild's wood-speaker, could also find evidence from the tree, but I'd let Samson handle it his way. At least until he hits a dead end.

We rode the antique elevator to the third floor. It is tiny and intimate in the metal cage, and you could cut the sexual tension with a tree saw, even now, after our talk about being just friends. The elevator is also slow, dangerously slow.

The door finally opened, and I jumped out, my marriage vows still intact. I led Samson to 303 and unlocked the door with the old-fashioned key.

The room was dark with the curtains and blinds closed. The cloying smell of patchouli hung in the air. I remembered suffering through that scent while I sat beside Mrs. Ogglethwarp in front of the tree.

The ghost wasn't around. I would have sensed her if she was.

Pulling open the curtains and opening the blinds, I looked around the room. Bella hadn't come in yet to pack the belongings which cluttered the room.

"I assume you already checked her handbag and phone for calendars?" I asked.

"We did. Her phone was unlocked, and there was nothing on its calendar for last night. She didn't have a paper calendar, so I'm looking for one here."

We quickly scanned the items atop the desk and dresser. There wasn't one. Nothing in the bathroom, either. I didn't see any sticky notes.

"I guess she kept the appointment in her mind only," I said.

"And that's where you come in."

He meant my psychometry. It was up to me to look for memories she left on her belongings.

"Okay," I said. "If you don't mind stepping out so I can have some privacy in order to concentrate. Or does that violate the rules?"

"It's not a crime scene, and I've already visually inspected the room. We're good. I'll meet you downstairs."

"Oh, Mike, wait. I'll need her handbag, too. It was with her when she met this person for dinner. And the folding chair she used in the park, too. I want to read her memories right before her death."

Samson hesitated. "The handbag is logged in as evidence. Same with the folding chair, which was damaged by the tree, so we have to keep it in case there's a lawsuit. You can come by the department to check it out."

I thanked him and turned my attention to the task at hand. It was time to enter the world of Mabel Ogglethwarp.

CHAPTER 2

MEMORIES OF A SPIRITUALIST

M abel was a bona fide spiritualist, that was for sure. Scattered across all her possessions were memory frag-ments of her paid work as a medium conducting seances and as a spiritualist consultant. The latter included advice about ending hauntings and insight into clients' previous lives.

When I say bona fide, I mean she made a real living off her fees. Whether she truly delivered the goods, I couldn't say from my cursory survey of her psychic energy left on her belongings.

As I've come to terms with my paranormal abilities and those of others, I've had to open my mind and accept things I used to believe were only folklore. Like vampires. Clairvoyance. Talking gargoyles. The list goes on.

At the same time, I needed to hone my skepticism. Not everything people claimed to be paranormal truly was. For instance, Gloria of the Memory Guild was a highly effective medium and had genuine psychic abilities. On the other hand, the woman in the shop near the tourist zone, the place with the neon "psychic" sign in the window, was not legit. She could impress marks using her Tarot cards with the skill of a hustler playing three-card Monte on a street corner. But she couldn't really see anyone's future. She got arrested last year for "cleansing the evil" from clients' cash. Meaning she took bags with wads of cash and returned to clients bags with wads of newspaper. After serving time in the county jail, she was soon back in business.

I needed to read more of Mrs. Ogglethwarp's memories before I could ascertain her legitimacy.

I scanned a hardcover book on reincarnation, a large quartz crystal, a paperback shifter romance novel, a bottle of stool softener, and a bag of dark-chocolate candies. None seemed to hold coherent thoughts.

I'm afraid to say she had ADHD.

It wasn't until I touched her hairbrush on the bathroom counter that I felt some powerful memories. The image of her in my mind, of dark blonde frizzy hair, explained why. Her hair had required tons of brushing. And there was a lot on the brush. I grabbed the black plastic handle, and I became her, I—

—can't believe he called so early. He knows I'm not awake before seven. And he expects me to drop everything and meet him for dinner. Tonight, I planned on trying to communicate with Great-Aunt Bessie. Now it will have to wait until after dinner. And he knows I couldn't say no. He always holds the threat of calling in my debts.

His voice sounded threatening, even though he tried to act casual. I hate it when he tries to be sweet and friendly. That's not him at all, no way. Is he going to make more demands on me? (Frustration at my hair.) This is hopeless. I have to leave soon. Dinner better not go long. I told Darla I'd meet her at 8:30. Guess it doesn't matter if I'm late, but I don't want to spend any more time with him than I absolutely have to. Okay, let's get this show on the road. Lord, how I dread this—

—She put the brush down, and the memory ended.

I learned absolutely nothing useful from my reverie, except the fact I needed to learn more.

"Mike, I need to read her handbag," I barked the moment I found Samson waiting downstairs.

"Can you elaborate?" he asked sarcastically.

"I didn't get any useful details from her room, though I learned she was meeting some guy who was threatening to her. He seemed to have some leverage over her, money she owed him. I don't know. But this dinner engagement was not with a friend, I can tell you that. We need to find out more."

"Did you learn his name?"

"No. His name didn't come up in her thoughts."

"Okay, you know the drill," he said as he left. "They're closed during lunch. Stop by at one."

I did, indeed, know the drill. Tommy, the evidence clerk, knew me almost as well as if I were a coworker. His unruly beard often contained the evidence of where he had lunch. Asian food today, by the rice grains caught in the bushy brown hair. At least, Tommy had requested healthier brown rice today.

"Ms. Chesswick, what brings you here today? Another serial killer?"

"You know we can't discuss the case," Samson said. I needed him with me to authorize my visit.

Tommy glanced at the paperwork.

"Good thing you came right away. We still have her handbag. Without a murder investigation on the books, we'll have to give it up to the family as soon as they request it. But the legal department secured two folding chairs, whatever good they might do."

"We want to see it all," Samson said.

I nodded. As if my opinion meant anything in this building.

I went to a table by a window at the edge of the large room

while Samson remained at the front counter. Tommy disappeared into the warren of steel shelves loaded with cardboard and plastic boxes.

He brought me the Louis Vuitton bag I recognized as Mrs. Ogglethwarp's. Next, he returned with the two folding red-canvas chairs. One of them was mangled. The other one had been mine.

I cringed at the thought of experiencing her memory of the limb falling. So, I began with the handbag. It was old and well-worn. Tons of memories were on it and in it.

This is where psychometry is not just an ability, but also a learned skill. I had to sort through this haystack of psychic energy to find the relevant memories. Sure, more recent ones were usually stronger. But older memories could be just as powerful if they were of intense experiences.

The problem was, they were all present, useful ones and junk, mixed together like a stew. I needed to find the tender morsels while skipping the chewy root vegetables that were only there because they were good for you.

I began scanning for memories, using the technique Laurel had taught me in which I kept my distance slightly above the memories, so I could peruse them like going through the index of a book. This way, I wouldn't be drawn into a full-blown reverie in which I virtually become the person, reliving her memories as if they were mine.

There was much to search through. This worn-leather bag had been hers for several years. I sensed financial difficulties. Making a living as a spiritualist in Cassadaga meant you had tons of competition. She had frustration about that, with all the psychics, mediums, clairvoyants, telekinesis performers. . . and, yes, there was some fraud going around. The big-name celebrity spiritualists had plenty of business. They hosted expensive seances and public-speaking gigs. Plus, even more expensive personal consultations.

The rest of the fish in the pond had to fight it out to feed upon the more clueless tourists who wandered into town without having done prior research. Mabel was not above resorting to shady practices. Phony seances, the usual grifter tricks of fake psychic readings.

I zeroed in on more recent memories, ignoring the irrelevant. There were just so many memories accumulated in the leather of this bag.

Her home was a Victorian, like my mother's, but much smaller and in disrepair. A shutter hanging crookedly. Pine needles and Spanish moss covering the roof shingles. She's looking at it for the last time as she backs down her driveway before driving to San Marcos.

Good, I found the most recent thread of memories.

She's checking into the Esperanza Inn and notices right away that I have psychic abilities, just as I did with her. She has positive thoughts toward me, which is a relief. That's not always the case, believe me.

As she rides to the third floor, she senses something disturbing in the elevator. Someone died in there years ago.

This was news to me. I never enjoyed riding the small clanking contraption that was at least a hundred years old. But I never knew someone had died in there. I needed to look into this. Thankfully, the death wasn't during my tenure.

Now at room 303. Mrs. Ogglethwarp was not a psychometrist, but she picked up some spooky vibes the moment she touched the doorknob. She is pleased. She enters the room and—

—the ghost is territorial. She knows I can sense her. She's young and sad and frightened. Still angry at her paranoid husband and his crazed

expression when he accused her of cheating on him—on their honeymoon, for crying out loud. The utter disbelief and horror when he pushes her out the window. Must not dwell upon her death. Think happy thoughts so she's not threatened by me.

Oh, this girl's a hard case. Lots of anger. Is she a threat? Don't think so. But it's been a while since I interacted with a genuine ghost instead of just putting on a show for the tourists.

There she is! Half materialized. When she drifts past the window, she actually becomes opaquer.

"Pleased to meet you," I say. "You can feel safe with me."

Quiet weeping.

"There, there, girl. It will be all right. You don't need to linger here on earth anymore. The peace of Heaven awaits you."

Anger radiating from her. What did I say wrong?

I think it's time to give her some space and head into town for the day. I'll unpack later.

"Goodbye, dear." I close the door softly and head for the stairs. Not getting into that elevator—

—That was interesting. Maybe I should consider inviting more psychics here to tell me things about my inn that I haven't learned yet.

Back to the task at hand. Let me find the memory of her dinner with the mysterious man.

I ran my index finger along the bag's leather handles until I found a very recent memory of exiting a ride-share car. I grasped the handles and dove—

—into the restaurant, the enticing aroma of paella, chorizo, and fresh fish. He already has a table for two near the bar. I cut through the tightly packed tables toward him. He's all in black, as usual, his pentagram necklace's silver standing out against the black. His goatee, shaped into a point, is trying too hard. The bad toupee is trying too hard. Everything about him is. He gives me insincere kisses on both cheeks.

"I'm glad you agreed to come," he says, as we sit down. "We must come to an agreement this time." An insincere smile. "It would be so damaging not to."

Putting my handbag on the floor beside my leg—

—Drat! The memory was cut off when she stopped touching the bag. I search for when she picks it up again. I—

—grab my bag and get up.

"Thank you for dinner. I'm late for an appointment, but I'll be in touch."

"My pleasure," he says. "You made the right decision tonight, I assure you."

I hurry outside where the car is waiting for me. I need a shower after all the lies and malarky I heard tonight. But Darla will be waiting, and I'm late—

—and she deliberately forces herself to not think of tonight's agreement. Because she was ashamed? I think so. And angry, too.

Man, even as I get better at psychometry, it never fails to frustrate me, too. I want to know what deal she made!

The handbag didn't have any other valuable memories. Or perhaps I was losing concentration. In any event, it was time to read her folding chair and see if it held any secrets.

Picking up the mangled aluminum chair frame made me shudder. What the tree did to the chair, it did even worse to Mrs. Ogglethwarp.

The chair's arm rails were covered by canvas, creating armrests more uncomfortable than they looked. I remembered Mrs. Ogglethwarp clutching the diagonal support bars, so I placed my hands directly upon the—

—tree is old and wise and there are more spirits in here than Great-Aunt Bessie for sure. And the tree itself has a great and powerful spirit, but so different from the human ones. It's not as I

expected. Not exactly benign. Trees are supposed to be totally passive and cooperative, right? Not this girl. It's hard to explain, but I guess if you've lived for hundreds of years through frosts and hurricanes and droughts and parasites and stupid humans' weedkiller, you'd be pretty cranky.

But where is Bessie? I'm calling her name, but she's not responding. I know she's in there. Not just because Jonathon said so, but I remember her from when I was a kid and I definitely sense her in there.

Please, Auntie Bessie, please respond to me. I'm told you left me an inheritance, but your will was never found. What did you leave me? Is it still around? Where can I find it? I've been under a lot of financial stress lately, Auntie. Anything could help me. Money, heirlooms. Your house is still standing and Henry, from your brother-in-law's family, lives there. Doesn't deserve it, though. But whatever you left me could still be in the house. Please, send a message to me. Please, I beg you.

You always liked me, Auntie Bessie. You said I was the cutest little girl. I loved your sugar cookies. Remember, you spent one Christmas with my parents and me?

This isn't working. No, wait, what was that?

A spirit is stirring inside the tree. This is for real. It's been a while since I found an actual spirit, and now I've found two in in the same day.

Auntie Bessie? Is that you?

Wow, it's powerful. So much energy.

Will you show yourself to me? I know you have the power to. Come on, reveal yourself. Show me a sign. Come forth and make yourself known.

Chanting aloud will help. Darla looks at me like I'm a nut. I don't care.

Show me a sign. Any sign.

"Bessie, show me something, anything, to let me know you hear me."

Wait, who are you?

What are you?

I come in peace. I mean no harm. Why are you angry? Please don't harm me!

What was that bang?

Oh, my sakes, what is happening? Oh, my—

—I released the aluminum, and the chair clattered upon the tile floor.

Tommy looks up at me from the front desk.

I experienced Mrs. Ogglethwarp's memory of the giant tree limb cracking and dropping upon her. I broke away just before it hit her, so I thankfully avoided experiencing the pain.

Even so, I felt her horror. Every drop of it.

My hands were shaking. Who cares if I'm actually safe here in the police department headquarters? I just experienced being about to die. And it was horrible.

Mothers, don't let your girls grow up to be psychometrists. Trust me on this.

CHAPTER 3

THE DAVENPORT DUO

"Hello? Is anyone here?" a male voice said in the hallway.

He had to be a guest, because the outside door would have rung a chime in the kitchen if someone came in from the street.

I hurried to the kitchen entrance, where a prim and proper elderly man stood. He wore a pink dress shirt and khakis. His thick white hair was carefully trimmed.

"Sorry to bother you. Are you the owner of this establishment?"

"Yes. I'm Darla Chesswick."

"Ah, excellent," he said, smiling. "I'm Jonathon Davenport in Room two-oh-two. Pleased to meet you. You already met my wife, Franny, when she checked in earlier in the week. I was off exploring the town at the time."

"Nice meeting you. Have you come down for Teatime?"

"Actually, I had some questions for you."

"I need to finish preparing for tea. Why don't you meet me

in the dining room, the breakfast room as I call it, after four, and we'll chat then."

"Perfect. I'll see you at half past."

I rushed back into the kitchen to get the scones out, but my daughter, Sophie, had beaten me to it. They looked perfect: lightly browned with a bumpy surface. This batch had cranberries and honey added.

Sophie was slicing the finger sandwiches, both egg salad and cucumber. Two kettles were heating water on the stove. I decided not to bring out any of the sweets, since attendance would be so low today.

"I'm supposed to meet with that gentleman from two-oh-two at four-thirty. Can you take over serving then?" I asked Sophie.

"Sure. It will be easy since hardly anyone will be there. I think our inn has more ghosts than guests."

"I think you may be right." I was certain there were more ghosts I hadn't met yet.

As I was wondering what Mr. Davenport wished to discuss, I remembered something.

His name was Jonathon. Could this be the same Jonathon who told Mrs. Ogglethwarp about Bessie's spirit?

In that case, our little chat could be uncomfortable, to say the least.

JONATHON DAVENPORT SHOWED UP IN THE DINING ROOM without his wife. I poured cups of hot water for both of us and offered the wooden box with the tea bag selection. You might believe tea bags are barbaric, but when you serve the public, you can't brew only one or two teas. You need choices. He took an Earl Grey and so did I. He politely declined any food.

"I'm sure you're wondering what this is about," Jonathon said. "Sorry if it is a delicate subject, but I wish to discuss Mabel Ogglethwarp. We learned only this morning of her passing. She was a dear friend of ours, and we were extremely concerned when we didn't see her yesterday, and she didn't respond to any of my calls or texts."

"I'm so sorry for your loss," I said.

"Thank you." He blotted the corner of his eyes with a napkin. "The three of us were going to investigate a haunting at the fort together."

"Which one? There are many."

"Yes, I know. Mabel was looking into some of them on her own. Together, we were going to look into the ghost of a woman imprisoned at the fort in the eighteenth century. The wife of one of the commanders, sealed inside a wall of the dungeon with her lover. We wanted to try to communicate with her."

"Oh, yes, I've heard of that haunting. Now, are you the one who told Mabel about her great-aunt's spirit being in the tree?"

He blushed. "She told you about that?"

"Yes. And I went with her to visit the tree. I was nearly hit by the same limb."

"I almost feel as if her death was my fault," he said.

"Don't feel that way. Many people hang out beneath that tree. It's a great photo opportunity. This was simply a terrible accident."

"Maybe it was."

Did he know something I didn't know?

"Tell me about the spirit in the tree."

"She wasn't shy. Very easy to communicate with. I told her we were from Cassadaga, and she mentioned her great niece, Mabel, lived there. I said it was a wonderful coincidence, since Mabel was in town. The spirit then mentioned an inheritance.

She didn't say what it was. She was eager for Mabel to visit the tree. I think the spirit was starved for attention."

"Did you speak to any other spirits in the tree?"

"No. I didn't know there were others. It seemed such a wonderful turn of events that we found Mabel's great-aunt. I couldn't wait for them to meet."

"You were going to visit the tree with Mabel?"

"I thought so, but she cancelled on me at the last minute with no explanation. It hurt my feelings. And then, to have Mabel taken away in such a horrible fashion."

"I know, I'm sorry."

"I spoke to the police," Jonathon said. "They were investigating her death, as if it were deliberate and not an accident. But then, they said there was no evidence of a homicide."

"A homicide would have been awfully tricky to pull off."

"I know. The reason I mention this is I wasn't surprised the police first thought it was murder."

"I don't understand."

"Mabel had enemies back home in Cassadaga. I never believed anyone would actually kill her, but I wouldn't have been completely surprised."

"Why would she have enemies?" I asked.

"Fraud. It's one thing to rip off tourists who want their palms read or to attend a seance. It's another thing altogether to defraud locals. That's what the rumors say about her."

This information would be useful for investigating her murder. Perhaps she had defrauded someone, who retaliated by using a spell to bring down the tree limb. How should I broach the subject of magic with Jonathon?

"Do you believe in magic?" I just went with the direct approach.

"What do you mean? What kind of magic?"

"You know, like witches casting spells."

Annoyance crept into his face. "Just because I'm a spiritualist doesn't mean I believe that people who claim they're witches or warlocks actually have magical powers. That's all claptrap, in my view."

Okay, so we're not going to discuss a witch or warlock killing Mrs. Ogglethwarp.

"You're right," I said. "It was just a rhetorical question."

He took a large gulp of tea, as if to cleanse his mouth of the claptrap.

After a long, awkward pause, he cleared his throat.

"The reason I wanted to speak with you is to find out if you know whom she had dinner with the night of her death. I was supposed to go out with her before visiting the tree, but she cancelled that, too. She said she needed to meet with someone else. Did you see anyone come around to pick her up?"

I, too, was curious about the man she met. So, I told a white lie, hoping to draw information from Jonathon.

"I don't know who it was except that it was a man younger than her with black hair, a goatee, and black clothing. He wore a pentagram on a chain around his neck," I said, describing the man I had seen via Mrs. Ogglethwarp's memories.

Jonathon's eyes widened.

"You say a pentagram?"

I nodded.

"Was he wearing a black turtleneck, which is really not a good look for him, because it emphasizes his pot belly?"

I recalled the mental image of him.

"Yes, he was."

"I think his name is Sykes," Jonathon said. "Don't know his first name. He showed up in Cassadaga recently. He purports to be a spiritualist, but I actually believe he's a Satanist. And we're not that kind of town. I didn't realize Mabel knew him. This is disturbing."

"He's that bad?"

"He's held at least one lecture in town about that claptrap you brought up—something about magic. I think he's a Satanist trying to recruit people to a cult or something. It bugs me to think Mabel was having dinner with him. She actually cancelled with me to go out with him? That means he has some sort of power over her."

"Does he have anything to do with her defrauding people?"

"Maybe they have some scheme together. But the rumors that she was involved in fraud were going around long before this Sykes character showed up in town."

Frankly, the more I learned about Mrs. Ogglethwarp, the more I believed her death was intentional and not the random result of a vandalized tree limb.

Jonathon stood up.

"Thank you for the tea. Franny and I aren't checking out early. We're staying for the remainder of our reservation, so if you learn of anything, let us know."

"I will. I'd love to see you at Teatime tomorrow."

"We'll see. Maybe."

"Oh, there you are," said a woman's voice behind us.

A well-dressed woman around Jonathon's age stood in the doorway. I recognized her as his wife from when she checked in. In her lavender pants suit, she certainly didn't look like the typical San Marcos tourist wearing shorts and a fanny pack.

"Franny, have you met Darla Chesswick?"

"I have."

"I finally met your husband just now," I said.

Franny frowned.

"Um, have y'all met the ghost in your room yet?" I asked.

28

"Unfortunately, not," Franny said. "We haven't had time for a seance."

"You don't need a seance to reach this guy. He's a real ham. He'll be singing Elvis tunes for you soon, I'm sure of it."

"It hasn't been top of mind, honestly, not with the mortifying news about Mabel."

"Yes, I understand. I'm sorry for your loss."

"Would it be possible if we packed her belongings?" Franny asked. "I'd rather a stranger didn't do it."

She frowned at me again.

"Okay," I said. "I mean, I should contact her next of kin."

"There is no one except a distant cousin. We were as close as family with her."

"Okay. I'll get you a room key."

Why hadn't Mrs. Ogglethwarp told me she was visiting San Marcos with the Davenports? And Franny didn't mention anything about Mabel when checking in. There was so much about Mrs. Ogglethwarp to arouse suspicions. And curiosity.

The problem is, I tend to get into trouble when I'm curious.

CHAPTER 4

THE TREE OF KNOWLEDGE

"Um, do you have a lost and found office?" I asked the lady on the phone.

She was the receptionist at the Parks and Recreation Department of the City of San Marcos.

"Yes, we do. Let me transfer you."

The on-hold music made me feel like I was lost in the 1970s.

"Gilroy," said a gruff man.

"Is this lost and found?"

"Lost Property Division. What did you lose?"

"I didn't lose anything. I'm calling about something that was found."

"How could it be found if it wasn't lost first?"

"If you hid something, then someone else found it," I explained.

"Then it wouldn't be lost. It was deliberately concealed, then someone accidentally found it. Or, you might say, stole it. Unless the item was stolen in the first place, hidden by the thief, and then stolen from the thief by someone who was acting like a thief. If a stolen item was stolen, it's still stolen in my book."

I sighed aloud. "It's a giant pearl. It was found inside the Southern live oak tree that lost a limb in the little park between Bayfront Avenue and Cortez Street."

"The tree that killed the lady?"

"Yes."

"Oh. Why didn't you say so? We don't have it anymore. The arborist who found it said it was hidden in the tree so long ago the trunk had completely grown around the object. So, he said the person who hid it—and note that I'm not calling this person a thief—wouldn't be alive today."

Interesting.

"Okay, so where is this object?" I asked.

"The arborist gave it to the city museum."

I thanked him and hung up.

When I had free time in the middle of the day, I hopped on my motor scooter and rode across Old Town to the city museum, which was housed in a former luxury hotel built during the Gilded Age, in the late-nineteenth century when San Marcos was Florida's tourist hot spot. At the reception desk, I didn't know who to ask for, so I tried to explain what I knew about the pearl, leaving out the part about lost vs. hidden and found vs. stolen.

"You'll have to speak to the Acquisitions Department," the elderly man at the information desk said. "I'll ask someone to come down for you."

Several minutes passed as I stood in the cavernous central hall that had once been the hotel's lobby. Voices of tourists echoed off the marble floor and the groin-vault ceiling two stories above. Finally, a woman in her twenties walked up to the desk. She wore her hair short and straight and had large-rimmed glasses. Her expression was one of suspicion.

"Can I help you?"

I explained the story all over again.

"Why would you like to see it?" she asked.

Good question. I couldn't explain that I was curious about it because it was discovered when the tree killed my guest, and I wanted to learn if my guest died accidentally because I had too many guests of my inn dying lately. Nor did I want to mention I had a paranormal ability that would allow me to learn, possibly, why the pearl was placed in the tree.

"It involves a friend," I lamely obfuscated.

"The item in question is not available to be viewed by the public," the woman said in a very official-sounding voice. "First, we must establish its provenance and then create the context for its display setting."

"Can I have the name of your manager?"

She frowned. "Marianne LeBoeuf. Who would be me. I'm the manager of the department."

I thanked her curtly and left. It was time to bring in the big guns. Dr. Sven Noordlun and the Memory Guild.

WHEN I RETURNED TO THE INN, SAMSON WAS WAITING FOR ME in the foyer.

"Hey, Mike. What brings you here today?"

"Scones, if you have any left from breakfast."

"I do. And if you come back at Teatime, you can have fresh ones."

I was pleasantly surprised to hear he liked them so much. They're made with Mom's recipe, but she has to add magic to hers to make a police detective addicted to them. I apparently didn't need the sorcery with my detective.

"Oh, the leftovers are fine," Samson said. The tray was on the butcher block island. I removed the aluminum foil cover and offered them.

"Want me to heat them up?"

"No, thanks." He grabbed two and gulped down half of one while leaning against the island. "The real reason I came by is to tell you the report says there's no evidence of explosive material on the tree in the park. Which means the limb breaking wasn't triggered remotely. That torpedoes the possibility someone deliberately murdered Mabel Ogglethwarp. For the city to avoid liability, we're going to need to prove a manslaughter case against whomever sabotaged the limb by cutting the notch. If that's really what he did. I saw the surveillance video, and it looks convincing, but I'm sure a defense attorney could shoot holes in it and say the guy was carving his initials into the tree with his chainsaw, or something even stupider. Assuming we catch the guy, of course."

"So, you're saying he weakened the limb, not knowing when it would break and if it would land on anyone? Mrs. Oggleth-warp wasn't the intended victim?"

"That's a possibility. It could simply be a case of vandalism turned deadly."

"What if the breakage was triggered another way?"

"Like how?"

"Through magic. Or telekinesis."

"I was afraid you were going to bring that up again. We can't use that in court."

"I don't care. I only want justice for Mrs. Ogglethwarp."

"Since she was a guest, wouldn't you rather the word be that she died in a random accident rather than murder?"

"As a member of law enforcement, wouldn't you rather know the truth?"

"Ouch. Yeah. But I was hoping not to get dragged into another paranormal odyssey."

"You go where the investigation takes you, Detective Samson. By the way, I heard the arborist believes the pearl he found in the tree was in there for many, many years. So, it's very unlikely the vandal was trying to find it."

"Right. I already knew that."

"Thanks for telling me."

"I didn't realize you were playing detective again."

"Well, I am. I told you why."

"Are you getting the Memory Guild involved?"

"Yeah. They'll help me learn about the pearl. And also, about the tree. You have an arborist and a surveillance video to work with. I have a wood-speaker who can communicate with trees."

"It looks like we're going to be collaborating again," Samson said with an ironic grin.

"It does, doesn't it?"

IT TOOK ME ONLY A HALF HOUR TO AWAKEN ARCHIBALD, AND I didn't even have to use my cat, Cervantes, to smack his stony face. My resident gargoyle passed my message on to Dr. Noordlun. He authorized Summer, our wood-speaker, and Gloria, our medium, to meet me at the live oak tree to see what we could learn.

Dr. Noordlun also called the president of the city museum and leaned heavily, with all his weight as history chair of the city's college as well as renowned historian in his own right, to get me permission to examine the gem found in the tree. They wanted to run some more tests on it, but I could come by at the end of the week.

It pays to have friends in high places.

WE MET AT THE LIVE OAK AT DAWN, WHEN THE SPIRITUAL world was still active from the night, and the trees would be waking up to the sunlight.

I wondered if I should bring a watering can or fertilizer as a hello gift for the tree, but Summer only laughed in response. She believed I was joking. I wasn't.

Gloria sat on a blanket beneath Old Courage and leaned back against its trunk. She immediately went into a trance in order to seek which, if any, spirits resided in the tree. Gloria was in her midlife, like me, yet her face looked years younger, free of wrinkles, and only her silver hair gave away her age. Her eyelids twitched, indicating her rapid eye movements beneath them.

Summer placed her hand against one of the tree's large boughs, not as thick as the one that had broken off. Live oaks do not grow especially tall, but their meandering limbs spread horizontally for long distances. Old Courage had tiny ferns coating the larger limbs and clumps of Spanish moss, like gray hairs hanging from many of its branches, making it look as old as its size suggested it was.

"Those trees across the street are part of her family," Summer said. "The roots of live oaks spread much further than their branches. Hers are interwoven with her family's. They communicate with each other all the time."

"Communicate?"

"Absolutely. If you want a scientific explanation, they use

mycorrhizae, partnerships between their root systems and fungi, that send impulses from tree to tree."

"I didn't know that."

"She feels lonely out here by herself. She misses being close to family members. But at least, they can talk."

"It's a female? How old is she?" I asked.

"Oak trees are monoecious. Each has both male and female flowers. But I would call her a she, because she has engendered many other trees with her acorns. This wise soul is older than the tourist guides say. She's nearly 400 seasons old."

She approached the massive trunk, on the opposite side of where Gloria was sitting. Running both hands up and down the bark, Summer hummed a low, unfamiliar tune. It was a song that sounded ageless. It could have been sung by the Druids in ancient Britain, or the earliest Native Americans.

The leaves of the tree rustled, though no wind was blowing.

Summer wrapped her arms around the trunk, too large for them to encircle, and rested the side of her face against the bark. This must be where the term "tree hugger" came from. She continued humming.

I stepped back and glanced at Gloria. Her eyes were closed, and her head was tilted back against the trunk. Her lips moved soundlessly.

A young couple who looked like tourists cut through the tiny park. They stopped and stared at my friends' odd behavior, then looked at me questioningly.

"We're an improv theater group," I said. "Warming-up exercises."

Based on the expressions on the couple's faces, my explanation was not sufficient.

I returned to Summer's side of the tree. She clearly had established a deep connection to the tree. It's hard to explain. The position of her body mimicked the gentle curves of the trunk and main limbs. Though Summer was fair-skinned with straight blonde hair, I half expected her to turn into the color and texture of the tree. It was as if she had become less of a mammal and more of a plant.

I was still fairly new to the Memory Guild and only knew a few of its members fairly well. Summer was not one of them. She had angular, elfin features. At first glance, she appeared quite young, but as you studied her, she looked more like she was in her forties. If the light struck her a certain way, you could be excused for thinking she was a youthful-looking sixty-year-old. Most of the time, though, she simply seemed ageless. I knew she worked, fittingly, at a tree nursery. But I knew little else about her. I needed to correct that.

The minutes ticked by slowly. I wanted to sit down, but there wasn't a bench in the tiny park. Sitting cross-legged on the grass in the tree's shade was what I resorted to, staying cool as the sun rose over the bay.

At last, Summer detached herself from Old Courage. Her face showed the struggle to disconnect herself from the tree's consciousness and return to the human world.

"The poor tree is traumatized," she said.

"No doubt. Losing a large limb like that must be terrible. Was it painful?"

"Trees don't feel pain like we do, but they strongly sense when damage is inflicted upon them. First, a human cut a section from the groin below the limb. The tree knew its limb was vulnerable and sent extra nutrients to the wound to help heal it. The limb would have survived, unless a strong windstorm came along. In several months, it might have healed well enough to withstand even that. But then the power snapped it off. The poor tree reacted in agony, and all its family trees around here suffered in sympathy."

"What power snapped it off?" I asked.

"Magic of some sort. Trees don't understand magic the way we do, but a tree as old as this one has sensed it in the atmosphere before, just like it senses any kind of force, from weather to air pressure to human-created forces such as explosions and bullets. And, of course, saws. Old Courage even has several bullets embedded in her trunk, from musket balls to modern bullets, from hunters, invaders, and vandals."

"Wow. Did she tell you anything about the magic?"

"Only that it was a powerful, concussive force that struck downward. It came out of nowhere and was extremely violent. It was also precise, attempting to knock the limb at a certain angle toward the east, instead of directly downward."

It was aiming for Mrs. Ogglethwarp. Whoever had engineered this would know she would sit beneath the limb because of the layout of the park. But the killer wouldn't know exactly where she sat, so he or she would need to aim the falling limb toward her.

That meant the killer had been here, observing us. Or, perhaps, was watching us magically.

"Is there any way Old Courage could help us identify the person responsible?"

"Not who cast the spell. The person who cut the notch, maybe. Obviously, trees can't see, but they receive chemical warnings of damaging pests. From insects to humans. But we would have to bring the person to the tree for her to identify him."

"One last question. Does the tree remember the pearl being placed inside it?"

"Yes. It was over a hundred years ago. The tree had a knothole that squirrels and birds sometimes sheltered inside. A human came along and stuffed the object inside. It was handled by the human again, then left alone. Eventually, the trunk healed over it, and the object was nearly forgotten, like the bullets."

"Thank you," I said. "That was very enlightening. I want to learn more about trees."

"I'll gladly introduce you into their world."

Now, it was Gloria's turn to report her findings, but she was still in her trance. She suddenly moaned and twitched.

"Did she encounter a hostile spirit?" Summer asked.

"I hope not. Should we try to wake her?"

"Wait. Do you feel that? Sage is here."

The only member of the Memory Guild who was a spirit, Sage was like Gloria's alter ego from the other side. If Gloria was being harassed by a hostile ghost, Sage would try to defend her.

Gloria calmed down.

Sage materialized in the shadows beneath the tree, smiled at us, then disappeared.

Gloria's eyes shot open.

"Are you okay, Gloria?" I asked.

"Yes. I wasn't in danger of getting hurt, but I suffered a torrent of verbal abuse."

"Who abused you?" Summer asked.

"The deceased's Great-Aunt Bessie. What a character!"

"Why was she giving you a hard time?" I asked.

"She was upset about the death of her great-niece, of course. Wouldn't you be?"

"Yeah, but I'm not a ghost living in a tree. Why is she living there, anyway?"

"Kind of an odd story. She died in a home not far from here. Her spirit lingered, to make sure all the family showed up and expressed a suitable amount of grief. Well, it turns out she

39

lingered too long, enjoying watching everyone cry over her loss. When she tried to ascend to Heaven, she had problems finding her way out of the house. Once she was out, she accidentally went into the body of a squirrel eating an acorn in a tree outside the window. The squirrel, now possessed by a domineering old lady, freaked out, and scampered away, going from tree to tree until he ended up in this one. Great-Aunt Bessie realized she did not want to spend any more of her afterlife inside a squirrel, so she left and ended up inside the tree. There are other spirits here, who warmly welcomed her, and she never left."

"This tree is better than Heaven?" I asked.

"I guess she still had some of the squirrel's point of view, which was that this is a heavenly place to be. Plus, it has a wonderful view of the bay, which appealed to her human side."

"I see. So, is it true there's an unclaimed inheritance for Mrs. Ogglethwarp?"

"Not exactly. Bessie left her vast collection of vintage coffee cans for her great-niece. Not exactly a windfall. You see, she didn't particularly care for Mabel."

"Then why is she so upset about Mabel's death?"

"She enjoys the drama. Plus, it was disturbing to see it happen right here, caused by the tree. The other spirits weren't happy about it, either."

"Who are they?"

"A Spanish soldier and a Native American of the Timucuan people."

"Summer learned from the tree that magic was used to break the tree limb. Do the spirits have any insight on that?" I asked.

"The Timucuan had been a shaman, so he was quite aware of the magic. The others sensed something weird was going on but didn't realize it was a magic spell at work."

"What did the shaman say about it? Did he know who cast the spell?"

Gloria seemed uncomfortable about the topic now.

"No, he didn't know who cast the spell," Gloria said. "Except that it came from a powerful magician. An experienced one. The shaman was surprised that someone of such abilities would make a mistake."

"What do you mean by mistake?"

"The shaman's spirit was very clued in on the spell. Spirits exist in the same spectrum of the universe that many magic spells operate in, so they have a front-row view of the inner workings of magic. It's hard to explain. The spirit doesn't speak English, so he's imparting this knowledge to me in a non-verbal way. Sort of like osmosis."

Gloria acted as if she had more to tell but struggled to do it.

"Okay," I said. "You were saying that the magician made a mistake."

"Yes. I don't know how to tell you this, but when the bough landed on Mrs. Ogglethwarp, it wasn't as intended."

"Are you kidding me? I don't understand what the magic was doing if it wasn't supposed to kill her."

"It wasn't supposed to kill only her, it was meant to kill you, too," Gloria said in a thick voice. "The spirit said the limb was supposed to land on both her and the person with her, but the magician aimed wrong, and it landed on Mrs. Ogglethwarp alone."

No one spoke for a long while.

"Oh," I said. "Good to know."

CHAPTER 5

PEARL OF WISDOM

W e sat on a bench along the promenade that lined the bay. It was a beautiful morning, and a flock of pelicans in a V-formation glided past us, low to the glistening water.

I was completely immune to the morning's beauty. Because my world had been tipped upside down.

Summer and Gloria had refused to allow me to drive home alone, since I was reeling from the news I had narrowly escaped murder.

"It's partly why Great-Aunt Bessie was so nasty," Gloria said, "when she learned her great niece wasn't the only one who was supposed to die, and you were spared."

"I'm sorry for disappointing her," I said.

"Why would a magician try to kill you?" Summer asked.

"How would I know?" I swear, talking to trees and twigs and two-by-fours all the time made her a little dense. "If I knew that, I wouldn't be hanging out beneath live oak trees."

"Isn't your husband being held captive by a wizard?" Gloria asked. "Maybe the wizard sees you as a threat."

"There are a million other, more effective ways to kill me with magic. Why use such an indirect, sloppy method? That wizard is said to be super powerful. If he wanted to kill me, he could do it like that."

I snapped my fingers.

My two friends jumped, startled.

"How do we find out who did it?" Gloria asked.

Summer and I both stared at her.

"Hey," she said, "I'm only a psychic and a medium. I'm not some Magic Eight Ball with the answers to everything."

"The first thing we should do is notify the Magic Guild," I said. "They need to know a murder was committed using magic, and they're the best ones to investigate it. We're supposed to use official channels, so I'll ask Dr. Noordlun to contact the Arch Mage of the Magic Guild."

"How will you stay safe?" Summer asked.

"I have two witches in my immediate family and a cousin who's one. Hopefully, their magic will protect me from the evil magic."

"Hopefully," Gloria said in a voice completely lacking confidence.

I CALLED SAMSON. THERE WAS A LOT OF INFORMATION TO download to him, and I hadn't yet had the opportunity. I also kind of dreaded the drama that would ensue when I told him I was one of the targets of a homicidal spell.

Now, I should first add a disclaimer. If you're considering making reservations at the Esperanza Inn, rest assured, I practice absolute discretion with your privacy. Just because I'm friends with a police detective and collaborate with him on cases, does *not* mean I blab stuff about my guests to him. As long as you're not a murderer or actively engaged in a crime, your privacy is absolute. If, however, you fall into one or both of the above categories, let's save everyone a headache—don't book a room here.

Now that I've got that off my chest, I'll admit I did a lot of blabbing to Samson.

"Hold on, hold on," he commanded.

"Sorry. I talk fast when I'm nervous."

"I'm trying to absorb the fact you were an intended victim. I'm freaked out about it, okay? Wouldn't you expect me to be?"

"It wasn't my idea to be an intended victim."

"You say the spirit of a shaman from hundreds of years ago told you this?"

"He told Gloria, our psychic and medium."

"Just because he's a spirit, doesn't mean you have to believe what he says."

"Exactly! Because the more I learn about Mabel Oggleth-warp, the more hinky stuff I'm learning. She's been accused of fraud and was involved with suspicious characters. But as for me, I don't know any practicing witch, wizard, mage—not any kind of magician—who wants me dead."

"That you know of."

"That's what I said."

"The people who want to kill you whom you don't know about are usually the ones who succeed."

"Oh."

"Yes. What are you doing to find out if any magicians want you dead? I'll do my best to help, but remember, I'm a cop in a world that doesn't believe in magic. If you find an evil magician, I'll do everything I can to mess him or her up. But I don't have the tools or abilities to investigate and prosecute magic criminal acts."

"I know, I know. We've been through this talk so many times before. The Magic Guild should be looking into it. I just get antsy doing nothing while waiting for them."

"I'll help you any way I can. As long as it's legal."

"I have one thing I can do: check out the pearl found in the tree."

"I thought you said it was in the tree too long to be related."

"The vandal who cut the notch wouldn't know about it. But a witch or wizard might."

"Yes, possibly."

"And speaking of whom, have you had any headway in finding out who the vandal was?"

"No," he said sheepishly.

"You'd better get busy."

I WAS IN THE INN'S KITCHEN, PREPARING THE DAILY HIGH Tea, trying to keep my mind focused on the task at hand so it wouldn't go wandering into fear and paranoia.

"So, someone is trying to kill you?" asked a male English accent.

It was Archibald, perched on the tile wall of the kitchen. So much for keeping my mind from scary things.

"You're not supposed to animate and wander about the inn where guests could see you."

"As usual, you hardly have any guests. I would also point out that I'm being quite discrete. Guests are not allowed in the kitchen."

"One could peek in or wander in here by accident."

"I would instantly return to my stone form. I would appear to the guest as a wall decoration."

"And I would appear to be a kook who talks to herself. Besides, I don't know many people who would hang a gargoyle on their kitchen wall. But anyway, how did you hear about me?"

"The Memory Guild is all abuzz about it. No one ever wanted to kill our members until you joined. Suddenly, there were how many attempts on our members' lives?"

"That was an aberrant case. I'd rather not talk about it."

"Well, this time, we'll be ready for the mayhem you'll bring us. Dr. Noordlun has already contacted the Magic Guild. I expect they'll sort things out."

"Do you really?"

"Alas, no," Archibald said, lowering his impish face. "They've never been able to police their members well. But," he tried to sound cheerful, "the Memory Guild is on top of it. We have Diana, our own witch, who has vowed to do a forensic analysis of the magic used on the tree."

"Really? The spell left traces of evidence she can read?"

"She said she hoped it did."

"Okay."

My batch of scones was almost finished baking, filling the air with their buttery, slightly nutty scent. Usually, when the aroma spread throughout the inn, it lured guests down to the dining room. Today, only two rooms were booked, and I was afraid their occupants were out and about in town.

Sophie strolled into the kitchen. I didn't have to worry about my scones going to waste anymore.

"So, someone is trying to kill you?" she asked as she opened the oven door a crack. "I think the scones are ready."

"You don't seem very concerned."

"I am. I don't want you to overcook them. They're too yummy."

"I meant concerned about my life."

"Of course, I am, Mom." She kissed my cheek. "Do you have any idea who would cast that spell and why?"

"Nope. Do you?"

"Why would I know?"

"You're a witch now, Sophie. You're part of the club. I would imagine you'd have a sense of what your fellow witches are up to."

"You sound bitter, Mom. It's not my fault the witch gene skipped a generation."

She was right. I did sound rather pathetic.

"My cousin, Missy, can often tell when a spell has been cast. It's like she has a nose for it."

"She's a highly experienced witch. I'm just a beginner. Maybe Grammers can help you."

"Your grandmother is little more than a hobbyist. I can tell you're destined to be much more powerful than her."

"I've only begun training."

"Ask your tutor, Hugo, if he can help."

"Mom, the Magic Guild will look into this and find the rogue witch or wizard."

"Are you really that certain?"

She met my eyes, and I saw she was not.

"I'm scared to death," she said. "I don't want anything to happen to you. But I don't know who else can help us."

I didn't either.

MARIANNE LEBOEUF WAS NOT PLEASED TO SEE ME. I WAS waiting in the reception area on the museum's third floor where the offices were. But thanks to Dr. Noordlun's request to Marianne's boss, she had no choice but to humor me.

"Come with me," she said, without so much as a hello.

I followed her down a hall, past offices, and into a large room with worktables and shelves filled with boxes and random objects, such as carved wooden masks and the steel helmet of a Spanish musketeer.

She showed me an open plastic container, the kind you put food leftovers in. It held the largest pearl I had ever seen in my life, about the size of a tennis ball.

"Wow," I said. "That's amazing!"

"We ran some tests, and radiometric dating indicated it probably came from a prehistoric giant oyster thousands of years ago."

"May I touch it?" I asked.

"I was told you're some sort of psychic?"

She said "psychic" with the disdain scientists and people with fancy degrees have for the paranormal.

"I am."

"I'll leave you alone to do your little ritual. Please be careful with the pearl, and it is *not* to leave this room."

"Gotcha."

She walked briskly away, her shoes clicking down the hallway like a tap dancer with OCD.

"What an insufferable little snot," Archibald said. He had appeared on the nearby concrete-block wall.

"What are you doing here?"

"What do you think? Come now, bring me the pearl so I can examine it."

I carried the open plastic container to him. He snatched it

48

up and held it in both palms of his little clawed hands. He rolled it around between them and closed his eyes.

"She is correct. It came from a marshy saltwater creek near here. An early Native American tribe, the predecessors of the Timucuans, found it and treated it as a magical object. Then, it seems to have been lost or forgotten for centuries. I detect no handling by humans over those years. But, ah! I sense other creatures handled it—from a race of magical humanoids. Most recently, about a century or two ago, it was mounted on a wooden object of some sort. Then, years later, it was removed and placed into living wood—a tree, I presume."

"Is it truly magical?" I asked.

"Yes, of course. It's not my specialty to identify magic, but I most definitely sense quite a bit of power inside the pearl."

"Interesting. That would make it worth hiding and protecting."

"Absolutely."

Archibald returned the pearl to the container.

"I must go now," he said, "lest I be discovered by a human."

In a blink of an eye, he was gone.

It was my turn to use my own ability. I hoped my psychometry would pick up the memories of who had last handled it and explain why it was hidden in the tree. Though it had been placed there more than a century ago, I wanted to find out if there was any relevance to today. It seemed too coincidental that an iconic old tree used by a magician to try to kill me would also have a rare giant pearl inside it, a gem that had some magic in it.

I placed the container back on the table and sat on a stool beside it. The glum Ms. LeBoeuf could return at any moment, so I had to work quickly.

Hovering my hand just above the shiny white ball, I picked up plenty of psychic energy. Most of it was extremely old. There were murmurs in an ancient language I couldn't understand, and images of rituals performed by torchlight.

But there was a more recent memory. It stood out because of the urgency and desperation of the person who left it on here. I placed my hand upon the pearl and—

—*wrench it from the golden prongs that attached it to the end of the staff. The gold is pliable enough that I can do this without tools. I glance around nervously and listen for any approaching footsteps. All is quiet in the house.*

This is his secondary staff, so I hope he won't notice what I have done for quite some time. If he accuses me of doing it, I won't know what to say.

His primary staff is one for wielding power over others, of making people submit, and attacking those who don't. He uses it as a weapon. This staff, though, is protective. He told me once, the pearl contains a healing magic that will cure him of potions or poisons used upon him. It will even dispel certain spells. He claims it can summon help from other beings, such as angels and the Fae.

It might be my only way of escaping the magic he uses to bind me to him.

I don't know how to use the pearl and might need much time to learn its secrets. It must be hidden somewhere I can access it and where he can't find it. I've already scouted out just the right place.

With the pearl in my pocket, I go downstairs and walk out of the house he rents. The power of the magic that binds me to him is such that I feel as if I were free. I can wander anywhere in town, within a certain radius of him, when he doesn't need me.

But I can never leave his sphere of influence. And the moment he needs me to serve him, the spell drags me back to him like a magnet, leaving me at his beck and call. Lately, he has been more permissive as his power grows and he needs less of mine. But I can't assume it will continue like this. At any time, he can keep me trapped at his side like before. It's a living hell for me.

The park is just ahead. A hansom cab with no passengers rattles past, its horse rearing its head, the driver sitting atop the compartment seemingly enjoying the warm weather.

The beautiful live oak tree is smaller than its older version in my time era, but it is still gigantic. I discovered the knothole only a few days ago, and the idea of hiding the pearl in it came to me instantly. I scoop out decayed wood and leaves to carve out this space in the bottom of the hole where I place the pearl. And no one can see it. It fits perfectly.

I will return here regularly and handle the pearl, trying to assess its power and how to use it. It's my only chance of breaking his hold upon me. Then, I will be able to enter a gateway as soon as I find one. Once I'm in the In Between, I can return to my own era. To Darla. Now, I must—

—drop the pearl into the container in my astonishment. It makes a loud *thunk.*

Yes, you guessed it correctly: I was reading Cory's memory. I had sensed it was him even before he thought of my name.

Cory placed the pearl in the tree, which was revealed only when the limb broke off and nearly killed me.

What did this mean?

Based upon what Cory saw around him in this memory—the clothing people wore, the signs on shops, the horses, and carriages—he was in a year in the late nineteenth century.

Was he still there now?

The concept of time travel really messed with my head. Over a hundred years ago, at the time of this memory, Cory could still be accessing the pearl and working on its powers. The fact that the pearl had been sealed into the current-day tree did not mean he failed to escape the wizard. It only meant he hadn't done so yet. Back in his time period, the pearl was still accessible to him. Since there were no more recent memories of him studying the pearl, he must not have done so yet. He's still working on mastering its powers.

This pearl I'm touching with my hand, sealed for all this time in a tree, is still accessible to my husband. He might be touching it now, right at this moment.

I placed my hand on it again, hoping to connect with him somehow. But I came up empty. Cory, existing over a hundred years before my current time, is still simultaneously existing with me. He has yet to touch the pearl again. But he will.

I was doubtful Ms. LeBoeuf would let me back here to check for more recent memories. Should I try to time travel again via the In Between?

I had been unnaturally lucky to have found him when I traveled back to 1580. It's unlikely I would be fortunate enough to find him again in whatever year he was in. I couldn't go there unless I knew which year. And I wouldn't be able to help him even if I did.

This pearl sitting before me in the plastic container will hopefully be the key to Cory returning to me.

From a hundred-plus years ago.

CHAPTER 6

DWELLING IN THE PAST

It was the second night that Texas Tom had not returned. Cory enjoyed it whenever Tom went away, though the dread of him returning, and not knowing when it would be, always added anxiety. Gone were the days when the older wizard would torture him with painful magic. Cory was an obedient captive now. But he knew if his plans to escape were ever discovered, the punishment would be brutal and possibly fatal.

Cory left his small, spare bedroom with the narrow metal-frame bed and searched the house to make sure Tom was not there. Whenever Tom left for more than a day, he told the servants not to come and sealed the small house with a barrier spell to keep Cory inside. Tom was not in his bedroom, or downstairs in the parlor, the study, dining room, or kitchen.

Predictably, the front and back doors wouldn't open, even when unlocked.

Cory had hoped to investigate the giant pearl, but that would have to wait until the barrier spell was lifted, and Tom was distracted enough that Cory could slip out and visit the Southern live oak tree.

Tom kept his magic books in the study: grimoires, reference materials, and histories. The house in San Marcos, in the year 1891, appeared to be Tom's main residence with the bulk of his possessions. Cory had first met the wizard in the In Between, that world that was neither here nor there, heaven nor earth. The only way a human could survive there was with magic, and Tom brought him back to earth regularly so their bodies wouldn't sustain molecular damage, he said. The wizard could choose any time period to arrive in, and usually, they came to this era. Though, they had visited different eras and cities before.

When they were in San Marcos in the year 1580, Darla had made a brief surprise visit. Cory had been ecstatic ever since, knowing his wife still loved him, and that she had learned the trick of traveling to the In Between, then returning to earth in a different era. It was a sign that events were in motion, and Cory's liberation might be on the horizon.

As soon as they returned to 1891, Cory stole the pearl from Tom's second staff. He needed to find a way to use the pearl's powers to defend himself against Tom's magic.

In the kitchen, he lit the gas stove and boiled water for tea. The icebox held bacon, eggs, cheese, and two dubious-looking pork chops. The block of ice in the top compartment was half melted. Cory wondered why the wizard hadn't used a cooling spell. He hoped he wouldn't be sealed in the house longer than the food lasted.

When his tea was ready, he brought it into the study and searched the bookcases for a tome that might be helpful. There, beside several volumes on alchemy, was an ancient book on crystals, gems, and other precious minerals. Listed in the Table of

Contents were a few chapters on pearls, so he brought it to the wingback chair to read.

He flipped through the book to the first chapter on pearls, then stopped. It was as if this portion of the book was glued together.

The chapters were magically sealed.

Cory was both amazed and appalled. Did Tom actually have the foresight to block Cory from ever studying the secondary staff? Or did prying the pearl from the staff somehow trigger this spell?

He returned to the bookcase and found another book, *The Magickal Properties of Precious Stones*. In here, a chapter on pearls was also sealed. This was maddening.

The only way he'd be able to activate the pearl's powers would be to learn from it intuitively. He would have to use the limited spell-casting he had learned and somehow leverage his innate magical energies.

He had been a promising student of Texas Tom, until the tables turned, and the wizard used Cory as a source of additional power, like a cow to be milked. Tom had, at first, been a savior to a disoriented Cory, thrust unexpectedly into the In Between. He fed Cory with his magically created food and water. He gave him shelter. And he recognized the magic in Cory's genes, offering to make him a protege and teach him the craft.

Cory had only wanted to return home. But Tom had lied, convincing him the gateways couldn't be controlled and would send him back to earth only when they were good and ready. In the meantime, why not learn magic?

Once Cory got a taste of the power magic brings, it was difficult to turn away from it.

The memory was so strong of that first trip to the In Between. Reading a book in his and Darla's small living room, glancing up to rest his eyes, and noticing for the first time an extra door. The one on the left was the bathroom. The one in the middle was the guest bedroom. And the one on the right . . . it was a closet, right? But he didn't remember a closet in this room. However, with all the nonstop work running their bed and breakfast, Cory rarely had time to hang out in the living room. It was perfectly possible that this was a linen closet he never opened and thus it never drew his attention.

But it bothered him. He got up to open it. Just as he turned the knob and pulled the door toward him, nausea swept through him. Not enough to send him running to the bathroom, but unsettling, nevertheless. When he opened the door, he saw only darkness, as if it was the entrance to a mine shaft. Deep, solid-black darkness.

An unseen force seized his body and sucked him into the closet. And into oblivion.

The next thing he knew, he was lying face down in grass. Grass that had no scent. He pushed himself up and saw he was on a flat plain covered with shallow grass that stretched to the horizon in every direction. The sky was a dull white with no sun or clouds visible. There was no wind, no buzzing of insects. It was eerie.

It must be a dream, he had thought.

He was unsure what to do until he saw movement in the distance. Someone or something was moving toward him.

Cory didn't know if he should flee from, or walk toward, the creature.

As it gradually drew closer, it was clearly a human. A man in a cloak and wide-brimmed hat.

It took a while, but he trudged determinedly toward Cory, as if he had been expecting him. The man was old, with a long white beard. He looked like someone dressed as a wizard for Halloween, the spitting image of Gandalf.

Finally, he stopped an arm's length away. His face was gaunt and wrinkled. Beneath his tattered cloak he wore a woolen workman's shirt and trousers, old-fashioned looking ones. He smiled, but his gray eyes remained cold. The man was frail, but emanated strength, enough to kick Cory's butt. He had an air of malevolence to him, though he widened his arms in a gesture of acceptance.

"Welcome to the In Between," he said. "My name is Tom."

"I'm Cory."

"I know."

"Where is this?" Cory asked, trying to hide the anxiety in his voice.

"Oh, the In Between is an alternate plane of existence. Recently deceased souls rest here before they're sent up to the good place or down to the bad place. Living creatures also come here for brief visits, usually to escape danger on earth or wherever they live. Me, I come here for the solitude and to avoid my enemies. I, unfortunately, have many."

He laughed bitterly.

"How did I get here?" Cory asked.

"Via a gateway. Strange creatures with agendas all their own, but in your case, it was by accident. But when it saw what you are, it notified me."

"What do you mean? What I am?"

"Yes. You have magic in you."

"No, I don't."

"You're probably unaware of it," he said, pointing the head of his staff at me. The object affixed to it was the skeleton of a human hand. "Living on earth, it's difficult to see magic, let alone recognize it in yourself."

"What kind of magic do I have?"

"We shall find out. All we know is you have magic in your blood. In your genes, to be precise. Doesn't mean you can do anything with it. It needs to be trained, controlled, and strengthened."

Cory looked at the wizard-like old man and asked the obvious question, "Are you a wizard?"

"No, I'm a cavalry officer. Of course, I'm a wizard," he broke out in rough laughter. "Isn't it obvious from my wardrobe?"

"Well, yes."

"I don't always look like this. I change my appearance whenever I wish. But today, this suited my fancy."

He was correct. He changed his appearance all the time. Not only his style of wardrobe, but also his age. On that day, he appeared to be in his late-seventies. But the first time he and Cory returned to earth, he transformed into a forty-year-old. Once, he appeared as a child, and it truly freaked Cory out when he realized it was Tom. Cory believed that was why he did it, to tease him.

That first day in the In Between, Tom took him to a canvas tent. He said it wasn't real; he'd conjured it with magic. But he claimed he couldn't sleep without the feeling of shelter, though it never rained here or turned to night.

He gave Cory a tin cup filled with water and a wooden bowl containing an unnamed stew with unrecognizable ingredients. All of these, he said, were created with magic.

"There is no sustenance for humans in the In Between," he said. "Nothing here is real, except the creatures. Be careful, some of them are dangerous. Don't wander away from me."

"I want to go home," Cory said.

"It is up to the gateways to decide if they want to bring you home."

That wasn't entirely a lie, since a gateway did bring Cory to the In Between for its own reasons. But Tom wouldn't let them bring him back. It was a while before he realized that.

Cory pulled another volume randomly from the bookcase, an old, dusty tome called *The Power of Ley Lines*. This book didn't have any chapters blocked. After all, ley lines were among the topics Tom gladly taught him. Tom couldn't teach this in the In Between, of course. They had to return to earth to find one of these conduits of natural energy that run underground, criss-crossing the landscape between manmade holy sites or natural cores of elemental power.

It was easy to learn how to draw power from ley lines once you got the hang of it. The hard part was using it to cast spells. Tom taught him only rudimentary spell-casting techniques, to whet his interest and keep him cooperating.

He didn't have to worry about Cory running off when they returned to earth. Each time, he brought Cory to a totally different era than the one Darla and he lived in, where he would have difficulty surviving on his own. Once, they visited San Marcos in 1580, when it was a small garrison town. On another occasion, it was before Europeans had discovered North America. Once, it was before any humans were on the continent at all.

Now, in 1891, when it would be easier for Cory to adapt to the culture, he kept him tethered to his home with magic.

The truth was, there was no point in Cory escaping if he couldn't return to Darla.

Before long, Tom admitted Cory wouldn't be freed until his "education had reached a sufficient level." What this level was, he never said.

Cory finally realized he would never learn to be an accomplished witch or wizard under Tom. The lessons focused more on harvesting energy from the elements of earth, water, fire, air, and spirit. The intention was to teach Cory how to soak up power.

Power that Tom then drained from him to supplement his own. Cory was livestock, being fattened for Tom's nourishment.

Cory did not participate in this passively. The first time he resisted in a fit of anger, he tackled Tom and pummeled him with his fists.

But only for a few seconds before the crippling pain of a hundred migraines pushed Cory into unconsciousness.

In another incident, after Cory was filled with energy from a ley line, he tried to repel Tom with a simple version of a warding spell.

The wizard deflected it back into Cory's face, rendering him deaf and blind for several horrifying hours.

Finally, Tom dropped the pretense of training Cory. He simply forced him to absorb magical energy before draining it from him.

Cory didn't know what Tom was doing with the energy he stole. He sensed the wizard was storing it to be used later in massive magic attacks.

"You've grown to hate me, my dear Cory," Tom had said to him, smiling in his middle-aged, pudgy face. "But someday, you'll be grateful you could serve me like this. Because when I rule, I'll look upon you kindly and grant you favors."

Cory didn't know what megalomaniacal goals Tom had, and whom exactly he planned to rule. But Cory doubted the promise of special treatment.

In fact, he believed that when Cory outlived his usefulness to the wizard, he would no longer be allowed to live.

The front door opened and slammed shut. Cory jumped in his chair. But he refused to run upstairs and hide in his room. He propped up his feet on the ottoman and continued flipping through the book.

Tom walked past the study with the afternoon paper under his arm. He stopped when he saw Cory inside.

"Have you been a good boy while I was gone?" Tom asked. His voice had the slightest softness hinting at a Southern drawl, but it wasn't pleasant. It always carried a touch of malice.

"Of course. And where have you been?"

"One should not ask one's master such a direct, impertinent question. But to answer you, I was conducting business. Someone has to pay the bills around here, you know."

Whenever they showed up in a new time period, Tom always brought a considerable amount of money. Usually, it was in the form of gold, because of the constant evolution of currency over time. Our modern money didn't look much like the greenbacks of 1891.

When you used the In Between and gateways to deliver you to another time in history, you could only bring what you could carry. This often involved a very awkward and dangerous period of trading the gold for the local currency and then buying the clothing of the era. Next, you scrambled to find lodging. The late nineteenth century was a regular stop for Tom, so he maintained his house and a suitable wardrobe, always ready for him to drop in from another time.

They had never traveled to a time in the future. Cory didn't know if it was even possible, though he suspected it was. The concept frightened him.

Tom had shaved his beard while he was gone. Today, he looked like a man in his fifties, which Cory believed was his true age.

Tom stared at Cory's book.

"I would like to learn more magic," Cory said.

"In due time. I need you to build up your power again. I have big plans, Cory. But they will surely involve some hostilities."

"Violence?"

"Of the magical kind. And if we prevail, we won't have to be on the move all the time. We'll be able to stay in San Marcos in our native time period. And I'll be the one running the entire show."

Mrs. McHugh showed up not long afterwards and cooked them a chicken dinner. Afterwards, Tom sent Cory out to the tobacconist for Tom's favorite brand of cigar.

"I've lengthened your leash, but you're still wearing one. Remember that," Tom warned.

Cory hurried to the shop. In modern times, the space was a small ice cream store serving tourists. He purchased the box of cigars. On the way back home, he stopped by the park.

No one was around in the darkness. He crawled into the elbow of one of the live oak's giant limbs and reached a hand into the knothole. Pushing aside the concealing cover of Spanish moss, he held the pearl in his hand.

At this point in his training, he was skilled at finding and extracting energy from a variety of natural sources. He just wasn't good at doing much with it.

From the pearl, he absorbed a benevolent energy. It was protective and healing. Like all energy, it made him feel stronger, but this was different. He felt safer, too.

As the minutes ticked by on his pocket watch, he hid the pearl again and hurried home. Hopefully, there would be another opportunity to visit the pearl again soon.

When he returned home, Tom called out and said he was in the study.

Cory walked through the darkened foyer toward the open door of the study, bright with light from the gas jets on the wall.

The wingback chair was empty. Cory entered the room to hand the cigar box to Tom at his desk.

Tom was not at his desk.

The blow hit Cory on the back of his head and neck with a loud *crack* of wood on flesh.

Cory fell to the floor, but his anger overcame his pain, and he sprang back up to attack Tom in the darkened hallway.

But a powerful wind threw Cory against the opposite wall, almost knocking the wind out of him. He stayed suspended there like a bug on flypaper. All four limbs were paralyzed.

"You stole the pearl from my staff!" Tom screamed and hit him with the staff again, the one that used to hold the pearl. "I know it was you."

"No," Cory whispered through a bloody mouth.

"Tell me where you put it, or I will kill you."

"A sorcerer bought it from me. He knew you had this staff."

"You're a liar," Tom said, spittle spraying Cory's battered face. "I'll make you tell me where it is."

While Cory remained on the wall, Tom waved his hands and silently intoned a spell. Cory recognized it as a truth-telling spell. He conjured up his own spell, a simple one that strengthened the concentration. The energy he had received from the pearl enhanced it.

He steeled his mind as Tom's spell tried and failed to penetrate it. Cory made his face slacken, pretending the spell had worked.

"Where is the pearl?" Tom demanded.

"A sorcerer has it," Cory said in a monotone voice. "I don't know his name. He said he is staying at a small inn."

Tom narrowed his eyes in suspicion. "I should torture you to make sure you're telling the truth."

But he didn't. He waved a hand, and Cory fell to the floor. He remained there until Tom left the room.

Cory suspected Tom would ask again where the pearl was, but he vowed not to tell him. For he knew the pearl might be his only way to escape his servitude alive.

CHAPTER 7

YOUR WILDEST DREAMS

When I get summoned to a Memory Guild meeting, it's a summons. Not an invitation. Actually, it's more akin to a kidnapping. I had just finished up in my bathroom when I found myself soaring over a landscape covered with forests. Yes, I was astral traveling to the meeting, though I was freaking out about the timing right after my potty break. In truth, even if I had still been sitting on the throne, my body would have stayed there while my spirit-self would show up at the meeting all buttoned, zipped, and presentable. But still, I felt as if my privacy had been invaded.

This trip was as much of a travelogue as they usually are. I flew over a pristine Florida and North America, where forests and savannas still flourished before humankind came along to ruin them. It was an inspiring experience, seeing the majesty of nature without highways and subdivisions.

Then, with no transition, I stood in the torch-lit stone chamber where our virtual meetings were always held. Including me, ten of us stood on the floor, sat in our wheelchair, or perched upon the wall, facing each other.

"I called this meeting to discuss some recent developments," Dr. Noordlun said. "I'll get directly to the point. The equilibrium of magic has been disrupted in San Marcos, and the Memory Guild, unfortunately, cannot remain uninvolved."

Everyone gave me a side-wise stare. Hey, it's not my fault!

"As you probably all know, Darla was very nearly killed by a limb that fell from the live oak tree known as Old Courage. A spiritualist sitting right beside her was crushed. Gloria communed with a spirit in the tree who claimed magic was involved, and that it was intended to kill Darla, as well. Of course, we reported this to the Magic Guild, and, in typical fashion, they have been slow in identifying the culprit."

"They must have suspicions," I said.

"Indeed. Arch Mage Bob is obsessed with his biggest threat, the wizard known as Texas Tom. He's the one holding Darla's husband captive. Bob believes Darla was targeted to keep her from helping her husband escape."

I laughed mockingly. "If I could do that, I would have done so ages ago."

"Right." Dr. Noordlun nodded. "Nonetheless, this Texas Tom is emerging as a major threat to the Magic Guild. Its members are reporting the disrupted equilibrium and strange interferences with their routine spells."

"I can confirm that," said Diana, our astral witch, and a member of both guilds. "The energy I get from the stars has been blocked sometimes. It's a miracle I could get you all here today safely."

Not something I wanted to hear when I still had to travel home the same way.

"Summer, do you want to share your observations?" Dr. Noordlun asked.

"Something is odd with the trees and the more advanced bushes of the understory," she said. "The woods don't care about rivalries between wizards. But something has gotten them aroused more than I've ever witnessed in my life. And I've been alive for two hundred years."

"Wait a minute," I interrupted. "What did you just say? You've been alive for two centuries? Are you a vampire?"

"A vampire would be undead, not alive," Diego corrected.

Summer grinned. "You didn't know I'm part elf?"

"I guess I'm not surprised. But no one told me."

"Because you're the new kid," Archibald said.

I glared at him.

"My Elven blood is what enables me to be a wood-speaker and commune with trees," Summer said. "I don't live in the forest, of course. I live in a one-bedroom condo on Córdoba Street. Still, the trees know I'm an elf, and they trust me."

In the spirit of diversity, being a member of a magical race shouldn't matter. But it did right now.

"The trees in the city and countryside are all buzzing with energy," Summer continued. "As I told you before, trees within a given area communicate, even between species. They warn each other of parasitic insects and even help protect each other from dangerous weather. But this is different."

"Please explain," Dr. Noordlun said.

"I can't assign an emotion to what's going on in the trees— alarm or anger or fear—but it's similar to what happens when a forest faces a threat. But there's also something empowering about it, as if they're rallying together."

"This makes no sense," I muttered.

"My intuition is they feel the threat from the disruption of the magic and the seeping in of evil magic," Summer said. "Yet, at the same time, when the giant pearl was discovered and jostled inside Old Courage, the benevolent magic in the pearl spread throughout the tree and to her nearby brethren. And it kept spreading to other trees."

"What does that mean?" I asked. "What will it do to the trees?"

"Give them strength. Cure disease. I don't know what else to expect."

"Team, we can't wait to see what happens," Dr. Noordlun said. "It is not our purview to manage the world of magic. But we can do everything in our powers to protect Darla. Whoever or whatever tried to kill her is still out there and might try again."

That made me feel special. But not in a nice way.

"Am I free to use our team's abilities to help me track down the murderer?" I asked Dr. Noordlun. "Since the Magic Guild isn't providing much help."

"Certainly. You seem to take pleasure in detective work."

"Oh, no. There is no pleasure in it. That, I can assure you."

WHEN I RETURNED TO MY COTTAGE, I REJOINED MY corporeal body as it was just leaving the bathroom.

Cervantes sat on my bed, staring strangely at me. He knew something odd had happened. He meowed, sounding like, "*no*."

"No, it's not normal," I said to him.

It was time to banish thoughts of magic and the occult from my mind and concentrate on the details of running my inn.

Bella, the housekeeper, had the day off. I had a part-time housekeeper who occasionally filled in for Bella, but my occupancy rate was too low to afford her at the moment. So, it was up to the innkeeper herself to grab a mop and vacuum cleaner. And her daughter.

I found Sophie in the kitchen, only halfway through cleaning up after breakfast. She stood beside the counter, her hand on an unmoving sponge, her face lost in thought.

"Are we still sleepy this morning?" I asked.

Sophie didn't answer. A faint smile appeared as her eyes stared at an imaginary distant object.

"Earth to Sophie, do you hear me?"

"Yes, Mom," she said in a sleepy voice. "I was daydreaming."

"Please finish up in here, then I need your help to turn over the Honeymoon Suite. We have guests arriving today, and I also need to take care of two-oh-one."

"Will do."

She remained unmoving.

"Time's a wasting," I said.

She took a deep breath and tore her gaze from its distant focus, turning toward the counter. She moved the sponge in a lazy circle.

Sophie once had problems with a substance-use disorder. She went through a successful recovery. But, as a mom, I was immediately fearful that she had relapsed. I'd never seen her behaving like this before.

I approached and touched her shoulder, looking closely at her eyes. They didn't appear stoned at all.

They looked, well, in love.

"Is there a new man in your life?" I asked.

She shook her head no. "In my dreams. I know this sounds weird, but I dreamed of a man last night, a gorgeous hunk about my age. Tall and broad shouldered, thick blond hair that hung below his jawline. Stunning green eyes. He was someone I felt I knew for all my life, and he was beckoning for me to come to him, to be hugged and to rest my head against his perfect pecs."

"My word. He does sound attractive."

"I moved toward him in the dream, but I never touched him," Sophie continued. "It's left me feeling haunted by him all day."

"It's not unusual to have a dream that stays with you,"

"It seemed real, though, not like a dream. And today I feel so empty. I can't stop thinking about him. I miss him."

I was relieved Sophie wasn't using again, but as I was completely in the mundane real world today, I had little patience for her subconscious getting in the way of her work.

"Do you need some more coffee? There's a lot of work to be done. I never promised you working in an inn would be romantic."

"I'm sorry, Mom. I'll snap out of it shortly."

She moved the sponge a bit more deliberately, as if she actually wanted to clean the crumbs from the counter. I turned away and went to the workroom in the back of the building facing the alley. This was where we did the laundry and stored supplies. I put fresh linens and towels in the cart and rolled it to the elevator.

Never forget how strenuous it is for a housekeeper to turn over your room. Changing the sheets, remaking the bed, vacuuming, dusting, cleaning every nook and cranny in the bathroom. Plus, doing it as quickly as possible. It took me way longer in 201 than it should have. I have great sympathy for housekeepers in larger hotels who have to do dozens of rooms each day. Tip your housekeepers, people!

When I returned downstairs, I took a peek in the Honeymoon Suite. Sophie had only started in here. She wasn't moving much faster than she had in the kitchen. I was beginning to worry about her.

I had promised Mom help in unloading a new batch of junk from her SUV. I didn't want to send Miss Enchanted Princess to do it in her current state, so I hopped on my motor scooter and made the quick trip through Old Town to the Victorian-era neighborhood of our family home.

Of course, my childhood home was only recognizable from the outside, with its turrets and gingerbread accents along the roof lines. Inside, it had been transformed into Mom's antiques store, or, more precisely, her junk depository. Where some pieces were sold, more than that were added regularly, and space for humans rapidly diminished.

An old Ford sat by the curb in front of the house. Detective Billy Reyna was making his nearly daily visit. I drove the scooter up the drive beside the house and parked it by the back door to the kitchen.

"Will you stop your pouting?" Mom said to Billy when I walked inside.

"But you *always* have scones when I visit," Billy said. "Freshly baked, enticingly delicious. Sometimes, I like to believe you make them just for me."

Billy stood beside the stove, empty of baking sheets, instead of his usual seat at the kitchen table in front of a mug of coffee.

"I told you, I've been too busy this morning," Mom said. "Distracted. If you have an hour to wait, I could whip up a batch right now."

Oh, no. Mom had a strange look in her eyes. A look just like Sophie's.

"Nah, I got a bunch of calls to make," Billy said. "Since you don't have any merchandise you think is hot, I'm going to move on. I'll check back in tomorrow. At nine-thirty." He held out his wrist and tapped his watch. "On the dot. Oh, hi, Darla."

"Hi, Billy. How are you?"

"Hungry," he said as he stepped out the door.

"I don't know what got into me," Mom said. "My daily routine has just fallen by the wayside. I haven't even opened the store yet."

"That's okay. Antiques shops open late."

I studied her as she sat at the table, an empty mug near her hands. She stared past me, through the window, out at some distant cloud.

"Are you feeling okay, Mom?"

"I feel wonderful." She smiled beguilingly.

"You didn't happen to have a strange dream last night, did you?"

"Funny you ask. I had a most remarkable dream. About a remarkable man."

Oh, boy. "Tell me about it."

She sat up in her chair and clasped her hands beneath her chin.

"In my dream, a man walked into the store, the most handsome man I've ever seen. He was tall, like your father, but much more muscular. Short, gray hair, gray eyes. A chiseled chin. He looked like a movie star. He told me he'd finally come for me, and he held out his arms for a hug. I got up from the counter and walked toward him, but it was like I was wading through water, and I could barely move. I wanted so badly for him to hug me, and to rest my head upon his massive chest. But I never reached him. I've been haunted by this dream all morning."

"I think we have a problem," I said. I explained Sophie's suspiciously similar dream, though with a different dreamboat man matching her ideal.

"Oh," Mom said, embarrassed. "That's odd."

I snorted. "You think so? Is sorcery at work here?"

"I was thinking my dream was a premonition of finding the new love of my life. Hoping it was."

"Same with Sophie. Remember, I told you about the wizard who is holding Cory captive? Arch Mage Bob has worried this wizard is coming to take over the Magic Guild and rule San Marcos. Maybe rule witches everywhere. Strange things are afoot in town. The equilibrium of magic has been disrupted."

She had already heard about the death of Mrs. Ogglethwarp. Now, I broke the news that magic had been involved, and I was an intended target.

"Good lord!" she said, her dreamy expression fading fast. "Who would want to kill you?"

"Well, there have been a few individuals in recent times who wanted to. I know, because they actually tried. But they're out of the picture now."

Or were they? Esmerelda had been a sorceress and was now serving time in state prison. She didn't have the power to kill me with magic, nor the resources to hire someone to do it. Another threat to my life was in the county jail awaiting trial. She had unsuccessfully tried to kill several members of the Memory Guild. She probably still wanted to. But she'd lost access to the demon who had supplied her power. A third person, werewolf actually, who had meant to take me out, was taken out himself.

So, no, I couldn't think of anyone else who would want the demise of Darla.

"Mom, does it feel like your dream was influenced by magic?"

"No. And what would be the point? To get me to fall in love with the magician?"

"Basically, yes. To be in thrall to him so he can manipulate you."

"Let me think for a moment. There might be a spell I can use to detect the magic."

She pursed her lips and furrowed her brow. I poured coffee for her and myself, then took a seat at the table. I stared out the window at the backyard. An oak tree stood near the detached garage, a much younger and smaller tree than Old Courage. A swing I had enjoyed as a kid still hung from the largest bough. The chains supporting the swing had been partially absorbed into the bough where they wrapped around it. The things that restrict us can be overcome even if they can't be broken.

Mom cleared her throat. Against the light coming through the window, her frizzy poof of black dyed hair looked electrified. Her expression was still dreamy, but more lucid than before.

"The spell affected both Sophie and me in different locations. Is he going after members of our family or all the witches in San Marcos?"

"Diana, from my guild, has had problems accessing astral energy, but she didn't say anything about a lust dream."

"It wasn't lust," Mom said. "It was romantic wish fulfillment."

"Whatever."

"I need to know if he's targeting our family, using a hair or something with our DNA. If he's broadcasting his spell to all the witches in town, then it would take tons of power. Where is he getting it?"

"No offense but targeting you and Sophie would only serve to scare me," I said. "You two aren't the ones he needs to fight if he wants to take over in San Marcos, so he must enchant all the witches."

"Then why did he try to kill you with the tree?"

"I'm not convinced the wizard did it."

"Okay, then we'll assume he's going after all the witches in town. I have a spell that can identify if energy that strong was broadcast over the city. I'll be back."

She left the kitchen, and the stairs creaked as she trudged up them. I assumed she was fetching some ingredients from her apothecary cabinet in the sewing room turned magic room on the third floor.

When she returned, she had several vials, a painted tin, and a blank piece of parchment. I watched as she boiled water in a small pot and added an assortment of unrecognizable herbs and dried flowers to it, as well as tiny bones from the tin.

She lit some candles placed on the stove around the pot with her witch's brew. When the water came to a full boil, she stirred it with deliberate circular motions while chanting something in Latin. I picked up only a few words here and there, courtesy of my Catholic high school education.

Finally, she dipped the strip of parchment into the brew, pulled it out, and held it aloft while she continued to chant.

The paper turned bright red.

"It's like a pregnancy test for magic," I said under my breath.

"Yes, an immense amount of magic energy is in the air. Some witches can sense it intuitively, but I need this potion to help me identify it."

"So, how do we find out who's casting the spell?" I asked.

"My potion isn't sophisticated enough to identify the magician. But really, how many witches have the power to send the spell across an entire city? And to tap into each witch's mind to create an image of himself they would fall in love with? This is big-time magic, Darla. I'm thinking ley lines."

"What do you mean?"

"The wizard would need to harvest the energy of a ley line to create a spell this massive."

"There's one in San Marcos?"

"There is. It crosses beneath the cathedral. In one direction, it heads inland at an angle. In the other, it heads out to sea."

I pulled up a map of the city on my phone.

"Show me where it runs."

"This isn't exact," Mom said. "It's a rough guess from my memory."

Her finger traced a diagonal line across my phone screen, intersecting the cathedral in the center. I zoomed in after she finished.

The section of the line heading toward the sea crossed through a tiny park.

The one where Old Courage stood.

CHAPTER 8

SPELLBOUND

I carried Cervantes into the front parlor and placed the sleek black cat atop the fireplace mantel. I needed to speak with Archibald and didn't have the ridiculous amount of patience required to rouse him from his stony slumber. This called for the heavy artillery.

Cervantes was pleased, his tail sticking straight up, because this was his favorite game. He crouched, leaned over the edge of the mantel, and smacked the gargoyle beneath it with his right front paw.

Then he hit him with his left. He picked up the pace, alternating between paws like a boxer with a punching bag.

"Will you get this cursed creature away from me?" Archibald whined, as he animated from stone to a living creature. "You know how he torments me."

"Relax. He can't hurt you. You're a gargoyle, for Pete's sake."

"He's a little monster, and I swear the Devil himself is inside him."

"Maybe if you didn't ignore me when I needed your attention, I wouldn't have to sic Cervantes on you."

"Very well. You've made your point. Now, why did you wake me?"

"I have a question about ley lines. Do you know anything about them?"

"Electro-magnetic lines running through the earth. Some humans claim they connect important man-made edifices, such as cathedrals. The truth is, they connect natural deposits of earth energy. The humans came along, sensed these deposits, and built their temples there."

"Who can I speak to with local knowledge of them?"

"Dr. Noordlun, of course. If you can worm your way into his schedule. And Diana knows a thing or two about ley lines. You should speak with her."

I thanked Archibald, who promptly calcified back to stone. I texted Diana, requesting a few moments of her time, but she didn't respond. She's usually very good at electronic communications etiquette.

I tried her again an hour later. Still no response. After getting lost in chores, I checked my phone, worried now about her. So, I called. It went straight to voicemail.

My last resort was to contact her via telepathy. Even if she didn't have the ability, my telepathy should be enough to connect us, especially since she had paranormal in her blood.

Diana, it's Darla. Can you hear me? I asked with my mind.

I repeated this several times before I received a response.

Darla?

Yes. Are you all right, Diana?

No. Please help me, her voice said weakly in my mind.

Should I call an ambulance?

No, no. It's magical. I need a little help.

I texted Sophie, who was somewhere on the property, to take care of things while I left to help a friend. Hopping into my car, I drove to the astral witch's home outside of the city.

It was an older home, right at the edge of salt marshes. She had a giant deck on pilings facing the creeks, pockets of water, and thick spartina grass that stretched seemingly forever to the Intracoastal Waterway.

I ran up to her front porch, dodging the wind chimes hanging everywhere. The doorbell and my pounding on the door didn't summon her. So, I tried the door and found it unlocked.

"Diana? Where are you?"

No answer.

I crept through the living and dining rooms. The home was small and older, originally a fisherman's house, but she had added larger windows and several skylights, improving the views of the marsh and flooding the home with natural lighting.

But it felt creepy since I knew something was wrong.

"Diana?"

"I'm in my bedroom."

I found the master bedroom at the rear of the house, but I didn't see her in there.

Until I looked up. She was suspended on the ceiling, her back, arms, and legs touching the plaster above her bed, like a human-shaped ceiling fan. And she was naked.

"This is more embarrassing than you can imagine," she said.

Diana was middle-aged like me, but stout and sturdy, unlike me. Gravity was not flattering some of her features right now.

"How can I help you?" I asked.

"Just peel me off here, so I'll land on the bed. The magic holding me isn't that strong, but I'm totally helpless against it."

I kicked off my shoes and climbed onto the bed

"My legs first," she said.

I grabbed her left calf and ankle and pulled. Her leg didn't move.

"Harder," she said.

I tried again, afraid that I'd tear her skin, but as I increased my pull, the leg finally popped free. Then, I did the same to her right leg.

Her legs dangled perpendicular to the ceiling, while her back, arms, and head remained attached to it.

Next, I hugged her legs and pulled.

I was not enjoying this one bit.

Her pelvis broke free, and soon her back detached, as well. She remained hanging by her arms and shoulders, looking like she'd been crucified. She swung her body back and forth and popped free.

She landed feet-first on the bed and fell onto her back. The bouncing mattress trampolined me off it, depositing me on the floor on my butt.

"How the heck did that happen?" I asked.

"What a nightmare. It actually began with a dream, a very naughty one, about a ravishingly handsome man. Believe me when I say I don't have those kinds of dreams anymore."

"Did he look like your ideal man?"

"Yes, the kind of man I dreamed about when I was a teenager and a young woman. But he was around my current age. It was a powerful dream, if you get what I mean. You know how sometimes when you're dreaming, you're aware it's a dream even while you're in the thick of it?"

"Sure."

"That was the case this morning, and I also knew magic was involved. Someone was turning me into a helpless admirer. I resisted and tried to wake myself up."

"What happened when you resisted?" I asked, handing her a bathrobe.

"You saw what happened." She pointed to the ceiling. "I've been stuck up there since five this morning."

"What does this magician want to do, other than make you horny? A similar thing happened to my daughter and mother."

"He's attempting to subjugate the magic folk of San Marcos. He doesn't have the ability to enslave us all right now, but he's softening our resistance, getting inside our heads, finding our fantasies and weaknesses. I can only assume that once he's able to, he'll command us to do things, like fight his enemies. Fortunately, the best he can do now is glue me to the ceiling."

"He's Texas Tom, right?"

"It has to be. Arch Mage Bob instructed the Magic Guild to be on the lookout for Tom, but none of us have known what to do. Now, he's actually making moves against us."

"Bob was also supposed to find out who tried to kill me," I said. "But I haven't heard a word from him. It's only logical that Texas Tom did it. But I don't know why he would, other than the fact he's holding my husband captive. It's not as if I pose a threat to rescue him. I don't even know where or when they are. It is an odd way for a wizard as powerful as he to try to kill me. Unless, like you said, it's because he's too far away to use more powerful magic. Namely, more than a hundred years away."

"His intentions might be to hurt your husband. By killing you, he would destroy your husband's hope. Your husband would be plunged into despair, so the wizard could more fully control him."

That would be incredibly cruel. But it made sense. If Cory was being harvested for energy, Tom might as well make him as docile as the vegetables in a garden.

I pushed the dark thoughts away and returned to the problem at hand.

"The reason I was trying to reach you is Archibald says you know a lot about ley lines."

"Yes, of course. I work with them all the time."

"Is it true Texas Tom would need the power taken from a ley line to be able to broadcast such a wide spell from afar?"

"That's what I assumed," Diana said. "There might also be black-magic methods of gathering such power, but let's hope he isn't going down that road."

"I'm told there's a ley line running right through San Marcos and beneath the park where Old Courage stands?"

Diana smiled. "I forgot the tree is on top of the line. It surely has benefitted from the power. But all the serious witches in town know of this ley line and many have drunk from it. I am told it is weaker today than in previous eras."

"Why? Is it getting tapped out from overuse?"

"Partly that. Also, because of the general degradation of the environment."

"Can this ley line help us monitor Texas Tom?" I asked. "I mean, even if he's far from the city, he could be tapping into the same line. If we put our finger on the pulse here, can we tell if something big is happening to it further down the line, or in an earlier time period?"

"I might be able to. And Dr. Noordlun, as an energy-speaker, can."

"Maybe we can even determine where Texas Tom is."

"You could be right. But don't get your hopes too high."

"What else do we have other than desperate hopes?"

Diana laughed bitterly. Her eyes were still slightly glazed from her dream attack, but she acted as if she had largely recovered.

"We need to tell Arch Mage Bob," she said.

"I don't need his permission to go after the guy who's trying to kill me."

"Not necessarily his permission. He'll just want to be in the loop. After all, he's the general of our army."

"An army that has barely put up a fight."

Diana was reluctant to visit Bob without an invitation, but I insisted she get in the car with me. Since she was a member of the Magic Guild, as well as the Memory Guild, Arch Mage Bob was as much an authority figure to her as was Dr. Noordlun. But to me, Bob was just Bob. Sometimes a foil, sometimes an ally. I could usually find him at the surf shop he owned, or on the beach. If he was elsewhere today, we'd simply come back later.

I pulled into the employee parking lot behind his shop on A1A, the beach road. Thankfully, his open-top jeep, outfitted for driving on the sand, was there.

"We're here to see Bob," I told the pimply faced young man behind the counter.

"He's busy," the punk said, after sizing us up and lumping us in with his mom.

"This is important," I said, and started walking through the rows of T-shirts and board shorts.

"Wait, you can't just go back there!"

"Watch me," I said.

Diana trailed behind me timidly.

The kid raced from behind the counter to cut me off. As if he could really stop me.

But I did stop when an enraged roar came from behind the office door past the racks of surfboards.

A scream followed. I pushed myself forward while the kid faded back toward the front counter.

I pushed open the door that said, "Employees Only."

A lanky man in his early thirties, with long blond hair and a deep tan, was strangling Arch Mage Bob from behind as Bob sat in a chair. The man was Aaron, Bob's top assistant and a well-known custom board maker. He was also pretty good looking, if you're into the surfer aesthetic.

At the moment, however, he was foaming at the mouth like a rabid dog. And Bob, a strong, heavyset dude, was turning blue as his windpipe was crushed.

Diana gasped behind me.

"You'd better cast a spell to help him," I said, wondering why Bob's magic hadn't protected him.

I had no magic myself, but I had two hands and a nasty disposition when I needed one. The nearest potential weapon was a paddle for a paddle-board. I slammed Aaron across the back of his head with all my might. Once, twice.

It was an expensive paddle, made with carbon for the lightest possible weight. In other words, it was useless for bashing in someone's head.

I dropped it and glanced at the nearby workbench. No way was I going to use a blade of any sort on this guy.

Bob gurgled as his brain reached the end of its oxygen. Diana mumbled an incantation but hadn't cast a spell yet.

I grabbed the nearest object, a two-handed belt sander. It seemed nearly as heavy as me. Holding it above my head with both hands, I charged Aaron, and brought the big block of metal down on his golden locks.

Aaron dropped like a tree and lay unmoving next to the chair where Bob slumped.

"I hope I didn't hurt him too much," I said, relieved to see Aaron's chest rising and falling with regular breathing.

"I'm giving you a freeing spell to help you breathe," Diana said to Bob.

He wheezed and gulped in air. Soon, his face went from blue to purple, and then to red, which was pretty much the normal color for him.

"I can't believe it," he said in a croak. "He just went nuts, like he was on bath salts or something."

"Is Aaron a witch?" I asked.

"A lower-level wizard."

"He was enchanted by Texas Tom."

I described the spell that was invading witches' dreams. Obviously, it had a different effect on Aaron. Or it could have been a different spell. But the objective was the same.

"He's attacking the Magic Guild from within," I said. He's far away now, but he's trying to soften your resistance before he shows up in town."

Bob shook his head and coughed. "He'll have a surprise when we start fighting back."

"And when would that be?"

"You can stay out of our business, dude," he said, glaring at me.

"I have two witches in my family who were both affected by a dream attack. And, in case you've forgotten, I was almost murdered. So, no, I'm not going to stay out of it."

"The situation is a lot more complicated than you think," he said. "You wouldn't understand."

"Then, you need to explain it to me."

He sighed. And started coughing again.

CHAPTER 9

THE LAY OF THE LEY LINES

"What exactly is the complication?" I asked.

"Business," Bob said. "I've got to make a living, you know. Being a witch doesn't bring in the big bucks these days. Like, what the guild pays me as Arch Mage is a joke, dude."

"I know. You've got this." I gestured at the popular surf shop around me. "And your paddle-sports rentals. I had the impression you're doing just fine."

"Yeah. Until my ex cleaned me out. So, I always have my eye open for new business opportunities."

"Sure. Why not?"

"Right. And, like, Texas Tom and I invested in a little scheme a while back."

"Wait. I'm sorry, you and an evil wizard were business partners?"

"This was before he was evil. He was only immoral at the time."

"Of course. But what does this have to do with the fact he's trying to take over the Magic Guild and enslave all the magicians?"

"Nothing. I mean, except he lost a bunch of money in our little venture. And I beat him in Texas Hold 'Em poker, and that's what he's famous for. So, he's kind of ticked off about that, too."

"Are you saying he wants to take over the city to get his money back?"

"No. He wants to rule the city because he's evil, and every evil wizard wants to rule a city. It's part of the package."

"Then who cares about your old business dealings?"

"Well, the Feds might. We, like, maybe broke some rules the Security and Exchange Commission might be kinda mad about."

"What did you do?"

"Have you heard of multi-level marketing?"

"You mean when you make a bunch of people sell your products to their friends out of the trunks of their cars?"

"Yeah, basically. You get your friends to join and pay you a membership fee, then buy a bunch of products, which they will try to sell to their friends. But they have to get *their* friends to sign up, pay the membership fee, and buy product. Your friends get to keep some of the money they earned from their friends, but most of it goes to you. Then, your friends' friends do the same with their friends."

"It sounds more like a pyramid scheme to me," I said.

"It sounded like that to the SEC, too. And they went after us."

"What were you selling? Just curious, don't want to buy any of it."

"Skin moisturizers. And my garage is packed full of them."

"I can't believe a wizard and a mage were selling skin moisturizers."

"It's living the American Dream, dude."

I shook my head. "It sounds too complicated."

"Exactly! That's how you're supposed to get rich, while everyone else is hosed. But remember, I said there were complications."

"You did."

"Like Texas Tom threatening to report me to the Feds."

"He's blackmailing you?"

"Maybe."

"But you need to fight him. You need to protect the witches and wizards of San Marcos. And you need to help me free my husband."

"Totally, dude."

"But you're not."

"I will for sure. If I find the right way to do it."

"Are you crazy? Don't you realize how immense the stakes are?"

"Dude, of course I do. Big fines. Maybe some jail time."

"No! The enslavement of all the magic folk in this city! You, Diana, my mother, and daughter. You told me before that Tom's ambitions are even greater than that, and he wants to be godlike in his powers."

"For sure. He's a determined dude. Sometimes, it's best to not fight bad hombres like him."

"You're the leader of the Magic Guild," Diana spoke up. "We depend on you to protect us."

"There are smarter ways to protect you than fighting and making Tom even madder."

Diana and I both let out exasperated sighs.

"Come on," I said to her. "We have better things to do. Oh, and Bob? I think Aaron needs an ambulance or a really good healing spell."

As we walked through the parking lot, Diana asked me what we should do.

"Let's check out the ley line," I said. "We need to find out if it can lead us to Texas Tom."

We left the beach and went over the Bridge of Memories into the center of town. I found a parking spot along Bayfront Avenue, and we crossed the street to the park where Old Courage stood.

"What makes this spot special," Diana said, "is more than the major ley line that passes through. It's the convergence of a minor ley line, too. See if you can find the convergence point."

"Me? I'm not a witch."

"Come on, Darla. You have paranormal abilities and are sensitive to psychic energy. You, too, should be able to sense electromagnetic energy."

I felt nothing at all at the moment, but I tried to clear all the daily trivia cluttering my brain. I focused inward and opened up my senses like I do when searching for memories on an object.

Sure enough, a thrumming of power in the earth vibrated beneath my feet.

Walking in widening concentric circles, I held out my arms, palms facing downward, and searched for a change in the power I was sensing.

I found it only about ten feet away from Old Courage: a massive surge in energy below me. In fact, a tingling immersed my feet and traveled up my legs. If I moved only a foot or two in any direction, the sensation lessened.

"Right here?" I asked, tapping my foot at the point of maximum power.

"You did it," Diana said, beaming.

"Right at the heart of Old Courage's root system. I wonder if this is why she's lived so long."

"I wouldn't be surprised."

I looked around to make sure no tourists were nearby.

"Can you tap into the ley lines and see if anyone else has been doing the same?" I asked.

"Remember, we magic folk derive energy from ley lines all the time. I won't be able to detect all those interactions. But hopefully, I can tell if there has been a major energy extraction. Give me some time to cast a spell to assist me."

I stepped away, into the shade of Old Courage, while Diana used a small stick she found to scratch a magic circle on the ground.

It was much cooler in the shade and felt a world apart. As a kid, I spent countless hours playing around the oak behind our house, not only using the swing, but climbing in the branches and building a rudimentary tree house with my sister. When I was younger, I would sit at the base of the tree and play with dolls and figurines, imagining they lived inside the tree where there was an entire city in miniature.

Today, I enjoyed being sheltered by Old Courage, smelling the bark and the herbaceous Spanish moss against the slightly briny scent coming from the bay and nearby ocean. Squirrels cavorted in the branches above me. Surely, many families of them could live among the enormous network of limbs and branches. A mockingbird sang a complex song a few branches above me. A trail of tiny ants streamed up and down the lower trunk from their ant hills on the sandy ground. It was a soothing world under here. And, somehow, I felt as if the tree knew I was here and welcomed me. The tree was the mother of an entire ecosystem.

Diana was on her knees at the center of her magic circle, her arms outstretched. With luck, any passersby would assume she was doing yoga, not casting a magic spell. Now, she bent at the waist with her palms pressed to the ground. Her lips moved with her incantations.

She looked up and caught my eye, beckoning me over. Just before I reached the circle, her raised hand stopped me before I broke it.

"There have been deep extractions of energy from the ley lines," she said. "Not at a distant point along the major line, but right here where it intersects with the minor one."

"But not in our current time. When I read the pearl Cory had touched, I picked up visual information that he was in San Marcos in the nineteenth century. I don't know what year. I can't wrap my mind around the notion that the wizard was right here in this spot, but over a hundred years ago, casting magic that affects us today."

"Yes, it's crazy. Time is not a line moving from left to right. It's more like layers, as you'd find in an archeological dig. Where we stand today exists now at this moment, but all the previous days, months, years, and centuries that passed right here are still here, at the same time. That is how the gateways made your time travel possible. It's as if we're on the upper floor of a skyscraper that is constantly growing taller. The gateways are like elevators bringing you to floors below us."

I had to think for a while to digest all that.

While I was doing so, Diana gasped.

"I just sensed a plunge in the energy levels of the ley lines."

"What does that signify?" I asked.

"Someone is feeding on the energy in a big way. Right here. It must be the wizard, back in his own era. This worries me."

"Does it mean he's preparing another magic attack?"

"Yes. I think so. I should tell Arch Mage Bob. Even if he's paralyzed by his unwillingness to fight back, he can warn the guild. Only he can spread the word to everyone almost instantly."

She left the circle, breaking the spell, and typed away on her phone.

"He's not answering. We should go back to the surf shop."

I nodded, and we jogged to my car. I drove as fast as I could without being pulled over for speeding. We went along the bay and back over the bridge, heading east toward the beach.

When we reached the surf shop, the parking lot was empty. A closed sign was in the front door, and it was locked. The back door was locked, as well.

"What the heck?" I said. "Did he go into hiding?"

"He has horrible timing," Diana said. "I will reach out to all the Magic Guild members I know, which is only a fraction of the total. You need to tell your mother and daughter right away."

THE ATTACK CAME OVERNIGHT. AGAIN, THE WITCHES AND wizards of San Marcos were enchanted by dreams of alluring lovers. No woman was induced to violence, as Aaron had been toward Bob. But, you know how males are: lust plus a few beers can lead to violence. The next day, the local news reported several arrests for disorderly conduct and assault. Who knows how many other witches called in sick to their human-world jobs because they were too lost in the fog? But mostly, the effect of this spell was a town filled with aroused witches walking around in dazes.

If Texas Tom had wanted to, he could have strolled into town and taken over without encountering any resistance. The magic folk of San Marcos were simply too drunk on love to care about anything else.

I had my hands full, with Mom and Sophie even more zoned out than the last time.

"Mom, I can't work today," Sophie said to me from her bed. "I don't even want to live, unless I can be with Tom."

"Don't you understand he's an evil wizard who's controlling you with magic?"

"He's who I'm destined to spend my life with."

"How can you say that? Texas Tom is a slime mold who's keeping Cory prisoner, feeding on his energy."

"If you saw how hot Tom is, you'd forget about Cory."

"That's not even what Tom looks like," I said firmly.

"How do you know?"

"I know because Grammers also dreamed about him, but he looked completely different from what you're describing. His magic allows him to read your mind and project the image of your ideal-looking man."

"Grammers is dreaming about someone else. Tom came only to me in my dream."

"Will you, at the very least, get out of bed and drink some coffee?"

"I don't want coffee," she whined. "Or anything. I don't want to breathe anymore if I can't be with Tom."

This was hopeless. I closed the door to her room on the third floor, and went downstairs, preparing myself for a day of twice the amount of work.

I called to check on Mom. She sounded as if she had just come off of anesthesia, but she assured me she was okay.

"If only Tom would come take me away."

"Mom, you fully understand his magic is messing with your head, right?"

"Yes, dear, don't worry." Her words were slurred. "That square jaw, my lord, let me kiss that square jaw."

93

I said goodbye. How were we going to stop Texas Tom? Frankly, I didn't care if he conquered the Magic Guild. I just wanted my daughter and mother back.

And it didn't look like Bob was going to step up and fight for his guild. If I gave him the benefit of the doubt, he had a reason to run away. Or maybe he was a big coward.

I needed to check on Diana. She didn't have any family nearby, and said she'd have a non-magical friend stay at her house last night to keep an eye on her. I should have asked for this friend's contact info.

I had just enough time to run over to Diana's house before it was time to prepare breakfast. When I pulled into her driveway, there wasn't an extra car that would belong to her friend. He or she must have already left. Diana must be fine.

She didn't answer the doorbell. I let myself in, my gaze instantly going to the ceiling to make sure she wasn't up there.

"Diana?"

No answer. Not again, I thought.

As I headed through the common areas of the house toward her bedroom, something caught my eye outside. A skiff was tied up to a narrow dock that snaked from her rear deck to a channel through the marsh grass.

The boat must belong to her friend.

I turned the corner past the kitchen and saw her bedroom door was closed this time.

"Diana?"

Giggling came from behind the closed door. Male and female giggling.

How fortunate Diana was that her "friend" was here when the lust-magic attack came last night.

With Bob out of the picture for the time being, I realized it would be best if I spoke to a powerful witch or wizard who might have the power to fight Texas Tom. Diana didn't practice that kind of magic. Mom and Sophie were nowhere near being powerful enough, and I would never put them in danger like that. My cousin, Missy, had plenty of might behind her magick, but this war was between Tom and the San Marcos Magic Guild. Only a member of the guild should have to face this danger, because the guild had everything to lose.

Mom might be able to refer me to the right magician. Since I was already out, I stopped by her house.

Uh-oh, Billy's car was parked out front. I went into the kitchen. It was empty. No scones, no coffee, no Mom or Billy.

I didn't need any more hints to get out of there.

Did Texas Tom realize the shortcomings of his spell? He could pump the witches of San Marcos full of lust for him, but if he wasn't around, they could obviously make other arrangements.

Or was this his plan all along: make sure no one would fight him because everyone was too busy doing the horizontal dance?

My stomach sank when I thought about Sophie. She'd better still be in bed. Alone. I raced home.

I arrived outside her door, out of breath from running up the stairs. I knocked.

"How are you Sophie? Can I come in?"

An indecipherable mumble came from within.

I opened the door with the passkey. Sophie was alone in bed, the covers pulled up to her chin.

"I will never leave this room again," she said. "The world is a dark, lonely place without Tom, and I don't want to be a part of it."

"Honey, please tell me if you're feeling suicidal."

"No, Mom. Because Tom is coming for me. I just can't bear the waiting."

That was a relief.

I wanted a witch who was up to the task of fighting, but I didn't know any others.

Wait, the only other local witch I knew was Hugo the Magnificent, Sophie's magic tutor. His ridiculous name came from the magic shows he performed at children's birthday parties. Frankly, I had my doubts that he was an actual witch at all, as opposed to a "witch consultant," which is another term for someone who takes your money. But maybe, he could advise me on what kind of magical tactics were needed in a battle like this.

I called the number on his business card. Yes, a witch with a business card.

"Hello?" His voice was foggy, as if he'd been affected by the magic attack. Maybe he was a real witch, after all.

I explained the situation and asked him if he had advice.

"I can think of nothing to do, nothing," he said. "My life has stopped moving, like a paused Hallmark movie, while I wait for Tom to ride to me on a white steed and take this damsel in distress away with him to his castle on the hill."

I thanked him and hung up. Perhaps I should wait until the effects of this latest spell faded and I find a witch to talk sensibly with me.

Unless Tom stepped up his attacks, leaving the city's magic folk in a constant state of delirious lust.

I had to go on the offensive.

Another memory-reading session with the giant pearl might be helpful. If I studied the details of Cory's memories more carefully, perhaps I would spot a clue to the specific year Cory and the wizard were inhabiting. Then, I could go there via the gateways and the In Between.

What I would do once I got there, I had no idea.

CHAPTER 10

POWER TRIP

Bound by magic on the tiny bed, completely dependent on Tom for food, water, and even bathroom breaks, Cory was in the depths of despair. He would have taken his own life if he had the means to do so.

Instead, he clung to memories of life with Darla. Her impish smiles, her sarcastic jokes, the way she laughed off difficulties and convinced him that the broken air conditioning unit was really not the end of the world after all.

She was the elixir that got him through the tough job of running a bed-and-breakfast in a party town like Key West. He had regretted his decision to quit teaching and forgo his meager earnings as a photographer. But Darla convinced him that running an inn with his best friend, lover, and soulmate could be the most rewarding work of all.

Just as today, she was like a guardian angel keeping him alive, even though he had only his memories of her, now that she was more than a hundred years distant from him.

But in the same city. It was maddening to think her inn was

within walking distance of him, but she wouldn't be there. Not for over a century.

It wasn't yet dawn, and slow, heavy footsteps came up the stairs, stopping outside the door of the tiny room. Cory cringed.

"Time to go to work," Tom said as he opened the door, letting in yellow light from the gas lamp on the wall atop the stairs. Texas Tom was an old man again. Cory didn't know if Tom was changing appearances at whim, or whether it signified he was weak and depleted of power.

"I need you to mine the ley lines again."

"So soon after last time?" Cory asked.

"Of course. I'm stepping up my attacks, softening the opposition. I need every bit of power I can muster, and I've found the perfect source of extra energy. We make a good team, you and me."

Team, ha! Cory thought. It wasn't teamwork; it was abuse and would eventually end in Cory's death, he was certain.

It was odd that Tom depended upon Cory so much for mining the ley lines. Tom had plenty of ways to amass energy, demonstrating quite remarkable feats of magic before Cory was enslaved. But he didn't seem skilled at getting energy from ley lines. He truly needed what Cory mined for whatever spells he was using to attack the Magic Guild in the twenty-first century.

Or perhaps Cory was especially talented at working with ley lines. Tom had said something to that effect. Cory wished he could use this to his own advantage.

The magic binding, which felt exactly like coarse rope, suddenly dropped away. Cory rose stiffly from bed and went into the bathroom, forced to relieve himself and clean up under Tom's supervision.

"Shake a leg, my friend. I want you to complete your work before sunrise," Tom said.

Soon, they walked the deserted cobblestone streets toward the bay front, light pooling beneath the gas lamps on each corner.

Old Courage was smaller than when Cory had seen it in present-day San Marcos, but the tree was still formidable. The point where the major and minor ley lines bisected was exactly twelve feet from the trunk. Cory could tell exactly where the point was, though there was no visible sign above ground. He'd located it the first time they'd come here with no help from Tom. This made a good argument that Cory truly did have an innate ability to work with ley lines.

"Come on, let's get going," Tom said. He was getting on Cory's nerves.

Cory stood upon the intersection of the lines. The grass beneath his feet looked no different from the rest of the small park, but his feet became almost unbearably hot through the soles of his shoes, and vibrations danced up his legs and into his heart.

The tricky part was getting his mind on the exact wavelength as the electromagnetic current and then focusing on a point in the core of his body where his own natural energies were centered. And if he could align this point with the wavelength—

The blast of power felt like his head was exploding, but in a good way. No drug in the world could produce this high and this euphoria.

Arms stretched out, Cory felt his body fill with electromagnetic energy powerful enough to kill a hundred men if it had come from a downed power line. Every hair on his body stood on end. His vision was pure white light, and every inch of him tingled. He sensed sparks flying from his fingertips.

He was in utter ecstasy.

Until Tom seized him in an embrace and placed his hands on either side of Cory's head, covering his temples.

Cory almost vomited from the feeling of violation as the power drained from him almost as quickly as it had filled him.

Dizziness overcame him. He dropped to the ground, absolutely devoid of the strength to stand. Lying on the ground, panting as if his lungs lacked enough air to breathe, he watched Tom cast his spell. His wizard's staff, the one with the skeletal hand, he held aloft. True lightning bolts shot from the bones at its tip into the sky. And through the gates of time.

As Cory watched, he realized for the first time the gateways, that took them to the In Between and different time periods, were assisting Tom's spell. He was using them to transport his spell to the twenty-first century. Cory sensed their presence and the lightning bolts of magic pass through them.

What exactly were the gateways and why were they helping Texas Tom? He desperately wanted to know if they came at Tom's request or showed up on their own when they sensed the immense power being pulled from the ley lines.

And would Cory be able to use them to return to Darla? Or would they thwart him in order to serve Tom?

I FELT LIKE I HAD THE WEIGHT OF THE WORLD ON MY shoulders. Well, the fate of the Magic Guild, to which I didn't even belong. But, there were still some loose ends I wanted tied up before I did anything reckless.

I thought back to the night Mrs. Ogglethwarp died. Samson believed someone had rigged the tree limb to fall on her. What led him to that hypothesis was the security camera footage of someone cutting a notch beneath the limb.

This person still hadn't been identified. I called Samson to confirm this.

"Nope," he said. "The guy is seen mostly from the rear, and this is not high-resolution video. He came up as a dead end."

"Can I look at the video?" I asked.

"You?"

"Yes, me. If I was an actual target, then the guy in the video might be someone I know. It's worth taking a look."

"Yeah, if you have time to waste, come to the department, and I'll play it for you. I'm not allowed to email it or anything."

"Sure, I understand. Are you going to be around in the early afternoon?"

"Yeah, stop in around two."

I didn't make a very good sleuth, with my sleuthing hours constrained by my duties serving breakfast, Teatime, wine hour, and guest requests all day and night. But this, I could do.

Samson had the video cued up on the monitor of his ancient desktop computer. The department had expensive state-of-the-art models, but an old gumshoe detective like Samson would never get one. Especially since he typed using only two fingers.

"I have it zoomed in as much as possible before it pixelates too much. Click here to replay."

I sat in his chair, still warm with his hot-blooded-shifter body heat. Clicking the play arrow, I watched a man run into the frame and move up to the tree. He actually had a small chainsaw. It seemed really audacious, but a quieter type of saw would take too long to cut out the wedge of wood. Might as well be loud but fast and get out quickly.

He made two cuts at different angles and stepped back when the wedge fell to the ground. It looked like he turned off the saw (there was no audio with the video), then he kicked the piece of wood away from the tree. He stuck his hand in the V-cut briefly, then ran away out of frame.

There was definitely something familiar about the man.

I played the video over and over, picking up more details each time: the man's height and build. His long hair. The leather cord he wore on one wrist. His tattoo on the side of his neck when he turned to one side. The type of shirt he wore.

Yep, I knew this guy.

It was Aaron, Arch Mage Bob's assistant. The guy I stopped from strangling him to death.

"Wow," I said. It was a word I'd been saying a lot lately. It made me sound stupid, but it was often the only thing to say in response to some of the bat-poop crazy things I'd seen lately.

"What, do you know the guy?" Samson asked.

"I do. It's Aaron, Bob McGuinn's assistant and custom board maker. I don't know Aaron's last name, but I just found out he's a witch."

I explained the strangling attempt and the magic Texas Tom had been broadcasting to the magic folk of San Marcos.

"Why didn't you tell me this before?" Samson asked in a testy tone.

"It just started happening, and I've been busy. Plus, you never seem interested in magical happenings."

"I should have been told about the strangulation assault. When all the other magic people were feeling lust, why did this guy feel homicidal?"

"How should I know? Maybe Texas Tom ordered him to take out his rival. And there are bigger questions. Like, did he cut the notch under Tom's direction? This happened before the magic attacks on the town."

"Or Aaron was the one responsible for felling the limb. He cut the notch, then later, cast the spell that broke the limb. He's a witch, after all. Only not good enough to aim the limb correctly."

"Remember, he works for Bob. Maybe Bob is the murderer," I said.

"Bob is skilled enough to kill the right targets, right?"

"Yeah, unless he deliberately used a less-advanced spell so it wouldn't look like he did it. He should be powerful enough to break the limb and hit both people without cutting a notch, but he wanted it to appear more amateur."

"Okay, we're just adding more theories and not eliminating any. Time to stop theorizing and hit the streets. Let me confirm Aaron's last name, and I'll have a little chat with him. If he doesn't want to talk, I'll bring him in on the vandalism charge."

Samson walked out of the detective bureau, presumably to find a database person. Not long afterwards, he returned with a sticky note with a name and address written on it.

"Aaron Bilksbier," he said. "Let's go."

"I can go with you?"

"Yeah, but you'll have to stay in the car when I talk to him."

I didn't mind, actually. I didn't know if Aaron would remember who bashed the back of his head in with the belt sander.

Since it was the middle of the day, we drove first to Bob's surf shop. The place was still closed.

"Pagan Surf Shop is open seven days a week, fourteen hours a day," Samson said. "It gets tons of business from tourists and locals alike. This is highly unusual for it to be closed at this time of day."

"It was closed yesterday, too," I said.

"Okay, so it's Bilksbier's residence next."

We drove along A1A, and, not far from the shop, Samson turned onto a residential street on the west side, away from the beach. It was lined with older, working-class homes. At the far end, where the street ended at the Intracoastal Waterway, I saw newer, larger homes on the premium real estate.

"You know, if we can't find Aaron here, we should check with the hospital," I said. "Remember the belt sander I mentioned?"

Samson gave me a sideways glance.

He stopped at the edge of the street in front of a modest one-story home with a pickup truck parked in the driveway next to a sail catamaran on a trailer.

"Wait here," Samson said, getting out of the car.

I watched as he walked up the front walk, which was large flagstones engulfed in overgrown grass. His right hand instinctively strayed to his holster, clipped to his belt just behind his right hip, then back to swinging at his side.

The front porch covered the length of the house and had its own roof. A paddle board and several surf boards leaned against the house.

Just as Samson mounted the first porch step, a large area of blurry air appeared on the porch in his path. I thought my eyes were playing tricks on me.

But then, I felt the familiar nausea creep into my gut. Panic filled me.

I opened the passenger door.

"Mike! Stop right now!" I shouted. "Don't go forward—"

Detective Michael Samson stepped into the gateway and disappeared before my eyes.

CHAPTER 11

MAGICAL MEMORY LOSS

I stifled a scream and ran from Samson's car toward the gateway. It shimmered above the top step of the front porch, the details of the porch blurry behind it.

Samson had never been to the In Between. He would need my help returning to earth. If I went through the same gateway as him, there was a good chance I'd land near him in the alternate world.

But as I sprinted toward the porch, the gateway faded.

"No!" I pleaded.

There was still a slight shimmer in the air when I dove toward the steps. I landed hard on the wood.

The gateway was gone. Samson was marooned in the In Between. There was no guarantee he would receive help there, as I had. He could die of thirst and starvation without it. I needed to catch the next gateway. But the only way I had ever summoned a gateway when I wanted one was with the help of Missy's magic talisman. Without it, what was I to do?

And what was a gateway doing here, anyway? The only ones

I'd encountered had been in the In Between, in my home, and the one that rescued me from my brief trip back to the year 1580.

While I sat on the porch steps pondering how to hail a gateway, the front door opened.

Aaron stood here staring at me through the screen door, a confused expression on his face.

"Ms. Chesswick? What are you doing here?"

"Oh, hi. I just wanted to ask you a couple of questions, if that's okay."

I guess I would have to fill in for Samson.

"Ask me? About what?"

"How's your head feeling?"

He looked surprised again and held up an ice pack. "Pretty darn sore. Did Bob tell you about the accident?"

"Yes." Thanks to Bob for keeping the truth from Aaron. "I was sorry to hear about it."

"I don't remember any of it. Supposedly, I bent to pick up something off the floor next to the board I was sanding, and the sander fell off and hit me in the noggin. Bob said I was knocked out for a while. The doc at the ER said it's a mild concussion."

"Feel better soon," I said. "Now, do you mind a couple of questions?"

"All right."

He opened the screen door and beckoned for me to come inside. The living room was small, but much cleaner than I'd expected. It had decent rattan furniture, and there weren't surfing posters on the wall nor empty beer cans and a bong on the coffee table like you'd find with a guy living alone. There were even matching pillows on the couch. Definitely signs a woman lived here with him, though his ring finger was bare.

"Can I get you something to drink?" he asked.

"No thanks, I'm good."

He sat down on the couch and put the ice pack against the back of his head. He looked at me quizzically, waiting for the questions to begin. I dove right in.

"The city's Parks and Recreation Department has security camera footage of you damaging the old live oak tree near the bay. The one known as Old Courage."

"Me?"

"Yes. Definitely you. You had a small chainsaw, and you cut a notch beneath the largest limb, weakening it so it would fall."

"But I—"

"Why did you do that?"

"But I didn't. I think that tree's cool."

"It was definitely you in the video."

"Man, another blackout when I don't remember anything."

"It was on the night of the seventh. Do you remember anything from that night?"

"You say I used a chainsaw?"

"Yes. A green one with a short guide bar. The brand name wasn't visible in the video."

"It's so weird. I remember that night waking up in my truck parked along the promenade. I had no memory of driving there or why. And there was a green chainsaw sitting on the passenger-side floor. It wasn't mine. I think it's Bob's."

Hmm. Sounds like magic did this to him. I would not mention Mrs. Ogglethwarp. If he hadn't heard about her death, I didn't want him to panic and refuse to talk more.

"I drove by there yesterday," he said. "A crew was cutting up a fallen limb. Did I make that limb fall? I would never want that to happen."

I didn't answer. "Do you know if Bob has any issues with

me?" I asked. "You know, like he was mad at me or saw me as a threat?"

"I don't think so. Why would he?"

"No reason I can think of. It's just that I happened to be sitting beneath that limb when it fell."

"No way, dude! I'm glad you're okay."

"Bob's magic could easily make the limb fall. You probably know enough magic to do it yourself."

"Whoa, dude, I never."

"Where has Bob been? Why is his store closed?"

"I don't know. When I showed up for work today, it was closed. No one told me it was going to be. I called up one of the other guys, and he said no one told him anything, either."

"Has anyone been in touch with Bob?"

"Nope. He's missing in action, I guess."

"Do you know anything about the wizard named Texas Tom?"

"Met him once at the store, visiting Bob."

"Okay, Aaron. One last question, and I'll leave you alone. The night before the day you injured your head, do you remember any strange dreams?"

He pondered it for a moment, then his face turned red. "Um, yeah. I dreamed about this really hot chick. She was totally out of this world. Hey, but it wasn't a dirty dream or nothing."

"I asked because there was an attack on the magic folk that night. All the witches had dreams like yours. I think Texas Tom was behind the attack. Do you know anything about it?"

"Nope." He shook his head in the negative. "Are you sure it's Texas Tom who caused my dream?"

"Pretty sure," I said.

"Then he's doing more than giving me dreams. My mind has

been all messed up for a while with the blackouts, like the one at the tree. I lost a customer because of one."

"I'm sorry. What happened?"

"It started one afternoon at work when I felt, like, totally out of it. Some old lady was asking me questions, and I couldn't help her at all. I didn't understand a word of what she was saying. My mind just turned to mush. She must have thought I was on drugs. From then on, I've been brain dead."

"Was she a regular customer?"

"Sorry, dude, I don't remember. Sorry."

"If you do, call me," I said, handing Aaron my business card.

"Stay safe and be careful, Aaron," I said as I turned toward the door to leave.

It sounded like the aftereffects of Texas Tom's spell were even stronger with Aaron than they were with Sophie.

Unless Bob be-spelled him, too.

WHEN I STEPPED OUT OF THE DOOR, I FELT SICK TO MY stomach again. And lo-and-behold, a vertical wall of air about ten feet by ten feet was shimmering in the middle of the lawn.

Was it the same gateway that took Samson? Did it come back for me?

I know it was rash of me, but I couldn't miss this opportunity. I ran down the porch steps and into the shimmering. The feeling of vertigo, of tingling, and of my insides being rearranged. And then utter darkness.

I hit the ground hard and rolled.

The smell of sulfur was overpowering. Looking around, I was pretty sure I had arrived in Hell.

The surface I had landed on was sandy, thankfully, but there were rocky patches all around with holes in the ground from which hot lava bubbled and oozed. The air was hazy with steam and smoke, and the lighting was dark like twilight, so I couldn't see far in the distance. But this infernal setting stretched in every direction. Low hills and valleys were pockmarked by rock-lipped openings from which bright red-yellow liquid fire poured.

For a few minutes, I debated whether I was in the In Between or truly in Hell, but the logical part of my brain won out. This had to be the In Between, only a region of it I had never seen before.

Okay, so I made it here. Now, how was I going to find Samson? I felt a little guilty. If I was going to be travelling to other planes of existence, I should be searching for Cory instead of the man who was essentially his rival. But I was convinced the gateway would never have appeared at Aaron's house if I hadn't been there. Therefore, it was my fault Samson was transported from earth.

I stood up, dusted the sand from my jeans, and did what I always did when arriving in the In Between. I walked in a random direction, hoping I'd be found by someone sympathetic and not bothered by something scary.

The heat here was different this time. Previously, the air had been a neutral temperature I didn't even notice. Now, thanks to the lava, it was uncomfortably hot. As I walked in the straightest line I could, while skirting the lava, I sweated profusely. And that meant I needed water.

And there was no water to drink in the In Between. Humans who spent time here had to create their own with magic.

Samson better not have wandered far, or we'll both die of thirst and dehydration.

"Michael!" I shouted. My voice sounded flat and puny. If he

wasn't in view, he wouldn't be able to hear me. Might as well not dry my mouth out screaming for him.

I continued walking for at least a half hour but had no way of telling since my watch and phone were dead. I prayed I'd enter a different environment that wasn't so hot. And that someone would magically show up to help me.

The thing that appeared ahead of me just now did not want to help me, I was pretty sure.

It was bat like, with large papery wings. It hovered in the distance, obscured by the steam and smoke. I changed direction, so my walking angled me away from it.

But it fluttered into my path again.

I stopped. Did it want to attack me, or was it simply being annoying and getting in my way?

The correct answer was "A." Because the thing was flying right at me now.

And it wasn't a bat or a bird. It had a human face and body, a face contorted in agony.

The creature flew straight at me, then climbed at the last minute, passing over my head as I ducked to avoid it.

Maybe I truly was in Hell. Because that's where a creature like this belonged.

It emitted a sobbing cry and flew back toward me. I ducked again, and it just missed me.

I remembered hearing that the In Between was not only where magicians and certain supernatural creatures from earth took refuge. The main purpose of the In Between was to function as a form of limbo, where certain recently departed souls waited until it was decided if they were going to Heaven or to Hell.

This creature could be a soul who was about to go downstairs.

Just beyond my vision, it sobbed and cried, "Help me," gibbering like a wounded peacock.

It fluttered just above me, not as aggressively this time.

"How can I help you?" I ventured to ask.

"I don't want to go to Hell," he or she said. Its gender was impossible to determine.

"The higher powers make that decision," I said.

"I did nothing truly bad when I was alive. Yeah, maybe I did nothing good, but nothing strictly illegal. My original intentions were good."

"What were you when you were alive?" I asked as it hovered far above me.

"I was a U.S. Senator."

"Ah, my condolences."

"I began my career wanting to make people's lives better. But lobbyists have too much money, and they're too convincing. I became a cynical, craven politician who only cared about being reelected and eventually being hired by one of the lobbyists. My speeches were empty and posturing. I passed no legislation."

"I'm sorry to hear that," I said. "Hopefully, Hell won't be so bad."

"I don't want to go there. I never harmed anyone. Well, not directly."

"You sound as if you've discovered self-awareness now that your eternal fate has been decided. Maybe if you show more repentance, the decision will be changed."

"I request an appeal," it sobbed as it flew away. For its sake, I hoped it got another hearing. Besides, Hell was probably too full of politicians, anyway.

I continued trudging ahead through the Hell-scape, with no sense of direction. Trying to avoid the senator's soul pushed me off my original course. Usually, finding politicians' souls is the hard part, not avoiding them. But I had no choice but to keep moving, all the while trying to avoid stepping too close to the spills of lava.

More time passed, measured only by my increasing thirst. In my previous visits to the In Between, I hadn't had to wander this long before someone helped me.

What if no one did this time?

My spirits lifted slightly when I saw a landscape ahead that was sand only, with no rocks and lava. I reached it much faster than expected. Strangely, when I crossed into the sand zone, I turned around and the Hell-scape disappeared, only a few steps after leaving it.

But now, I had before me a desert of rolling sand dunes, and no other features. Since there was no wind, the sand was completely smooth.

Except to my right, where I saw human footprints.

Excited now, I followed the prints over the first dune and up the next. The human wore hiking shoes of some kind, leaving distinct prints in the firm sand.

Cresting the second dune, I saw the prints go down the back slope and up the next. Despair crept back in as thirst and fatigue grew more intense.

Then, to my surprise, an approaching figure rose above the top of the opposite dune, and a second figure, too. They were men, and one was pulling the other along with him.

As they got closer and easier to see, my heart leaped. One of them was Samson!

"Mike!" I shouted, waving my arms above my head.

He waved back, and I started down the slope toward him.

"I can't believe I was able to find you," I said as our paths finally met. "Who is this?"

"This is Burt Boston," Samson said. "I was wandering around

this place, totally lost and disoriented. I only knew it was the In Between from what you've told me about it. And I was worried I'd die here alone. And then I ran into Burt."

"Yeah, so now we can die together," Burt said. He was a short, wiry guy with a blond buzz cut and heavily tattooed arms, handcuffed behind him, showing beneath his T-shirt sleeves.

"It was amazing luck running into Burt," Samson said. "He's the main suspect in a murder case from over a year ago. He went on the lam, and we couldn't find him. Now, I know why."

"Do you know magic?" I asked Burt.

He wouldn't meet my eyes. "No."

"He has to know magic," I said, "or else he wouldn't be able to survive here for long. Be careful in case he tries a spell on you."

"Fortunately, I could keep my weapon when I was transported here. His magic would need to be stronger than a nine-millimeter round."

I have an ethical rule that I don't use my telepathy in an invasive way. The truth is, I don't have enough control over this ability to pry information out of people whenever I wanted, anyway.

But since this guy was a criminal, it couldn't hurt to try. I focused my mind on his, opening my senses and trying to connect with his mind waves.

This lady is suspicious. Does she know magic? Tom said I have to keep my magic secret, no matter what. I can't use it until he brings me back to earth. Then, I'll need to use it in battle.

"If you knew magic, you'd be able to create water for us before we die of thirst," I said.

"I don't know what you're talking about," Burt said. "I don't believe in garbage like that from comic books."

I caught Samson's eyes with a look that said the guy was lying.

"So, how are we going to get home?" Samson asked.

"I can't summon a gateway," I said. "We'll have to wander around and hope we run into one."

"That's not very encouraging," Samson said.

"What can I say? The good news is, the gateways seem to like us, or else I wouldn't have been able to follow and find you here."

So, we did the only thing we could: we walked. Along the way, I told Samson about my conversation with Aaron.

"He said it was Bob's chainsaw?" Samson asked.

"He thinks it was."

"Why would Bob want to kill Mabel Ogglethwarp and you?"

"I don't know. Maybe he's taking orders from Texas Tom now."

"It's odd that Bob would use that method."

"Not if he was trying to disguise his involvement. Even if the authorities didn't believe the limb fell of its own accord, and even if we suspected magic did it, we would never associate such a bumbling method with Bob."

Bob isn't as powerful as he seems, said Burt's thoughts. *The Magic Guild deserves a better leader.*

"I still haven't heard a convincing reason Texas Tom would want to kill the two of you," Samson said.

"Or Bob could have his own reasons. Though I can't imagine what they'd be."

As if it knew we were looking for it, a large square of shimmering air appeared on the top of the dune we were climbing.

I was elated, but both Samson and Burt hesitated.

"I know it can be an uncomfortable ride," I said, "but it's quick and it'll get us home."

Burt looked like he was thinking of bolting. Samson gave him a modest smack with his palm on the back of Burt's head.

"Don't even think of it."

Samson held Burt's arms tightly, and they disappeared into the gateway. I followed right behind.

WE LANDED SPRAWLED ATOP AARON'S YARD. WE'D GIVEN HIS neighbors a lot to talk about today.

Burt made a half-hearted effort to run away, but Samson tackled him easily.

"Thanks for giving me a grass stain on my trousers," he grumbled to Burt. He locked the accused murderer in the back seat of his car, which had waited faithfully in front of Aaron's house while we jaunted to another plane of existence.

Now that Burt couldn't hear us, I said, "I read some of his thoughts. Texas Tom was holding him in reserve before coming here to overthrow Bob. There could be other magicians like him."

"I wish I could help, but I can't. Not officially, that is."

"As the attacks ramp up, you might have to."

CHAPTER 12

FINDING THE TIME

Marianne LeBoeuf didn't even attempt to hide her distaste for me and having to let me into the hallowed ground of her cataloging room. But Dr. Noordlun had a lot of pull with her boss. Did my sweet smile come across as sarcastic when she handed me the plastic box?

I touched the pearl again, seeking Cory's memory. When I found it, I held the gem in both hands, immersing myself in his memory. It was sweet for me but so short.

This time, I tried to ignore his conscious thoughts and concentrated only on the sensory input the memory contained.

I watched what his eyes saw as he walked to the park where Old Courage stood. He was focused only on getting to the tree as quickly as possible and hiding the pearl in it without being caught by Tom or witnessed by an overly curious person. He didn't think about what he saw as he walked there. Yet, his eyes absorbed the images, and his brain recorded them in his memory. His other senses also sent inputs to his brain.

I studied all of them as I relived his journey: detaching the pearl from the staff, walking through the house, going down the few short blocks to the park. He didn't see any details in the house that would help, such as the daily newspaper.

He didn't look back at the house he was staying in, but I took note of the neighboring homes he passed to aid me in finding it if I ever traveled to this time.

During his walk to the park, he smelled meat cooking and the horse manure left behind by the passing carriages. But he had no olfactory information that would help me.

Two women crossing his path wore clothing that helped me peg the time period as the late nineteenth century. I made note of the cut of their ankle-length skirts, shirtwaists, and jackets, as well as the broad-brimmed hats adorned with feathers. Their outfits could help me narrow the dates, but not nail the year, because even if I found the fashions introduced in a contemporaneous magazine or catalog, I wouldn't know how long the women owned the clothes.

How I wished he would look at something with the day's date printed or written on it, but life is never that easy.

He turned at the end of a block and headed east toward the bay and the park. Something passed through his vision which didn't catch his eye, but it caught mine: a brand-new building.

I replayed the few seconds of his memory over and over. It was a three-story brick Victorian building with scaffolding on one wall where a paint job was nearly complete.

For less than a second, he saw a sign that said, "Opening soon."

This could be the clue I was looking for. The building wasn't a private residence, but most likely a small hotel. Too bad he hadn't seen the main sign for the business.

Fortunately, I had a phone with the internet. And the

internet can actually be good for something other than spreading conspiracy theories.

I pulled up a satellite map and zoomed into where I thought Cory had seen the building. It was on the corner of a street a block from the park.

I zoomed in. It looked as if the building still existed, rounded turrets and all. I zoomed in even more. The building was a business with its name listed in my browser's database.

The Bayview Inn Bed & Breakfast. I checked the street view of the address and, sure enough, it resembled the building Cory had passed, though now it was a different color.

I didn't know if I could access county real estate records on the internet from so long ago, so I began by simply searching the internet for the Bayview Inn. I found its website easily and prayed the owners had written about its history.

There! In the story behind the inn, the page said it was originally built in 1891, as the Larchmont Hotel.

Assuming this information was accurate, I now knew what year Cory was inhabiting.

Did I have the guts to go there?

"I NEED YOUR RED DRAGON," I BLURTED OUT TO MISSY THE moment she answered her phone.

"I beg your pardon?"

"Your Red Dragon talisman."

"I know what you're talking about. But why?"

"I need to make another trip back in time. To rescue Cory."

"Not so fast there, girl. Are you out of your mind?"

"I always am. I figured out he's in the year eighteen ninety-one, right here in San Marcos."

I explained how I figured this out, about the pearl, and about Mrs. Ogglethwarp.

"Oh, my," Missy said. "What kind of mess are you in now?"

"I'm worried about him. What if the wizard discovers Cory stole his pearl?"

"You need to slow down and think this through, Darla. First, how in the world are you going to free him from a wizard? Next, how can you be sure he's still in eighteen ninety-one? And last, don't you remember what happened the last time you time traveled? You were arrested by the Spanish Inquisition. I can't believe how lucky you were to be released."

"Maybe because if they kept me it would have changed history, so they were somehow prevented from doing that."

"Maybe you were just lucky."

"I admit travelling back across more than five centuries made it pretty difficult for me to fit in. But eighteen ninety-one can't be that different from today, can it?"

"Oh, you mean when women weren't allowed to vote? You'll stand out. It's too dangerous for you to do this. And remember, the wizard will be extra vigilant about you now. He could hurt you even worse than the Spanish Inquisition could."

"I promise I'll be careful with the Red Dragon."

"I can't in good conscience lend it to you."

"You did before, and I returned it to you."

"I believe it was freak luck. And I couldn't let you go alone."

"It's not such a big deal."

"I would have to go with you," Missy said.

"No, don't risk your life for me."

"You just said it's not such a big deal."

I sighed. "Okay, when would you be ready to go?"

"The day after tomorrow. I have a dentist appointment tomorrow."

"I see you have your priorities straight."

I WAS HANGING OUT WITH CERVANTES IN MY COTTAGE, WHEN suddenly his ears pricked up and he stood on his hind legs like a prairie dog, trying to peer out the window. He gave me a knowing look.

"Ah," I said, "Missy is here."

I opened the door, and he shot off like an arrow through the courtyard.

As a witch's familiar, preordained to belong to Cory if he returned, Cervantes was especially attuned to people with magic. He got on quite well with Sophie, for instance. While I was his cat mom, server of food, and massage therapist, Sophie was his peer. They communicated telepathically.

Yes, I was jealous. But I won't go into that now.

I went inside the inn and opened the front door just as Missy walked up, wheeling a suitcase. No, make that two suitcases.

We hugged and cheek-kissed.

Cervantes rubbed against Missy's legs and purred when she scratched him under the jawline. He was probably complaining to her about me telepathically.

I stared at the suitcases. "You're welcome to stay as long as you wish, but really?"

"We don't know how long we'll be in 1891. I brought some outfits I borrowed from the local theater company, from a recent production of Ibsen's *Hedda Gabler*. They're from the right era, though perhaps too European."

"San Marcos had European tourists back then, too. But if we're going to be there long enough to need to change outfits, are we staying in a hotel? How will we pay?"

"We'll pay in cash. And since the U.S. currency looked different back then, my theater company friends also supplied this."

She pulled out a stack of greenbacks in different denominations. At first glance, they looked like contemporary dollars, but were slightly larger with different designs.

"Is this money real?" I asked.

"Not exactly. But my friend assured me it's as good as counterfeits get."

"We don't need to be arrested. I've already been through that last time."

"Being arrested for counterfeiting is the least of our dangers."

It was time for the evening wine hour, so Missy joined me and the small number of guests. After I cleaned up, I drove Missy to Mom's house, since Mom had insisted on having her for dinner. Sophie was already there.

Missy and I planned to ride the gateways to 1891 in the early morning before dawn, in order to avoid being seen when we appeared. We also promised not to tell Mom and Sophie about our dangerous plans.

"How is the investigation going on the spiritualist's death?" Mom asked as she carved a roast chicken.

"Um, it's basically nowhere," I said.

"You never fully explained her death to me," Missy said.

I gave the basic outlines of the story.

"You left out the part about you," Mom said.

The part I should have never mentioned to her, and that I wished Sophie hadn't heard.

"The Memory Guild's psychic and medium conferred with a spirit living in the tree who said Mrs. Ogglethwarp's companion was supposed to be killed, as well," I explained. "That companion happened to be me."

"Don't downplay it, Mom," Sophie said. "This is serious."

"I know. I just can't find anyone with a motive to kill me."

"Texas Tom," Mom said. "To keep you from trying to rescue Cory."

"Why would he think I would try to do something so absurd?" I dishonestly asked.

Mom gave me an ironic look. She was probing me with her telepathy, but I easily blocked it.

"And Texas Tom is a powerful wizard," I added. "He wouldn't have allowed the limb to miss me. And he wouldn't have needed to pre-cut it."

I explained to Missy about the video footage of the V-cut notch.

"The man who cut it works for Arch Mage Bob," I said.

Missy raised her eyebrows. She knew Bob, and they had once been antagonists. Now, they were more like frenemies.

"And why would Bob be involved?" she asked.

"He's deathly afraid of Texas Tom incriminating him for fraud and taking over the Magic Guild."

I explained the mounting dream attacks against the magic folk of San Marcos.

"Bob has been acting totally passive during all of this," I said. "So much so that I suspect he's submitting to Tom to save his skin. He could have promised to kill me for Tom. And doing it this amateurishly would make it seem he didn't do it, so he wouldn't be breaking his own guild's rules."

"Have you pursued this avenue?" Missy asked.

"Bob's assistant has no memory of cutting the notch, so the culprit obviously erased his memory or something. Bob denied knowing anything about it. And now he's disappeared."

Mom and Missy both nodded knowingly.

"He's in hiding," Mom said. "From you."

"And from Texas Tom," I said.

Platters of chicken, mashed potatoes, and vegetables were floating around the table so each of us could serve ourselves.

"Can't we have a non-magical dinner?" I asked. It bothered me being the only one of the Chesswick women to not have inherited the magic gene.

"Don't be such a stick in the mud, dear," Mom said as she sent the potatoes platter to me. To rub it in, she magically dropped a scoop of mashed potatoes on my plate with a big splat. A chicken thigh rose from the platter that currently hovered in front of Sophie. The thigh circled Sophie, then Missy, then came from behind me before landing on my plate.

"I know you prefer dark meat," Mom said.

As I gritted my teeth, the gravy boat flew across the table and carefully poured upon my chicken and potatoes.

"Sophie, do you want to break the wishbone with me?" Mom asked.

"Sure, Grammers."

The thin V-shaped bone, the fusion of two clavicles, hovered over the middle of the table. Mom and Sophie closed their eyes, and the bone snapped. The broken section Sophie held was the longer one.

"You get to make a wish," Mom said.

"I wish whoever tried to hurt Mom is caught and punished. And I wish Mom won't do anything dangerous."

"You only get one wish," I said under my breath.

BEFORE I WENT TO BED, I GAVE SOPHIE SPECIFIC instructions for handling breakfast for the guests in the morning. I used the excuse that Missy and I were going to visit the ley lines before dawn. Maybe I'm a terrible mother for keeping our planned travel secret, but I didn't want Sophie to worry about me. Besides, no matter how much time we spent in 1891, very little time would pass here in the present. For all I knew, we'd be back in time for breakfast.

Long before dawn, Missy met me at my cottage. Missy wore skirts and shirtwaists that looked a lot like those in Cory's mental images of passersby. We were pretty convincing, right down to the shoes.

"The waists of these skirts are way too tight," I complained.

"The costume-maker at the playhouse said they're actually much looser than they would have been back in their era."

"Didn't ice cream and buttered popcorn exist back then?"

"Okay, where do you want to do it?" Missy asked.

"Let's do it here, if a gateway will agree to come."

"My spell and the Red Dragon will compel it."

Missy took the small metal talisman from her pocket. But before she even began building her spell, a shimmering appeared in my living room.

"Wow," I said. "There's never been one in here before. Only on the third floor of the inn. The Red Dragon sure is strong, because you didn't even cast your spell yet."

"But that's not the way the Red Dragon works. It's almost as if the gateway knew we wanted it and it came proactively."

"It's odd," I said. "They've been unusually helpful lately. They must like me, or something. I recently learned they're sentient creatures."

"Really?" Missy looked freaked out.

"Maybe it's best if you don't think about that," I said, fighting my nausea and walking toward the gateway.

Missy caught up to me, and we entered it together.

And my vision went black.

WE TUMBLED INTO THE IN BETWEEN, LANDING IN A PLACE familiar to me: the endlessly wide beach of the sea without waves.

"I've been on this beach before," I said. "Watch out for the kraken in the water. And the giant ghost crabs in the dunes."

"I've been here, too," Missy said, "but didn't have the pleasure of meeting those creatures."

"Oh, the pleasure was all theirs."

Now that we were here, we needed to take a ride through a gateway back to earth. But we had to make the gateway take us to 1891, rather than sending us right back to where and when we came from, which was the default behavior of the gateways.

"Look, the gateway that brought us is still here," Missy said.

She was right. It hovered behind us. It must have never left, which was odd.

"Maybe there is some truth to what you said about them liking you. But let's hitch a ride before it changes its mind. Let me direct it."

Missy clutched the Red Dragon and recited the spell:

Oh, portals of magic, doorways of light,
You wondrous beings of wisdom and might.
I beg your help in sending us from here,
To land again upon our earth so dear.
Return me not from where I came,
But to this time that I shall name.

"I command you to take us to San Marcos, Florida, in October of the year eighteen ninety-one."

Missy offered me her arm. "Shall we?"

I hooked my arm through hers. "We shall."

We stepped into the shimmering air and the stomach-churning journey.

CORY SEARCHED FOR THE INTERSECTION OF THE LEY LINES near Old Courage in the pre-dawn darkness. The location had moved from where it had been last time.

"Come on, hurry up," Tom said impatiently. "It's getting late."

Tom seemed to have forgotten about the pearl or had other priorities. He'd been giving Cory slightly less supervision lately, but still much more than before he discovered his pearl had been stolen from his other staff. Nevertheless, Cory had been able to slip away last night and visited the gem hidden in the tree. He'd learned more about its healing and protective powers. It was becoming clearer that the pearl could serve as a defensive weapon against Tom. He wasn't sure how to use it, though.

"Let's get this show on the road," Tom said, "or I'll be forced to hurt you."

Cory finally found the junction, his feet and legs tingling with the electro-magnetic power. He focused on the ley lines running dozens of feet below ground and clicked his mind into the same frequency.

His body sang like a tuning fork as the power poured into him. He held his arms outstretched as every hair on his body stood on end. Sparks crackled from his fingertips.

Tom came up behind him to steal the power, as he always did. The gateway materialized in front of Cory, as it always did, to transport the massive amount of magic Tom would create from the energy. But this time was different.

This time, Cory spun on his heels and pushed his hands into Tom's face.

Tom screamed as the electricity coming from Cory's fingers shot into the wizard's eyes, ears, nose, and mouth. He staggered backwards.

Cory continued transferring the energy from the ley lines, through his solar plexus where it was concentrated, and against Tom's face like a weapon.

And then Cory went for it. He turned and raced for the waiting gateway. Tom screamed at him to stop and come back.

Just before he passed through the gateway, Cory had the oddest sensation. It was like a change in air pressure, and it tugged at his soul.

Darla? Is it something about her? Is she all right?

He continued wondering and worrying what it meant as the gateway whisked him away.

We landed in the courtyard of my inn. Fortunately, we didn't slam face-first upon the cobblestones. We just sort of found ourselves standing there in the dark, knees flexing to maintain balance.

It was my courtyard, but there were big differences. Notably, my cottage wasn't there. Nor was the tiny swimming pool on the other side. The plants and flowers in the brick planters were different from the ones I had planted. And the wooden gate to the street was in much better shape than mine. Otherwise, it looked pretty much the same.

Except, this was how it looked in 1891.

I was about to remark upon this to Missy, when a trembling

took over my body. It only lasted for a moment. I felt an odd sensation of displacement, of loss, of emptiness.

In my head, I heard Cory's voice say, "Darla?"

And that was all.

"I have this horrible feeling that Cory just left this time period," I said to Missy. "I think we may have crossed paths to and from the In Between."

"Then let's return immediately," Missy said. She seemed uneasy being in another time before she existed.

"Since we made it here, let's check the wizard's house just to be sure Cory's not here. I could be misinterpreting that weird feeling I got."

Missy looked at me doubtfully.

"Cousin, don't worry so much," I said. "We can talk our way out of anything, hop a gateway and be out of here."

"You've time traveled before. I haven't."

Yeah. I did it once. And it wasn't exactly a cakewalk.

CHAPTER 13

STUCK IN THE PAST

Before I could open the latch on the heavy oaken gate, a man cleared his throat.

"Ladies, may I assist you?"

Roderick stood in an open French door to the inn's living room.

I remembered Roderick was the owner of the inn at this time in history. He was a vampire even this long ago, having been turned decades before. He looked just like he did in contemporary times: pasty white complexion, sparse white hair parted on the side. His suit looked similar to ones he wore in my inn. I wouldn't be surprised if he still wore this particular suit.

"No, thank you, sir, we were just letting ourselves out," I said.

"Are you guests here?"

"Yes, we are. We are going out early to take in the sunrise at the seawall."

"Forgive me for not recognizing you. Are you really quite sure you are guests here?"

"Room three-oh-three," I said. "The day manager checked us in."

I knew Roderick wouldn't be awake during the day. He pursed his lips.

"We don't allow ladies of the evening to come onto our property."

"How dare you, sir! Let us go now, Missy, before this cad insults us further."

I got the latch open, and we scurried through the thick coquina wall and onto Cadiz Street.

"Is he your resident vampire?" Missy asked.

"Yeah, and I didn't want to interact with him and possibly mess up the future. Hopefully, he'll forget about this."

"He's not very friendly for an innkeeper."

"No. Especially when you consider he used to feed on his guests. Instead of a bed-and-breakfast, it was more of a bed-and-bloodshed. No wonder he defaulted on his mortgage."

We walked briskly along the cobblestone street.

"Do you know where we're going?" Missy asked.

"Yes. Well, sort of. I saw, through my psychometry, the street Texas Tom lives on and the neighboring homes. I should be able to figure out which is the right one."

"And then what?"

"We talk our way into the house."

"We do? How?"

"Okay, maybe this is where your magic comes in."

"So, then, it's all up to me to fight this powerful wizard?"

"I don't know. We didn't plan this mission adequately."

"We didn't plan at all."

"Look," I said, "the main objective is to find out if Cory's being held in the house, and my feeling of crossing paths with him was wrong. First, I'll do a psychometric reading of the doorknob and any handrails. Then, I'll try to read the thoughts of whomever answers the door and see if I can pick up Cory's thoughts from inside. If he is here, you can cast a sleeping spell on the bad guys, and we'll rush in and get Cory."

"On the bad guys? How do we know who the bad guys are?"

"Then just cast the spell on everyone."

"If we know he's inside," Missy said, "it would be smarter not to knock on the door. We'll try to help him break out."

"Yeah, maybe you're right."

"And we need a cover story explaining why we're poking around the house."

"How about we're going door to door soliciting support for women's suffrage?"

"That's as good as any."

As we neared our destination, it got trickier to navigate. My knowledge of present-day San Marcos didn't always square with what we beheld here in 1891. The basic street grid was the same, as were many of the buildings, but so much was different now, from unpaved streets to the lack of sidewalks on some of them. The store signs were different, trees were smaller, and the lighting at night was very poor, relegated to only gas lamps that were few and far between. In the distance, looming above the surrounding structures, was the Alhambra Hotel, where the wealthy from northern cities stayed during the winter tourist season. It was ablaze with electrical lighting generated from its own power plant.

When we reached the street I recognized from Cory's memory, I grew excited.

"This is the street," I whispered to Missy.

A faint, rosy light from the sunrise illuminated the scene, making it slightly different than Cory's view when he left his memories on the pearl. But I walked along the street, turning my head at different angles, until I zeroed in on Cory's perspective as he stole away from the house and headed for the park.

There—I saw the wrought-iron fence in front of the home Cory passed immediately after he left the front door. The nondescript, two-story brick home beside it must be where Texas Tom and Cory were staying.

Lights were ablaze on the first floor.

Realizing my initial thoughts about taking a bold approach were too risky, I crept up to the house to gather whatever intel I could find.

I cut through a tiny front yard and stood in the shadows at the corner of the house. Missy stayed back near the house next door. The wizard's house was silent.

I cleared my head, slowed my breathing, and eased myself into a semi-trance state.

And I listened. Not with my ears, but with my telepathy. I scanned the psychic frequency for other people's thoughts.

I came up with nothing, except Missy's fretting about how risky this was and some guy next door pondering whether he should have grits for breakfast.

Cory, are you there?

I sent my question out as a brain wave, over and over again, with no response. Cory wasn't telepathic, but if it worked with Diana, it might with him.

He didn't reply.

I went back to listening. Scattered, angry thoughts came from the wizard's house, probably from Tom. They were too guarded for me to decipher them.

But one thing was sure: this guy was furious. I hoped it didn't involve Cory.

Since my telepathy wasn't producing, I moved on to psychometry. It was a much more powerful ability, anyway.

Holding my hand above the handrail that ran up the short steps to the front door, I found many fast, perfunctory memories from an elderly woman. I got the impression she came by the house regularly to cook and clean. She leaned heavily on the handrail as she struggled up and down the stairs. I sensed a memory that was recent, so I grabbed the handrail and slid my hand along it as I climbed the steps and—

— (swing the bag of provisions up to the top step.) Praise be, the two of 'em don't eat much. You'd expect two men of middling age would indulge themselves more, but not these two. They're rather like monks, they are. Always studying the books. Haven't seen the clean-shaven one as much of late. I wonder what kind of relationship these two—

—the memory broke off as she reached the top step.

What I learned was encouraging. It did sound as if Texas Tom and Cory lived here. Checking the handrail for more memories, I held my hand just above it and moved back down the steps.

I sensed nothing except the old lady's random thoughts from her regular visits and older snippets from a previous tenant. There weren't any I could attribute to the wizard. I guessed he never used the railing.

Just before I gave up, I sensed something powerful at the very bottom.

Cory's thoughts. I grabbed the metal. I—

—am so depleted, I can't make it up the stairs without help. When Tom took the energy of the ley lines from me, he took all my natural energy, too. He drained me dry, leaving but a husk. I feel so exploited by this jerk. I wish I had the strength to stop him, but he always takes all I have. If he is successful in enslaving the entire Magic Guild, he'll be able to drain the energy from all of them. He'll have so much power, he'll be unstoppable. If I could kill him with a kitchen knife, I would have already, but he always

keeps a protection spell around himself, except when I'm magically bound and paralyzed. The only thing I can do is escape. In the few seconds between when I'm filled with all the energy I can handle from the ley lines and when he grabs me to steal it, that's when I can make a break for it. I'll be strong, and he'll be caught off guard. A gateway will be nearby, and I can dive in if I'm fast enough. Then, somehow, I'll make my way back to the time to which I belong. And to Darla. He's offering his hand to help me—

—cry. I don't mean to, but reliving Cory's memory just turns me into a mess.

A fear grips me, that what I sensed when we arrived here was him escaping. Don't get me wrong—if he escaped, I'll be elated. But doing so on his own could leave him stranded in the In Between. If I knew for sure that he escaped, Missy and I would leave here immediately.

Let me check the doorknob to see if it holds any important memories.

I went back up the steps and scanned the knob. It didn't feel promising. Doorknobs rarely retain much of value, since people hold them so briefly.

The door flew open. An old man stood there with long white hair and an enormous white beard. He wore a suit with an ascot tie.

"Ah," he said, "Darla, I presume?"

He grabbed me by the hair and yanked me into the house, slamming the door behind me.

FOR A PETITE WOMAN, I CAN BE PRETTY FORMIDABLE IF A MAN grabs me. I have done some damage to dudes half this guy's age. But he went directly into magic mode. Before I could so much as stomp on his foot, I was paralyzed with the sensation of rope wrapped all around me.

Then, I was levitating. I floated in a horizontal position down the hallway and up the stairs. The wizard walked behind me like a balloon handler at the Macy's Thanksgiving Day Parade.

"Your husband has been naughty and ran away," the wizard said. "But your visit won't be in vain. I'll find him and bring him back here. And he'll never leave my side again."

A bedroom door upstairs opened on its own accord, and I drifted inside. When I was above a narrow bed, I dropped, bounced on the mattress, crashed into the wall, and ended up lying on the bed, still bound by the invisible magic rope.

"Whoa, not a chick I'd expect to find here," said a familiar male voice.

Arch Mage Bob sat on a wooden chair at a small desk.

I strained my neck to look at him.

"Can you help me out here?" I asked.

"Yeah, yeah." He got up and grabbed my shoulders and legs, straightening me upon the bed so I wouldn't be in pain. As someone about to leave middle age behind, he sympathized with my recalcitrant body.

"How did you get here?" he asked.

"Same way you did, I guess. The In Between?"

"Yup."

"Did you come willingly?"

"Nope," Bob said. "He kidnapped me."

I wasn't sure if I believed him, but I'd accept him at his word for now.

"Okay. Give me a few moments for a mental-health break," I said.

I sent out a telepathic message to Missy. She, like Cory, did not have telepathy, but an urgent message from me should be able to appear in her head.

Missy, I'm okay for the time being. Block yourself so he doesn't sense your magick.

I did.

Good. Now try to stay hidden and safe. At some point, I'm sure he'll leave, and I'll need you to help us escape.

Us? Did you find Cory?

Sadly, no. I found Arch Mage Bob.

Yuck.

Yuck was the last word I heard from her for a while.

CHAPTER 14

MEGALOMANIAC

"Why did you let him capture you?" I asked Arch Mage Bob, who now, more than ever, didn't look very much like an arch mage. The person I beheld in the dim morning light was a defeated, old schlub who wore his hair like he was thirty years younger.

"You know, I used to be more powerful than him," Bob said. "He even looked up to me, back when we were training in magic."

"You've known him that long?"

"We were friends since grade school."

"Wait a minute. He looks like he's twenty, thirty years older than you."

"Tom has awesome magic. He changes his appearance all the time. Anyway, something drew us together in the beginning— must have been the magic gene, though neither of us knew at the time we had it. But we were always interested in magic. Stage magic, at first. In high school, we were partners in a magic show. Even got gigs doing birthday parties for little kids."

It sounded cute to me, two kids pretending to be magicians, still innocent of the strain to one's soul from using the power of magic to manipulate matter and other human beings.

"Sometimes, we discovered tricks we could do that weren't in the instruction books. They weren't sleight-of-hand or illusions. They seemed like real magic to us, like making a toad levitate. Or the neighbor's mailbox explode without using fireworks. We just thought it was cool. Didn't see the larger implications. Later, after college, we joined up again. We spent a year at the Lawner Institute."

"I thought that place was a training center for business executives," I said.

"Nope. There were some CEOs there, but not to learn business tactics. It was advanced magic. And some of them got even richer because of it. But Tom and I, we didn't really know what we wanted to do in life. You can't simply be a witch, wizard, or mage and make money that way. Magic can help your career, but it's not a career in itself."

Note to self: remind Sophie she still needs to find a career.

"I mean, look at me," Bob said. "I'm not a suit. I'm not going to use magic to make leveraged buyouts. Surfing is all I want to do. I managed to build a business around it."

"Did you use magic to do it?"

He smiled. "A bit. I make awesome surf boards. But being in the retail business ain't easy. Now, I have the biggest surf shop outside of Cocoa Beach."

"What about Texas Tom?"

"He had a harder time. Worked as a car salesman. Bought a dealership but got mixed up with organized crime and had to sell. Went into real estate. But I think the mafia dudes were never completely out of the picture. Everything changed for him when he captured the faerie."

"The *what?*"

"Faerie."

"You've got to be kidding," I said. "Faeries exist?"

"You don't know about the Fae?"

"Well, I do now. I recently found out elves exist, so why not faeries? I've been an ignorant human for too long. Everything changed once I developed my full paranormal abilities. Which, ironically, happened when I began 'the change.' Since then, I keep discovering that creatures I once thought were only in folk-lore are actually real."

"Duh. That's why they're in folklore."

"Are there a lot of them in San Marcos?"

"Not really. They were driven out by human civilization, like so many other things. But some faeries are around, and you don't want to mess with them, dude. They're like the mafia. And that's how Tom got involved with them, through his organized crime ties."

"How did the Fae help Tom's magic?"

"Well, they've got magic of their own, different than human magic. Probably more powerful. But they're like the mafia, you know? Like parasites. Instead of sucking money out of your business through protection payments, they drink your energy. They taught Tom how to do what he's doing to your husband. He's done it to me. And he's gonna do it to all the witches in San Marcos."

I tried to be delicate with my next question.

"If that's the case, Bob, why were you so reluctant to fight Texas Tom?"

His face reddened, and he looked away.

"I don't want to get into it."

"You're afraid he'll get you in trouble for the pyramid scheme you guys were running?"

"That's part of it."

"Only part?"

He nodded.

"We must defeat Tom," I said. "I need to know what he has over you. You can tell me. What the heck, we're both Tom's prisoners and not even in our own time period."

"Yeah. When we were younger, we were more than friends. You get where I'm going?"

"You were in a relationship?"

He nodded. "I was in love with him. I'd thought I put all that behind me. There were plenty of girlfriends. And then, I got married. That didn't turn out well."

"Are you afraid Tom will divulge your secret? I suppose the surfing world is very macho. Are they not tolerant?"

"That's part of it. But, you see, there are still feelings between us. Even though he's, like, trying to destroy me, overthrow me as Arch Mage, he's promised not to kill me. I don't want to submit to him, but I don't want to kill him either. Or hurt him badly. I guess I don't want to fight him at all. I wish he'd just go away and take over some other magic guild, or coven, or whatever."

Bob was being honest. I could see the hurt in his eyes and the conflicted struggle within.

"We still have to stop him," I said. "It's not just about you. My mother and daughter are witches. My husband, of course, is becoming some sort of magician. I don't want them to become enslaved to a power-mad megalomaniac."

"That description fits him to a tee."

"And think of all the other magic folk in the guild. They don't deserve this."

"I'm sorry for failing them. But no more. If I can't be, like, the tip of the spear, I'll still help in this fight as much as I can.

You're right, this is too important. I gotta forget about all my baggage."

"You don't have to personally hurt Tom. But you have to help us beat him."

"I will, I promise. I guess it's lucky, after all, that you got captured. This talk was very helpful."

"No, it wasn't lucky. I'm bound by magic and virtually paralyzed. And I have to pee. Can you help me get up?"

"Not now. Tom drained my energies, and he also put a blocking spell on me, so I can't use my magic."

"It's up to Missy to help us, then."

"Missy Mindle?"

"Yep. Are you guys still enemies?"

"We, like, had a bit of a conflict over a grimoire once. But we're over that now."

"I heard it was a brutal, abusive conflict."

Bob hung his head. "You could say I've not always been a nice dude."

"Yeah, I'll say. And that leads me to my last question. Did you try to kill me?"

He looked up, genuine bafflement in his face.

"What are you talking about?"

"The limb of the oak tree that killed my guest. I have reason to believe I was an intended target, too."

"I had nothing to do with it. Why would I?"

"There's security footage showing Aaron cutting a notch beneath the limb a few nights before it broke and killed my guest. Aaron acts like he was under the influence of a spell when he did it, and he used your chainsaw. Did you make him do it?"

"No way. Why do you think I would?"

"To make it look like an amateur magician did it instead of you."

"But I don't get it. Why would I try to kill you? There's, like, no reason."

"You could have wanted to appease Tom, to help him by offing his prisoner's wife."

"Listen, dude, Tom doesn't need anyone's help in killing people."

"Unless he wanted it to seem like someone else did it."

"What can I say?" he shrugged. "I had nothing to do with it. You can decide to believe me or not."

"We'll drop the topic for now and try to get out of here. What spells did he cast upon you besides blocking your magic?"

"He put a freaking tether on me. I can only leave this room to use the bathroom. Can't go any further than that or it yanks me back like a leash on a bad dog."

"Please don't bring up the bathroom."

"Sorry."

"Let me communicate with Missy and get her to help us."

"If she can. Tom's magic is pretty rad."

"Missy has come a long way with her powers. You'd be surprised. Is there anyone else in the house?"

He shook his head no.

I focused on her, picturing her face, feeling with my mind for hers, then sent my thoughts to her.

Missy, we need you now. We're imprisoned on the second floor. No one else is here.

Shortly afterwards, her words spoke in my head.

The front door is locked. I'll need some time to unlock it. I'm not too good at this kind of spell.

"She's on her way," I said.

We waited. Faint metallic clicks came from downstairs. Finally, footsteps rose up the creaky stairs. I had a sudden fear that it was Tom returning.

The bedroom door opened. Thankfully, it was Missy.

"Whoa!" Bob said. "Nice dress. Did you get it here?"

"Yes, I have an account at the local millinery," Missy snarked.

We explained to her the different spells Tom had placed on us.

"I can't simply wipe away a powerful wizard's magic," Missy said. "I need to cast negation spells. The binding and tether spells will take some work, but I can break them. The spell blocking your magic, Bob, will probably block mine."

"Try a liberation spell. There's one in the grimoire you stole."

"I didn't steal it. The book was passed down to me from my father. Don't antagonize the witch who's trying to free you."

That shut him up, no small feat.

"I don't know that one," Missy said. "And the grimoire is at my house in Jellyfish Beach."

"You gave me photocopies. They're in my office. We need to go there as soon as we get back."

CHAPTER 15

NEEDED

Cory landed face-down on a wet, spongy ground of ferns and large-leafed plants. He got to his feet and looked around. He was in a tropical rainforest of sorts. Smaller trees formed a canopy of leaves about two stories above, but the massive trunks of taller trees rose above this first canopy to heights he couldn't see.

But something was off in this forest. There were no sounds, no singing birds or buzzing insects. He glanced at the ground where he had fallen and realized there were no dead leaves as you'd find on any forest floor. The air was humid and smelled of lush greenery, but something was fake about the place. He'd been dragged by Tom to and from the In Between several times over the past year, but he'd never been to this rainforest before. Like all the In Between, it was an illusion, despite seeming so real.

He also knew that while the birds and insects were missing, he needed to be on guard. Because creatures did exist in the In Between. And they tended to be freakish and dangerous.

Cory had no plan except to find humans. A minuscule number of people traveled to and from the In Between, coming here to escape danger or persecution on earth. All magicians of one type or another, these refugees lived in different eras of human history and returned to those same times to repair the molecular damage that spending too much time in the In Between caused.

In Cory's case, he needed to return not to 1891, but to Darla's present day. The time and place where she was waiting for him.

If he ran into a magician here, could this person help him find a gateway and convince it to send him home to the present day?

When he had accidentally stepped through the gateway in Key West and came here for the first time, he hadn't known what to do. He had simply wandered through a large grassy plain until Tom found him. This time, he didn't know what else to do other than wander. He hoped if he did encounter someone, the person would be benevolent.

Cory weaved his way through the ferns and low bushes that lived in the forest's understory, where little to no direct sunlight made it through the canopies above. Though the air was humid, no water collected on leaves as you'd find in a real rainforest, because it didn't rain in the In Between. His chances of finding water were slim.

Most of the small amount of useful magic he'd learned from Tom wouldn't work here in the In Between. Cory had discovered that before. He could do very simple spells powered by the natural energies within himself, but he couldn't draw upon the elemental earth energies. He wasn't on earth. And the In Between didn't have those elemental energies.

This place itself existed because of magic, but it was a different sort, an ancient magic that predated the earth and the stars. The magicians who came here knew how to tap into it to create the food and water they needed to live, dragons who came here from earth tapped into it, the gateways fed upon it, and the souls who waited here in limbo were constrained by it. But Cory didn't know how to access it. Tom knew only as much as the other magicians. Yet, Tom wanted to learn more, because it was obvious this magic was vast and powerful.

Was it more powerful than earth magic? Tom believed it might be. And, as the most power-obsessed individual Cory had ever known, Tom would be the one who knew.

Cory trudged through the forest, ducking beneath vines, dodging the smaller trees, and making detours around the trunks of the larger trees. These trees had moss on the bark, as if it were a real rainforest.

Details such as this were hard to fathom. If the landscapes of the In Between were illusions, then who created them? Who would have added moss to the bark of trees in a forest without rain? And why? Was the In Between another of God's creations? Or someone else's?

He wondered if the place was created based upon images and memories in the human mind, seemingly real but always off a bit, like dreams.

He'd been moving through the trees for quite some time now when he noticed the sounds of something else coming behind him. There had been silence before, only the noise of Cory's own footsteps crunching through the brush. It was a somewhat muffled sound, due to all the vegetation. But these new footsteps alarmed him.

Was Tom hunting him?

Or was it something else?

He stopped and failed to spot the creature in the dark, dense forest. He held his breath and listened. The creature walked a couple of more steps before stopping, too. It sounded like a biped. Hopefully, a human. It was waiting for Cory to resume walking. The waiting was unbearable, so he continued his trek.

He hoped it was not Tom. But there was no guarantee it would be someone friendly.

The sounds of his pursuer were closer now, so Cory picked up his speed, but his boots kept getting hung up in tiny vines hidden in the carpet of ferns and leafy plants. He looked for a weapon lying on the ground, but there were no broken branches or stones he could use.

The forest had become smothering and haunting. He wanted to leave it and get out into the open and bright light so he could see his pursuer.

He considered turning around and heading toward his pursuer, to force the inevitable confrontation.

But then came sounds of another creature. It was coming toward Cory, but from another direction.

It was not a biped. It hastened toward him on four or more legs.

Cory turned in the direction away from both creatures and tried to run. He fell flat on his face, tripped by a vine, but scrambled to his feet and kept going.

Both pursuers picked up their paces, as well.

Cory scanned the trees behind and to the side of him. Still no sign of anything or anyone.

But wait—leaves were shaking on the small trees off to his right. Two saplings snapped in half, and something large and dark clambered over them.

It was a giant beetle. No, giant was not the right word. Colossal? Larger than a full-size SUV?

Cory turned and ran in full panic, crashing into trees, tripping on a vine and nearly falling. The giant insect galloped on its six legs, crunching through the underbrush, crawling sideways around the trunks of the large trees, pushing the smaller ones to the side.

It was almost upon him, its mandibles clicking in anticipation of a meal.

Though he knew it probably wouldn't work, Cory tried casting the most basic protection spell he knew, one he could invoke while running and unable to concentrate fully.

Nothing happened. He couldn't pull any energy from the environment, nor could he gather and concentrate his own energies. It was like flicking a lighter and seeing no flame.

Something caught the back of Cory's nineteenth century suit coat, pulling him backwards. He landed heavily on his back.

The beetle's mandibles clicked like infernal machinery as they descended toward his face.

The fireball knocked the beetle sideways and singed Cory's hair.

Tom was about twenty feet away, aiming his staff at the giant insect. It was his main staff, the one tipped with the skeletal hand. Another fireball flew from it and struck the beetle before it reacted to the first attack.

As soon as the fireball landed on its carapace, the giant insect disappeared. Black fragments sprinkled the ferns below, telling Cory that the monster had not been an illusion.

"I wouldn't run if I were you," Tom said. "These fireballs are especially nasty when they hit human flesh."

"Why did you come after me?" Cory asked.

"You're asking that of the man who saved your life?"

"I guess I wouldn't have minded dying if I could die free."

"Oh, come now. Let's not be melodramatic. You don't have it so bad being my assistant."

"Prisoner. And you tortured me."

"Please, it was a slap on the wrist compared to what I could have done. You needed to be punished for stealing the pearl from my other staff. Which you still haven't returned, I might add."

Tom finished closing the distance between them. No longer in the guise of an old man, he appeared to be in his actual age, in his fifties, a little older than Cory. He stood close enough to touch him with his staff, the head of which was still glowing red.

"I don't have it," Cory said.

"We'll save this discussion for later. Let's find a gateway and go home."

"Home, for me, is the time period when I used to live with my wife."

"And you will return there when we make our triumphant entry into San Marcos and rule the Magic Guild."

"I have the impression your ambitions are greater than that."

Tom laughed. "Indeed, they are. But one step at a time. Let's go now. You've been of immense help to me, and, as I've said, I'll be sure to reward you."

"Why do you need me? Is it only because of the ley lines? You can harvest them without me, right?"

Tom's face darkened. "Your companionship, I could never replace. Come, let's go."

Cory truly had no choice other than going along with his captor.

"How can your staff be so powerful here in the In Between?" he asked. "There's no energy to be used here for magic."

"This staff has tremendous power of its own. It doesn't need to draw upon elemental energy. And my organic energies have been enhanced over the years. They're what I use to activate the staff's magic. If you stole this staff from me, it wouldn't do anything for you."

It sounded credible, but Cory wondered if Tom was lying to discourage him from stealing the staff. It didn't really matter, because even if he escaped again from Tom, he didn't have a way to return to the present day, only to 1891 again. His only hope would have been to find another magician who could make a gateway take him to the time he wanted. And he couldn't do that with Tom on his heels in the In Between.

As a magician with experience in the In Between, Tom had a knack for finding gateways. He couldn't summon one, but he could sniff one out, eventually.

"Head this way," Tom said, pointing in the direction from which the beetle had come. Every direction in this forest looked the same to Cory, so he followed Tom's guidance.

Tom followed behind, close enough to touch him with the staff.

Cory had seen Tom use the staff when casting a variety of spells, but its main purpose seemed to be as a weapon. It did more than shoot fireballs. Tom had used it like a super-powered Taser to kill a pickpocket once in 1891. Tom merely touched the thief with the tip of the staff, and amid a crackle of electricity and the smell of burned hair, the man had dropped dead in front of them.

Cory did not want to be touched by it himself.

They walked silently through the forest for what seemed like hours. Finally, Cory couldn't bear his thirst any longer.

"Tom, could you make some water for me, please?"

"All right."

They stopped. Tom bent and plucked a leaf the size of a dinner plate, handing it to Cory.

"Form a cup with it," Tom said. "Yes, like that."

Tom closed his eyes, recited a verse in Latin, then touched the leaf with the head of his staff.

And suddenly, the leaf was filled with water.

Cory drank greedily from it. It tasted like real water, cool and with no aftertaste. Cory drank half the leaf cup and offered the rest to Tom, who took it and drained it.

"Thank you," Cory said.

Ahead, the forest floor sloped downwards slightly.

"There's a valley down there with a river running through it. Gateways seem to like that valley."

"You make it sound as if gateways were creatures."

"Perhaps they are."

After another long period of silence, Cory broke it.

"What do you want, Tom? I mean, really *want*. Why is ruling the Magic Guild so important to you?"

"I want to put Arch Mage Bob in his place."

"He's already your prisoner. There has to be more that you want."

"Power."

"For what? I guess I don't understand because I've never wanted power for power's sake."

"Money is one reason. You can understand that, can't you? I always seem to find myself with money problems. And the more power I have, the more money-making opportunities will open for me."

Cory still was not satisfied with this answer. But he remained silent, hoping it would allow Tom to open up more.

"Maybe it comes down to love," Tom said out of the blue.

"Love?"

"Yeah. I've never found true love, and I've given up waiting for it to come along. But I've learned true love comes from desire, and desire comes from need. What is the typical relationship other than two people who need things from each other? It could be as simple as your partner needing your body, your companionship, your help in parenting. Often, your money. When you come right down to it, love is the most common thing in the world and quite mundane, frankly."

"No, it's wonderful," Cory said. "You're so cynical."

Tom laughed. "Romanticize it all you want, but it's still mundane. I'll tell you what's not mundane. Absolute power. It's awe-inspiring. If you have the power to do nearly anything, everyone needs you. Everyone loves you, even if they hate themselves for it. Power creates need in others. And their need gives you even more power over them. It's so much better than love, I tell you. It's the ticket to glorious immortality."

"Then, isn't immortality what you ultimately want? Can't magic do that for you? Vampirism could."

"Who would want to live forever as a nobody? I want the constant need from everyone, the constant reminder of how much they want me."

"You ever think there might be a better way to get that, other than conquering the guild and turning its members into your energy slaves?"

"No, I haven't, frankly. That's simply the way it works. It will be a symbiotic relationship with the magic folk, but everyone else will simply admire me for my power."

"Everyone else?" Cory asked. "You're talking about ruling over more than the Magic Guild?"

"Good to see it's finally sinking in. You think too small. For me, the world is my oyster."

This guy is way too full of himself, Cory thought. But he's also really dangerous.

Cory glanced back at Tom. He didn't look like a charismatic leader. With a graying goatee, balding head, and potbelly, he looked like an overworked middle manager.

"Careful, or you're going to trip," Tom said.

The ground sloped more steeply now. And up ahead, the trees finally thinned out enough to allow glimpses of a river cutting through rocky banks. Cory knew the water would be poisonous and hold no edible fish, only monstrous creatures he couldn't even imagine.

He dug his boots into the rocky soil as he descended to the river. The noise of the rushing water was loud.

Tom joined him at the edge of the riverbank, watching the raging water.

"I feel a gateway not too far from here," Tom said. "This way. You go first." He pointed to his right.

Cory headed along the muddy, rocky bank, careful to not get too close to the edge where the ground was slippery.

The river was unnaturally straight. On both sides, the rainforest sloped down steeply. Though they were no longer stuck within the trees, the narrow valley was as claustrophobic as the forest.

They walked for a long while, Tom close enough behind to strike him with the staff.

But now, a familiar nausea crept into Cory's stomach.

"It's close now," Tom said.

About twenty feet ahead, a large section of air turned semi-opaque and shimmered. The gateway.

"Okay, my pet, let's hold hands going through," Tom said. "I don't trust you, of course."

Tom came up to stand beside him with an expression of sneering arrogance. Of mockery. Anger rose quickly in Cory.

At that moment, Tom looked like little more than a flabby, middle-aged jerk.

The anger, and the giddy anticipation of the release of it, swept through Cory. He couldn't help himself.

He swung his fist with all his might and clocked Tom in the jaw.

The wizard stumbled backward, completely off guard.

Before Tom could raise his staff in defense, Cory sprang and slammed into him with his shoulder and arms, like a linebacker savaging a quarterback. Tom went flying backwards.

Cory grabbed the ground to stop his forward momentum. And watched Tom, flailing his arms, fall off the bank into the river.

Cory leaped into the gateway and was gone.

CHAPTER 16

THE FAERIE QUEENE

M issy knelt within an improvised magic circle she'd
drawn on the bedroom floor with a pencil. She found
plenty of candles downstairs in the dining room, and five of
them were burning along the circumference of the circle, one at
each point of an imagined pentagram. She complained she didn't
have ingredients with her that were important in creating the
negation spells. However, I saw her clutching something under
her blouse between her breasts. I was certain it was the Red
Dragon. She would never want Bob to know she had it, because
he would want to steal it, but she would need it to undo Texas
Tom's magic.

As soon as she ended her incantation, I had the sensation of
severed ropes falling from my body.

"It worked!" I said. "Please help me to the bathroom. Fast!"

Missy helped me get my stiff and sore body off the bed and
into the bathroom next door. It looked like a modern bathroom,
except for an egregious lack of cabinets and counter space.
There was a quaint claw-foot tub, pedestal sink, subway tile, and

a toilet tank that was up near the ceiling. I had plenty of time to observe the décor before I was finished in there.

When I returned to the bedroom, Missy had finished negating the tethering spell that had kept Bob on a short leash.

"Remember, we have to do the spell to break his magic-blocker as soon as we get back," Bob said. "I feel naked without my magic."

"We will," Missy said. "I sure don't want to see you naked."

"I want to look for Cory when we're in the In Between," I said.

"We don't have time for that, dude," Bob said. "And Tom has, like, probably already caught him."

"You can go home without us."

"I need Missy to help me break the blocking spell. I can't do it to myself."

"You have plenty of witches to help you," Missy said. "I'm not leaving Darla alone in the In Between."

Bob sighed with exasperation. "Well, let's ditch this place."

"Not so fast," I said. "This is my one chance to search for memories on Tom's stuff. I might find something valuable."

"Are you serious? That will take forever," Bob whined.

In truth, I was anxious to go looking for Cory, but Bob was right: Tom had probably already recaptured him, as much as it hurt me to think so. I wanted to find information that could help us defeat Tom for good, so I could get my husband back, and the attacks on the magic folk of San Marcos would stop.

"His bedroom is at the end of the hall," Bob said. "And he spends a lot of time in the study downstairs. But please, hurry. Maybe you don't care when I get my magic back, but we don't want to be here when Tom gets home."

The bedroom was spartan, like the one where the prisoners were kept. I didn't know how much time Tom spent in the year

1891, but he had very few possessions in the room. Three suits and a half dozen shirts hung in the closet, along with six cravats. His dresser held a minimum of underclothes. A brush and hair tonic sat atop the dresser. The bathroom held only soap, cologne, a toothbrush, and a ceramic container of tooth powder.

In the interest of time, I was hovering my hand an inch away from the possessions, searching for powerful memories. Namely, memories of plotting to kill Mrs. Ogglethwarp and me. I found nothing promising, except on the hairbrush.

The man apparently spent a great deal of time brushing his hair. I grabbed the handle and felt the—

—thick old-man beard shrinking back into my goatee. Looking at my face. I could hide those gray hairs with a little magic . . . (gray disappears from goatee) . . . nah, people will think it's dyed (gray returns). Okay, then, back to modern San Marcos for some trendy food from a menu that doesn't have any blasted mutton on it! But I wish the gateways didn't make me feel so nauseous—

—the memory ended as he put down the brush.

Nothing deep revealed here, but the one thing I learned is extremely interesting.

The face he saw in the mirror is the same one I saw from Mrs. Ogglethwarp's memory. Texas Tom was her dinner date that fateful night.

What was the connection between them, the deal they were doing together? I wondered if it had something to do with the pyramid scheme Bob told me about. If that arrangement had become messy, it might be a motive for murder.

The murder of Mrs. Ogglethwarp. But what did I have to do with it?

This was a puzzle I'd love to solve, but not now. I needed to hurry and finish in this house before Tom returned, so I went downstairs to the study.

This was a modest home. The study was just as modest. It held a desk, two leather wingback chairs, and three of the four walls were covered by built-in bookshelves.

I sat behind the desk in a rather uncomfortable wooden chair with wheels. Since time was short, I wanted to find something about me—why I was an intended target of the tree limb. With both hands hovering above the desk, I moved them around and tried to feel for incriminating memories. I'm sorry, but there just wasn't enough time to scope out the multidimensional intellect of almighty Tom. I picked up lots of threads about magic and his power-mad desires, but I was looking for memories about myself. Yes, *me*. It was all about me.

And I came up short. Apparently, Tom didn't give a fig about me because there were no thoughts about me.

Without me in his thoughts, this poor man was missing out on life. But that was his loss.

Missy's face appeared in the study doorway. "I'm getting nervous sitting around here. Let's hurry," she said.

"Gotcha."

I ignored her and glanced around the small room. My eyes sized up the bookshelves, the one impressive feature of this room. Or of the house, for that matter.

I moved to the leather wingback chair closest to the shelves. Beside it was a small round table, just large enough for a glass of brandy and an ashtray for a cigar. On the other side was a floor lamp with a shade that had little frilly things hanging from it.

I'd assumed Tom didn't own but rented the place, so Tom was probably not the one who built up the nineteenth-century book collection. However, three shelves within arm's reach of the chair I was in held books about magic.

My eye was caught by the spine of a book on the magic of gemstones. I picked up fragmentary memories of Cory handling the book. I savored the thought that he had touched the leather I touched now, and I tried not to be overcome by the disappointment of having just missed him here in 1891.

A couple of shelves above sat Spenser's *The Faerie Queene*. It had a new significance now that I knew the Fae truly existed. What did they want from Tom, and what did he receive from them, other than the ability to harvest energy from magic folk?

I didn't believe this book belonged to Tom since it was such an old epic poem, but I had the strong urge to touch it. I held my finger near the spine and felt powerful psychic energy. It didn't feel like it was from a human. I'd never read a memory from a non-human of intelligence before, so the sensation was strange to me.

I pulled the book from the shelf safely, without being pulled into a reverie. Opening the cover, I read the inscription on the title page, written in old and faded ink in florid cursive.

To Tom,

It was such a pleasure meeting you. Please accept this as a gift from not only me but our entire race. It is part of our tradition of a gift for a power, a power for a gift, and blood for the most powerful gift. You'll come to understand its meaning someday. I look forward to our future partnership.

Sincerely,

Gleewight

It was dated in the year 1595, only five years after the original publication of the poem.

Had Tom traveled back in time to receive this book?

I opened the book to a page halfway through, pressed my right palm against it and my left against the cover. Books aren't great for holding memories, not in the paper at least. The leather binding would do better. But I sought a memory nearly 500 years old. How likely would it be to find—

—magic for your power, power for your children. Give us what we now struggle to produce. Give us what we need for our race to survive. We'll help you rule the human world if you give us their children. And through magic we will make them ours—

—the memory cut off like a hose deprived of water.

And if I understood it correctly, Tom had entered into a deal with the devil. Or, in this case, with the Fae. They would help him gain power to rule over humans. And he would help them get human children to keep their race from dying off.

Horrifying stuff, indeed.

"We really should get out of here, Darla," Missy said in the study's doorway.

"Right. I'm ready."

Missy, Bob, and I hurriedly left by the back door.

"It's about time we left," Bob said. "I thought I was being freed from this place, yet I was still here."

"Where are you going?" Missy asked as I reached the street and started walking in the opposite direction from which we'd come. "Your house is this way."

"We're not going there. Old Courage is much closer, and we know gateways show up there often."

"Where did you arrive here?" I asked Bob.

"In Tom's house."

"That's where he left from after he captured me," I said. "So hopefully, he'll return there and not near us."

We walked along the streets. The traffic of horse-drawn carriages and mule-drawn wagons was so striking to me. It was actually pretty cool to someone used to gasoline-powered cars clogging the streets. There weren't many pedestrians on the route we took, but they were a similar mix as today, locals doing their daily routines, while tourists wandered stupidly through them. The difference was, these tourists wore suits, bowler hats, ankle-length dresses. Not T-shirts and baseball caps like those of today.

My stomach growled, reminding me that nearly an entire day had passed by now. I hoped darkness would fall and the streets would clear before the gateway showed up and whisked us away. Three people disappearing into shimmering air would not go unnoticed.

Seeing Old Courage was like coming across a younger version of a good friend—familiar yet perplexing in its comparative youthfulness. Though it was hundreds of years old at this point. The limb that killed Mrs. Ogglethwarp was smaller now, of course, and healthy. The knothole that swallowed the pearl was barely visible, if you knew where to look.

For the briefest moment, I wanted to see the pearl, but disturbing it would break all the rules of time travel. So, I let it be. We needed to focus on summoning a gateway. They'd been very cooperative with me lately, but I figured Missy would need to use the Red Dragon to get one to come quickly. After it brought us to the In Between, we would have just one more leg of the journey back to the present.

To the east, the bay was taking on a purplish tone in the fading sunlight. Sailboats and small steamboats were moored at the marina, bobbing in the current.

I turned to Missy, about to whisper in her ear to summon a gateway with her talisman, when the air began shimmering across my view of the marina.

A gateway had arrived on its own accord!

A dark silhouette of a person appeared in the gateway. Then a man stepped somewhat unsteadily from it onto the grass of the park.

The man was my husband, Cory.

CHAPTER 17

A LOT OF CATCHING UP
TO DO

Cory stepped forward, as if walking onto a dock from a rocking boat. His eyes squinted in the setting sun. His straight blondish hair, parted on the side, was long and shaggy enough to call for a haircut. It had been several days since he shaved. He was way too thin and frail, adding to the ache in my heart. He'd been a prisoner, after all. But he wasn't dressed like one. He wore a long brown jacket over a red waistcoat with a matching red ascot tie. His slacks were a darker brown, ending atop cordovan dress boots.

His eyes darted back and forth as he assessed the situation. First, they went to the tree, Old Courage. A hansom cab rattling across cobblestones startled him.

It was only then that his eyes found me, widening with surprise.

"I came all this way to look for you, and you go off on a little adventure," I said.

He dashed toward me and grabbed me in a bear hug, pulling

me off the ground as he often did, his six-foot frame engulfing petite me.

"I feared I'd never see you again," his lips said against my cheek. His tears traveled down my cheek to my lips, and I tasted them.

Then his lips were all over mine. I forgot to breathe.

Finally, when he set me back on the ground, his face flushed, his eyes filled with delight, he noticed Missy and Bob.

"May I present Missy," I said, "the cousin I met for the first time after you were gone. And Bob, Arch Mage of the Magic Guild of San Marcos."

"Pleased to meet you," Cory said, looking like he was about to give them bear hugs, too. He resisted and shook their hands instead.

He took my hand as if he would never let go of it again.

"Wait, Magic Guild?" he asked.

"Yes," Bob said, "the very one Texas Tom is trying to take over."

"Do you know the guild because your mom's a witch?" Cory asked me.

"Yes, and, well, because I'm in a guild myself. The Memory Guild. A lot has happened since you left. My telepathy has strengthened, and I discovered a new ability, psychometry. Mom thinks the onset of menopause set it off."

It was a lot for Cory to take in.

"And Missy's a witch, too," I added. "So is Sophie now, though she just started."

"I guess you're into the paranormal now instead of inn keeping," Cory said.

"No, I'm still doing that. I sold our B&B in Key West and bought a historic inn in San Marcos. It used to be the Hidalgo Inn."

"I know that one. Wow."

"You guys have a lot of catching up to do," Missy said, "but we need to get out of here before Tom returns."

"He may have drowned in a river in the In Between," Cory said. "But I wouldn't count on it. If we go back there, we could run into him."

"We have to go there to catch a gateway to the present day," I said.

"You can control the gateways like Tom?"

"Well, Missy can," I said.

"How, exactly?" Bob asked.

"Oh, just a spell I've developed."

"Let's go," I said, trying to help Missy avoid mentioning the Red Dragon.

Before Missy even had to cast her spell, a gateway appeared. I tensed for a moment, worried that Tom would pop out. But he didn't. The gateway was just for us. I wished I knew why they seemed to be actively helping us.

The four of us walked toward it, Cory and I holding hands. Bob was more hesitant, being newer to this form of travel. But once he caught up to us, we went through together.

We landed on the top of a mesa in an arid Grand Canyon-like landscape. I'd been in this part of the In Between before, but only briefly. Because of the altitude, and the sheer drop off on every side of the plateau, we couldn't travel anywhere except via a gateway.

"I'm glad we didn't return to where I was when I escaped from Tom," Cory said. "He can't get us up here."

A fireball streaked up from the valley below and hit the side of the plateau, just below the lip.

"Okay, I take that back."

We all ducked as more fireballs rocketed up to us. Most hit

the sides of the plateau harmlessly, but some rose above us, then plunged downward, landing on the surface nearby.

"That one was too close for comfort," I said.

"He's firing them with his wizard's staff," Cory explained.

"Missy, help!"

"I don't have the ability to shoot back," she said. "You know I'm not that kind of witch."

"Please summon a gateway," Bob said. "Fast."

This time, Missy needed to invoke her spell. I guess the gateways were all busy at the moment. When one materialized a few minutes later, about twenty feet from us, a fireball arced into it and disappeared.

"I wonder where that one ended up," Cory said.

"Hopefully, not on my inn."

Missy finished the spell, ordering the gateway to take us back to the year in which we actually lived.

So, back into the stomach-churning chariot we went.

And when we arrived in my courtyard in front of my cottage, with the flowers I had grown in the planters, I sighed with relief.

Missy left with Bob to go to his store, where he had a photocopy of the grimoire in his safe. She'd use one of its spells to free Bob's magic.

And Cory and I, we had a year's worth of talking to do. But we also had other things to catch up on, we both knew, as I led him into my cottage.

Only to be blocked by a black cat, tail sticking straight up, eyes fixated on Cory.

"This is my cat, Cervantes," I said, "but I was told he's been chosen to be your witch's familiar. Cervantes, this is Cory, the guy you've been waiting for. I guess we had that much in common."

"A familiar? Is that really a thing?"

"I'll let you two decide."

Cory and I didn't have a pet in Key West, though both of us love dogs and cats. Right now, Cory seemed shy with Cervantes, too timid to do anything other than let the cat sniff him and rub himself against the human's legs. In fact, Cory seemed apprehensive, as if he was being judged before being approved or rejected.

The cat made a *mrrrmth* vocalization, then looked up at him.

A big grin lit Cory's face, and he pushed his hair aside and squatted beside Cervantes, rubbing the cat's cheeks and scratching his head.

"I completely agree," Cory said.

Cervantes purred as loudly as an idling motorcycle.

"It wasn't my fault," Cory said. "I was detained. But I'm here now, thanks to your mommy. You must continue to be nice to her, too. . . I see. I recall her snoring occasionally. Is it really so bad? No, that's good."

"Hey," I said. "It's impolite to talk about me when I can hear only one side of the conversation."

"He speaks in perfect English," Cory said. "With a bit of a Spanish accent. He seems very wise, and I think he's lived a lot longer than your average cat. Oh, really? He says he's lived in San Marcos since the second Spanish occupation."

"So, he has, like, nine hundred lives?"

"Something like that."

"Would he mind going off and hunting lizards to give us some privacy?"

Cervantes sauntered across the courtyard, and I dragged Cory to the bedroom.

Our time together was too precious to waste. We both knew the time for love would soon turn into the time for battle.

As we cuddled on the couch after dinner, Cory turned to me and asked, "Can we simply begin again where we left off? It's a different inn, but I can put my labor into it and make your life easier."

"If only it could be as simple as that. There are mysteries that must be solved and a war to be fought."

Cory sighed and stroked my hair. "Still no gray hairs."

"Stop trying to change the subject!" I said. "Someone tried to kill me, along with Mrs. Ogglethwarp. I need to find the killer. I thought it might have been Bob or his assistant. Tom remains the most likely subject, but I want to be sure."

"When you told me the story, something stuck out at me. You said the shaman's spirit who lived in the tree said the magic was meant to kill the spiritualist and the person with her."

"Right. Me."

"But what if it meant to kill someone other than you? Maybe Mrs. Ogglethwarp had planned on someone else being with her."

"Someone who cancelled on her?"

"Yeah. How far in advance did she invite you?"

"Um, earlier that day, I think."

"So, the spell could have been cast already before you made the plans."

"Or the spell was cast while I was there. Someone was watching us and broke the limb with the magic, like setting off a detonation. He or she was clumsy, and the limb didn't land the way it was supposed to."

"You could be right," Cory said, "but don't ignore my theory. If someone was supposed to be there instead of you, it could help you find out who the killer was."

"Okay," I said. "Duly noted. But that's only one item on the to-do list."

"What do you mean?"

"We have a wizard assaulting our city and our magic community."

"You don't need to get involved in that."

"Too late. I already am. Mom and Sophie are witches. And so are you."

"I'm not sure what I am."

"You have magic. You will be affected by Tom's attacks. And he might come after you and try to recapture you."

"So, what do you suggest? We kill Tom?"

"I don't want to kill anyone. But we need to stop him."

"If Bob won't step up and be a leader to the guild, we need to help the next in line. It shouldn't fall on our shoulders to fight this war."

"And there's another item on the list," I said.

"You've got to be kidding."

"Are you familiar with Tom's deal with the Fae?"

"What deal?"

"Did you look at the book, *The Faerie Queene*, in Tom's study?"

"I saw it, but, no, I didn't open it. I had to read that in college and I'm still scarred."

"There was an inscription in the book to Tom from one of the Fae. And memories on the book. They've been giving Tom power. Bob says they taught him how to drain power from others. In return, Tom promised that they could have human children to convert to faeries and add to their dying race."

"Criminy! That's barbaric."

"Right. When does Tom have to pay them? Or has he already? Another reason we have to stop him."

"If you stop him, or kill him, it doesn't mean the Fae will go away."

"So, how do we stop him?" I asked.

"Tom? Obviously I didn't have much luck at doing that."

"Bob has known him the longest, but you know him the best. At least, recently. What are his weaknesses?"

"Money. For all his great power—real or simply conjured up out of his braggadocio—he always seems to be struggling for cash."

"Some people are like that. Even wizards."

"You'd think. He has at least one other weakness," Cory said. "He's lonely and unloved."

I snorted. "He's an evil wizard. If he wanted to be loved, he shouldn't have become evil."

"I'm serious. He explained to me that the root of his lust for power is the desire to be needed. I know, this is amateur pop psychology."

"It's good to know what makes him tick. It will help us devise a trap for him."

"Tom's too smart," Cory said.

"No one is too smart if you fool them in the same way they fool themselves."

I HOSTED THE FAMILY REUNION DINNER AT THE INN, PUSHING together two of the breakfast tables in the dining room, with tablecloths, of course. Lots of candles. A fire roaring in the fireplace (this one didn't have any gargoyles beneath the mantel). I prepared snapper purchased at the local fish market with hush puppies, cheese grits, and asparagus. I was amply supplied with Pinot Grigio and Sauvignon Blanc.

Sophie had already had her reunion with Cory, complete with an awkward hug. She was from my first marriage and didn't live at home when I married Cory. When we moved to Key West, she had graduated college and had no desire to move down there with us, remaining in San Marcos with the wrong group of friends (that's another story for another time). Therefore, she didn't know Cory well, but definitely liked him. She told me he was still cute.

When Mom arrived, she gave Cory a rib-breaking hug. Her sobbing was a little over-the-top, in my opinion. She waited until the meal was served to launch into him.

"You know, I was so angry with you when you left," she told him.

He smiled uncomfortably.

"I wanted to track you down and shoot you."

"Of course," he said, "I don't blame you. You understand it wasn't on purpose, right?"

"Of course, she understands," I said.

"Why would you walk into a closet you'd never seen before?" Mom asked.

"Mom, you obviously have never been through a gateway before. They can suck you into them."

Mom looked at Cory.

"Yes!" he said. "That's what happened. The closet was too shallow for anyone to need to walk into it, anyway."

"When Darla told me you were being held captive, my heart went out to you," Mom said.

Cory's expression said he wasn't so sure.

"The wizard who kidnapped you is the one who's sending us the lust dreams?" Mom asked.

"Yes," Cory said. "Texas Tom is manipulating you before he comes and tries to take over."

"I don't think the lust dreams are so bad, actually."

"Mom! Will you please think before you talk?"

"I know the dreams are dangerous," Sophie said, but with a distant smile.

WARD PARKER

"He can shoot fireballs," I said.

"I bet he can!" Mom said with too much relish.

"He seems harmless now, but he wants to enslave you, suck all the energy from you, and give the children of San Marcos to the Fae."

"The who?"

"Faeries, Grammers," Sophie said. "I saw some once."

"You did?" I asked.

"Yeah. In the state park. I was camping with some friends and got up really early. The faeries were in a meadow, holding hands in a circle, dancing. I think they let me see them because they sensed magic in me. Though, that was before I knew I had any."

"They might have seemed harmless then, but they can kill humans. Be careful if you ever see any again."

CHAPTER 18

WORLD CHANGING

Another magic attack came that night.

I awoke to hear Cory moaning in the bed beside me. It had been a long time since anyone other than Cervantes had slept in my bed, and the cat didn't moan in his sleep. So, I felt uneasy, to put it mildly.

Cory groaned, followed by a whimper. It sounded like he was having a nightmare, so I stroked his back to calm him. It didn't help.

"No, no," he mumbled.

I kissed his cheek. "It's okay, darling. You're having a bad dream."

He mumbled something incoherent, rolled onto his stomach, and breathed deeply.

All was well again. I fell asleep.

But all was not well. An hour later, I woke again to find Cory's side of the bed empty. The bathroom door was open and the light off. I couldn't simply go back to sleep without knowing where he was.

I checked the living room to find it dark and without Cory. Pulling on shorts and a T-shirt, I stepped outside into the courtyard. The glow of the moon and the light in the fountain illuminated the area well enough to show no one was out there.

My anxiety rising, I entered the inn and checked all the common areas. He was nowhere to be found.

You must understand, a year ago, my husband disappeared one evening. I only just got him back. You could say I had become paranoid about disappearing husbands. Knowing that gateways frequently popped up in my inn, I naturally assumed he'd been taken away again.

I rushed up to the third floor, where the gateways usually appeared as fake attics. But there was no sign of one.

What should I do? Call the police and tell them my husband got out of bed and has been missing for one hour? Or tell them he might be in an alternate plane of existence?

I returned to the cottage and touched the inner doorknob of the front door, since that would be the last thing Cory touched before he left.

I did find something. A vivid image popped immediately into my mind.

Tom's face looking at me sternly.

Did that monster capture Cory again?

Desperate, I tried reaching out to him telepathically.

Cory, can you hear me? Where are you?

I tried this for a half hour, pacing back and forth in my tiny living room, debating whether I should get in the car and roam the city looking for a sleep-walking Cory.

But I forced myself to calm down and concentrate.

Cory, where are you?

At the ley lines, his voice said in my head.

I ran to my car and drove to the park where Old Courage stood.

The eastern sky had the rosy hue of dawn when I arrived at the park. A human form lay at the base of the live oak tree.

I rushed over and knelt beside him.

"Cory, are you hurt?"

"No, just drained," he mumbled, sounding half asleep and utterly exhausted. "Tom is here. He used me to harvest energy from the ley lines."

"Tom is in present-day San Marcos?"

"Yes. He said he's here to stay now. To rule over us all."

I DROVE CORY HOME AND HELPED HIM TO BED. HE'D NEVER looked so weak before. I made him drink a sports drink with electrolytes, not knowing if that would help, but it was worth the try. Then I put him to bed.

Sophie didn't appear while I was preparing breakfast, nor afterwards to help me clean up. I went up to her room, dreading what I might find.

I knocked several times before I heard a muffled response. Letting myself in with the passkey, I found her still in bed, the room dark with drawn shades.

"Are you feeling okay, sweetie?"

"I'm feeling wonderful, Mom. I'm going to meet the man of my dreams tonight."

"What do you mean?"

"Literally, the man I've been dreaming about, the most gorgeous, perfect man in the world. He sent me a message in my dreams to come to a meeting at the Wayward Hotel by the interstate."

"What? Don't you dare go."

"He'll be in the Imperial Ballroom. All the members of the Magic Guild are going. I can't wait."

Oh, boy. Tom has finally made his move to take over the guild. It seems he had already succeeded in taking over its members' minds.

THE IMPERIAL BALLROOM AT THE WAYWARD INN WAS ONE OF those giant spaces that was normally subdivided into rooms suitable for your wedding reception or Kiwanis Club meeting. This evening, it was fully open to maximum capacity.

I had no idea the Magic Guild had so many members. There had to be a couple hundred people here, of all adult ages, a variety of ethnicities, and all gender identities, though members identifying as women were in the majority. From the little I knew about the guild, there were mostly witches and some who called themselves warlocks, though that gender-based term has fallen out of favor. There was an elite number of showy wizards and sorcerers, and only a handful of mages.

Arch Mage Bob, incidentally, was not in attendance. Neither was Cory, who still needed to sleep off his power drain. It seemed Cory was useful to Tom only as a ley-line harvester.

All these guild members sitting in rows of banquet chairs were here to be Tom's foot soldiers in conquering whatever else he wanted to conquer.

I sat between Mom and Sophie in a middle row. No one checked if I was a Magic Guild member, probably because the invitation had gone out via dream spell to the members.

As the only person who wasn't affected by the spell, I assumed I was the only one who saw Tom for what he was: a middle-aged, paunchy guy with a goatee and a bald spot. When Mom and Sophie gazed upon him, they saw the ideal fantasy partner, with the age and characteristics they most desired.

Before the event, I wandered through the members as they stood around making small talk. It was creepy. They were all bug-eyed, head-over-heels in love with Tom. They each described him differently, the way he had appeared in their dreams. No one seemed to mind that those they spoke with described a completely different person than the one they saw. There was no dissonance at all when a male witch talked about Tom as a sexy, curvaceous woman, while the female witch he spoke with described Tom as a famous male movie star.

Tom had miraculously succeeded in brainwashing the entire Magic Guild and making them have a fanatical crush on him. So, my question was, now what?

"Please be seated," said an unseen person over the PA system.

The murmuring voices died out as everyone took a seat. When Tom appeared, they leaped to their feet and applauded him madly. Women screamed like the teenage girls at early Beatles concerts. Soon, the crowd united in "we love you" chants.

"Thank you, thank you," Tom said, waving to his acolytes. He signaled for them to sit down and be quiet. "Thank you all for attending. If you're wondering why this meeting was called, it was to announce a change in the leadership of the Magic Guild. I will be your new leader. I am the only one who can fix the problems and get things done."

You could barely hear the last part of what he was saying over the cheers and applause.

"Thank you so much," he said after the cheering had calmed down somewhat. "You can't imagine how much I appreciate your love and support. I feel inspired and stronger just by being here with you."

What they didn't understand was that he was being literal. He was sucking away their energies and powers for his own use. In fact, as the evening went on, the volume and enthusiasm of the cheering decreased notably. Don't get me wrong, all faces were still alight with rapture, but everyone was also getting more tired.

"It's important that we're all united in our purpose."

Cheers.

"We're not just practicing magic for our own gratification."

Applause.

"We're using our magic for a higher purpose than that. For the glorification of me!"

Cheers and applause.

I waited for him to give them their marching orders. Were they going to sack the city of San Marcos like the barbarians did in Rome? Was he going to run the guild like a crazy doomsday cult?

"Ladies and gentlemen, witches and wizards, I want to introduce you to your new life's work. It's called multi-level marketing. It's how you can get rich in your free time with hardly any effort at all."

Raucous cheers and applause.

"What's the secret? A new miracle product developed in Sweden that will make you rich."

From behind the lectern, he produced a white bottle with a minimalistic label.

"Blubber Buster. Forget about fad diets and dangerous pills. Forget about exercising. Blubber Buster takes the fat off topically. Just rub it into your skin and the weight comes off. Never before has it been so easy to lose weight.

This isn't just game-changing, folks. This is world-changing."

Enthusiastic cheers.

I couldn't believe I was sitting through this. And I knew what dreaded event was coming next.

Yes, a PowerPoint presentation.

A projector turned on and Tom used a remote control to click through slides projected across the bare wall above him.

First came all the Before and After photos of people who lost unbelievable amounts of weight.

Then came photos of the entire product portfolio. There were Blubber Buster creams for every part of your body that harbored fat. Big-Butt Buster, Belly Bulge Buster, Arm-fat Buster, Jelly Jowls Buster—you get the idea. On top of all these products, there were special toning creams and accessories.

The crowd loved the products like they loved the salesman.

Then, he moved into the hard sell. Basically, you paid a hefty yearly membership fee to be a Blubber Buster distributor. And you were required to buy all your inventory upfront. Several thousands of dollars' worth.

You were expected to sell products to your friends, family, and associates. Even better, if you convinced them to become distributors, you received a cut of their profits and membership fees. Then, *they* would do the same with the people they know.

As the network expanded, more and more money flowed to the top. To Tom, naturally, but also to the *magic folk in this room who got in early* and were in the top tier, the tip of the pyramid.

I was disgusted. This guy had powerful magic. I mean, he could shoot fireballs from his staff, for Pete's sake. And instead of doing wonderful things like curing sick people or evil things like hexing his enemies, he was using his magic to exploit these people in a pyramid scheme.

Cory and Bob were right—this guy was desperate for money. But was that all he was about—conning people out of their savings?

"But there's more," Tom announced to applause.

"Bonuses. Huge bonuses! Each month, the highest-selling members get bonuses of up to twenty percent of their earnings!"

The crowd was going wild.

"And here's the best part of all: The highest earners get a once-in-a-lifetime opportunity for their young children: free tuition to a private school. That's right, this academy will not only provide the best in academics but will also give them an education in magic that you could never match."

Oh no. This is where he tricks parents into giving up their kids to the Fae.

People cheered at this, not realizing what they would be doing. It was evil.

Magic strong enough to fool people like this was strong enough to bring about world peace. But instead, he was using it to con people out of their money and pay back the Fae.

"I'm glad Sophie and I are too old to be given up by our parents," I said. But Mom and Sophie were too swept up in the enthusiasm to hear my sarcasm.

Well, at least I knew our enemy better now and could work on a plan to defeat him.

But my immediate challenge might be even more difficult: keeping Mom and Sophie from handing their money to this grifter.

CHAPTER 19

RECRUITMENT

I t was just after my nightly wine social. I had cleaned up the glassware and leftover hors d'oeuvres. And I was in the process of cleaning up the nearly spent bottles by emptying them into my wine glass.

It was in my mildly buzzed state that I heard the cacophony from upstairs.

Elvis was belting out "Jailhouse Rock" from room 202. The ghost of the Elvis impersonator, that is. Except it was much louder than usual, allowing me to hear it down here in the foyer. The Davenports must have left the door to their room open. And something else was odd.

People were singing along.

It had to be the Davenports. They had enthusiastically taken part in the wine social, putting away one and a half bottles of Chardonnay between the two of them.

I couldn't resist. I crept up the stairs to get a better look.

Sure enough, at the end of the hall, the door to 202 was wide open. Normally, I'd be angered at the noise pouring out, but no one else was staying on this floor at the moment. No noise complaints would come my way, unless the noise reached the third floor.

I walked down the hallway softly and with trepidation. One does not stroll boldly into a room where supernatural activity was taking place, even if it was coming from the ghost of a fat guy with giant sideburns and a toupee.

Elvis had moved on to "Blue Suede Shoes." Based upon his girth, this impersonator was a dead ringer (no pun intended) for the latter-day Elvis, but he seemed to prefer singing the earlier Elvis hits.

So did the Davenports, apparently. They sat on the end of their bed, full-throatily singing along, while Elvis lounged naked in the hot tub built on a low platform in the middle of the room.

I couldn't help myself. I joined in singing along for the refrain.

Everyone looked up at me standing just outside the open door. Including Elvis. But he didn't disappear right away like he often did.

We finished the song.

"Thank you. Thank you very much," Elvis said before fading away. The hot tub remained running.

"I didn't mean to break up the party," I said, "but I couldn't resist joining in the fun."

"We're so happy you did," Jonathon said. "Virgil Bungroft is one of the most cooperative spirits we've worked with."

"As long as you call him Elvis and not Virgil," said Franny.

"Ms. Chesswick, as we've been about town, meeting other spiritualists and psychics, we've learned something interesting about you," Jonathon said.

Uh-oh. "I hope it's not derogatory. Some people in town think I'm a kook."

"Not at all. We learned you're a psychometrist."

"I didn't realize it was common knowledge."

"It's not," Franny said. "But you can't keep many secrets from psychics."

"True."

"We were wondering if you'd consider joining the Psychic Guild of Cassadaga. I don't know why there isn't such a guild in San Marcos."

"You know about our guilds?"

"I've heard you have a magic guild here," Jonathon said. "I've already expressed my view of so-called witches and warlocks and the like. But if you have a nonsensical magic guild, why not a legitimate guild for psychics and spiritualists?"

I was relieved he knew nothing about the vampire and shifter guilds. I thought it likely that there were additional guilds, but I've been kept in the dark about them.

"The problem is, we have too many illegitimate psychics in San Marcos," I said. "Unlike Cassadaga, which is known for spiritualism, San Marcos brings in all sorts of tourists who just want a good time. So, there are a lot of fake psychics who rip off the tourists. The psychics I'm friends with don't want to police who would be allowed into a psychic guild. Plus, there are many who aren't frauds, but they don't have true paranormal powers. They have good intuition and maybe a sixth sense. How do you decide who's invited into your guild?"

"We agree it's hard to define who's a psychic," Franny said. "I'm a spiritualist, but I don't have paranormal abilities. I have a spirit animal who helps me contact the dead, that is all."

"Franny is more talented than I," Jonathon said. "She's a hypnotist, too."

"We allow anyone in this field to join, as long as they don't intentionally commit fraud or misrepresentation," Franny said.

"What about Mrs. Ogglethwarp?" I asked.

Johnathon frowned. "She had true paranormal abilities. But her fraudulent activities would have gotten her kicked out of the guild if she were still alive."

"To be fair, she wasn't fleecing tourists," Franny said. "She was involved in some shady financial deals and pyramid schemes."

"Did she make any enemies?"

"She sure did," Jonathon said.

There was an awkward silence while the Davenports thought about Mrs. Ogglethwarp, and I wondered if the Native American spirit had been wrong or dishonest when he said the magic that felled the tree limb had been intended to kill me, too. Maybe the person who actually died had been the sole target.

"Our invitation stands for joining our guild," Franny said.

"Even though I live in San Marcos?"

"Yes, you would establish a chapter of our guild here, recruiting the people you want. Together, our towns would support all the psychics and spiritualists in Northern Florida."

"It sounds intriguing, and I'm honored by the offer," I said, "but give me some time to think about it."

"Of course," Franny said.

Frankly, I had way too many irons in the fire to have time for guild administrative duties. The inn and the Memory Guild were more than enough to drive me crazy.

It was getting awkward, with me standing in their doorway, them sitting on their bed, and the hot tub bubbling away between us. I bid them goodnight and went downstairs.

I HAVE A SMALL SWIMMING POOL IN THE EAST END OF MY courtyard, installed in the 1930s, I believe. You can't swim laps in it, but it's great just to plunk yourself in there to cool down. And guests who visit from up north expect to find a swimming pool in Florida at their place of lodging.

I bring this up, because the Davenports were out there in lounge chairs. But they were fully clothed. And not just clothed, Franny was in a business dress, and Jonathon wore a sport coat over a dress shirt. They didn't appear to be sweating at all.

Meanwhile, a couple in their forties from Ohio enjoyed the pool in the expected way: in their bathing suits while in the water. The wife wore a skimpy bikini. The husband, a really hairy guy, had on long bathing trunks. If not for the trunks, you could mistake him for a large-bellied Sasquatch.

The husband stood in the pool, arms resting on the edge, drinking from a can of beer while talking with Jonathon who was sitting nearby. They were deeply engrossed in a conversation. I couldn't think of anything they would have in common, but I was pleased to see my guests engaging with each other.

The two couples appeared at the wine hour that evening. Jonathon and the other man were again in a serious discussion. As I approached each guest carrying a tray of canapés, I overheard what they were talking about.

"So, I can only buy my merchandise from you?" the man asked Jonathon.

"Actually, it's *through* me. Your orders are fulfilled by the parent company."

"Oh, so you get a cut of it?"

"I do, in fact. That's the beauty of this system. The sales force you recruit has to order through you, and you get a cut. The more they sell, the more they order, and the more you make."

"How many bottles of back-hair remover can you actually sell?"

"The sky's the limit," Jonathon said. "American men—and a few women—are plagued by back hair."

"I sure am," the man said.

"I noticed. Bareback is a game-changing, world-changing product."

Speaking of hair, mine stood straight up when I heard that (and no, I don't have any on my back). Tom had used similar words when pitching his multi-level marketing scheme at the Wayward Inn.

And here Jonathon was, involved in the same kind of thing.

Were multi-level marketing companies and pyramid schemes suddenly popular in America again? I thought their moment in the sun had passed.

Or were they popular now only within a limited orbit? The orbit of one man.

I recalled reading Tom's hairbrush and seeing his face in the mirror matching Mrs. Ogglethwarp's memory of the man she had dinner with. And when I had described that man to Jonathon, he resembled the man named Sykes, who had arrived in town recruiting members for something. Jonathon said he thought it was a Satanic cult.

It looked to me like it was another of Tom's pyramid schemes. And with his magical influence, yes, it was pretty much a cult.

The old, rusty gears and cogs of my brain ground away. I needed some answers.

"Jonathon, Franny," I said after Sasquatch had gone upstairs, and the couple looked like they were about to leave for dinner.

"Yes, Darla?" Franny asked with a leisurely smile.

"I apologize for overhearing you, but how did you get involved in your, um, marketing adventure?"

"I'm a go-getter, always looking for new opportunities," Jonathon said.

"I mean, *who* got you involved? Who was the person above you on the pyramid—I mean, distribution hierarchy? The person who recruited you."

"Mabel," Franny said. "She gave us the opportunity."

"Are you interested?" Jonathon asked. "It's a game-changing—"

"World-changing product," I said. "I know."

"You don't realize how many people are suffering from an overabundance of back hair. They say it's caused by high levels of testosterone, but it keeps millions of people from their God-given right to go around shirtless in public. Or it ought to, if they have any sense of embarrassment."

"I know, it's a national tragedy. But let me ask, who recruited Mabel into the network?"

"That would be Tom Sykes," Franny said.

Texas Tom, in other words.

"Jonathon, you told me there was a cloud of accusations of fraud following Mabel around. Was it because of this marketing scheme?"

"I don't like the word 'scheme,'" Jonathon said.

"Mabel was involved in a lot of ventures, including real estate investing," Franny said. "This was only one of her ventures, and relatively harmless. Except for those lower down in the pyramid."

"Don't say 'pyramid.'" Jonathon said.

"Forgive me for my brazen question, but did you two lose any money because of Mabel?"

Jonathon and Franny didn't answer, though their eyes quickly met and then looked away.

"Being an entrepreneur involves both profit and loss," Jonathon said.

"Absolutely," I added. "Care for some more shrimp cocktail?"

"No, thank you," Franny said. "We're late for our dinner reservation."

"Sorry to delay you. Enjoy your evening."

As soon as they departed through the front door, I looked for their wine glasses. They left them, rather rudely in my opinion, on a shelf of the living room bookcase. Both glasses were empty. I touched the one with traces of lipstick on the rim and—

—*it's obvious she's suspicious of us, thanks to Jonathon blundering into yet another pyramid scheme. Why must he be such an idiot? We made money on the first one, the cosmetic company, but after that, every venture has been a disaster. We have a garage full of back-hair remover we can't unload . . . she's looking at us again. She knows something. I need to keep an eye on her. Let's get out of here—*

—the memory ended when Franny placed the glass on the shelf. I touched the other glass. All I found was a jumble of random thoughts, all tinged with the warm glow of alcohol. Most of them were in anticipation of dinner. The only coherent thought I found was:

Darla seems interested in our marketing efforts. Perhaps, she can be convinced to sign up.

Nope. Sorry, Jonathon.

They were the last of the wine-hour guests, and after I brought their glasses to the kitchen, I cleaned up the debris, gathered the leftover canapés to bring to the cottage, and finished up a bottle of Sauvignon Blanc.

I have to admit it was both strange and lovely to have a

husband again, waiting for me in my cottage. Normally, I'd devour the rest of the canapés, drink a little too much wine, and call it an evening. If there weren't enough leftovers, a frozen dinner would be my meal. Even after Sophie moved in, we had a proper dinner only two or three times a week, because she still worked occasional shifts at a restaurant.

Now I had to start planning proper dinners every night. Cory wasn't a bad cook. But when we ran our bed-and-breakfast in Key West, he worked twelve or fourteen-hour days doing maintenance and landscaping. So, I gladly took on the kitchen duties.

Now, he lay in bed, depleted by Tom, the energy vampire. Was this going to be our life moving forward? I needed to know, because the Esperanza Inn needed a heck of a lot more maintenance than our little inn did in Key West.

My husband was back. But he wasn't completely back. And I don't mean that he wasn't laboring for us. I mean, he was still under threat, and under the spell of an evil wizard.

And grifter.

CHAPTER 20

THE MISSING

"It was like a cult. All these people were no longer like themselves," I said to Cory, describing Tom's seminar the other night.

He reclined on the couch in the cottage, still not fully recovered from being drained of energy by Tom. Energy the wizard then used to brainwash the magic folk of San Marcos more deeply.

"It would have been comical," I went on, "if he hadn't slipped in an invitation for parents to give up their children."

We both knew the children would be sent to the Fae to be transformed somehow and brought up as their own.

"Tom must have a giant debt to settle with the Fae," Cory said.

"What does he need to repay them for? Arch Mage Bob said a faerie gave Tom the ability to take energy from others. Is that so great of a gift that they require children in repayment?"

"It doesn't seem like it to me. But Tom is incapable of harvesting ley lines. I don't know why I can do it while he can't."

"Maybe because you're an elemental witch, an earth witch, and he isn't."

"I think there's more to it than that. He gave me the impression that my ability is very rare. He said many witches augment their own energies with the power of ley lines, but only a trickle. But I, he said, can tap into it directly like drinking from a fire-hose. Taking in an amount of energy that would overwhelm, or even kill, other witches. Then, he steals it all from me."

"And I've seen the results. All the magic folk in the city turned into crazies."

"Back to your question earlier," Cory said, "the Fae gave Tom more than this ability. They also gave him a wizard's staff with the rare magic pearl on the end of it. The one I stole and hid in the tree."

"And which I read your memories from."

He nodded. "Tom never used this staff because it was for defense against magic and for healing. And the bearer of the pearl can summon the Fae for help. I stole it because I thought it might free me from whatever spell Tom has enslaved me with. But I'm not so sure anymore it would work, now that he's an ally of the Fae."

"It could free you?"

"That was my hope. The pearl is said to undo negative spells and poisons. But I think you need a spell or some sort of ritual to activate the pearl to do these things. And I haven't learned how to do it yet."

"Have you ever seen a faerie?" I asked.

"No. But Tom visited with them. No matter which period in the past we traveled to, they were there. The Fae have been on the earth longer than humans have."

"Are they good or evil?"

"Neither. Or both. They have their own agendas, and if it

suits them to be friends with humans, they will. If they have reason to kill us, they will. Most of the time, though, they simply can't be bothered with humans. They're completely indifferent to us.

"Well, we need to free you from Tom's influence. And if that means allying with the Fae, so be it."

BUT A COMPLICATION SOON APPEARED. A CATASTROPHIC ONE. Melissa Simpson, age five, was reported by her parents as missing. Mom told me her parents were witches. Did Melissa simply disappear, or did her parents send her to a non-existent private school while under the influence of Tom, and then snap out of it when they saw their daughter's empty bed?

"What is going on with the witches of San Marcos?" Samson asked when he called me the same day. "I've been trying to show my respect by staying away from you now that your husband is back, but I need some help here."

"You're a homicide detective," I said. "Why are you on the case?"

"Because we don't have 'abduction detectives.' And we don't want this case to turn out to be a homicide."

"Well, there has been a lot going on. And I'm sorry I haven't kept you up to date. But like you said, there hasn't been a homicide since Mrs. Ogglethwarp. I hope."

I gave him a summary of what had happened. Samson had already heard a bare-bones version of Cory's escape and my suspicion of Tom in Mrs. Ogglethwarp's death. But he didn't know about the magic dream attacks.

"You've got to be kidding me," he said. "That slime has the entire Magic Guild in his pocket?"

"Yeah. He may be slimy, but he has lots of power."

"The department can investigate him for fraud, but you need to lock up your husband at night."

"I beg your pardon?"

"Tom is draining him of the energy he pulls from the ley lines, and that energy is powering the spells that keep the guild under his control. If your husband can't get to the ley lines, then Tom can't get to the energy."

After Cory had finally escaped from Tom, the last thing I wanted to do was imprison him again.

"Tom will find someone else from the Magic Guild who can harvest ley lines," I said.

"But, your husband will be out of his direct control. I can't tell you what to do, I just don't want another child to be abducted."

"We have to stop Tom, not just cut off his access to power."

"First, we have to find the child. Do you know where the Fae live?"

"Not a clue," I said. I shared the little I knew about them, which was based solely on what Cory had told me.

"The last thing I need is to have to deal with another race of supernatural creatures I never knew existed," Samson said.

"I hear you. The only solution I can think of is the pearl that was inside Old Courage. It was given to Tom by the Fae, and it has the power to summon them."

"Okay, at least we have a place to start."

"If we can get our hands on it. The city museum has it. I received permission to handle it twice, but I think Ms. LeBoeuf, the manager of the acquisitions department, is tired of me."

"No problem. We'll subpoena it as evidence in an investigation if we have to. Give me her number."

Ah, if only life were that easy.

Samson called me back two hours later.

"You won't believe this," he said.

"Try me anyway."

"LeBoeuf said the pearl was stolen last night. She reported it to the department, but I didn't know. She said the museum's alarm didn't go off, and the security cameras didn't capture any footage of an intruder. I don't think we'll ever see the pearl again."

I PULLED UP TO MOM'S HOUSE, SHOCKED TO SEE PILES OF OLD furniture and junk piled up at the curb. If this had been someone else's house, Mom would have swooped in and stuffed her SUV with as much junk as would fit, then brought it here to her antique store with the stated intention of selling it. Of course, it probably would have sat for ages until she had room to display it in her shop, and by that time, she would have found even more junk to hoard.

So why was she abandoning this stuff? Was it merchandise she tried but failed to sell? On the rare occasions she gave up on a piece, she usually donated it to a charity store.

As I walked around the house, headed for the kitchen door, I noticed the detached garage door was open. No one ever went in there. It was too full of junk.

I approached it with dread. The interior light was on, and Mom was inside stacking boxes.

"Mom, what's going on?"

"Cataloging my inventory. It's heartbreaking to have to give up so many precious pieces, but I needed to make room for my products. They arrived earlier than I expected."

It was then that I noticed what was printed on the boxes.

Blubber Busters Variety Pack. "Say goodbye to your blubber."

The boxes took up half the garage and were stacked as tall as Mom could reach.

If that wasn't bad enough, on the opposite side were more boxes.

Bareback Back-Hair Remover. "Say goodbye to your back hair!"

"Mom. No. No. No."

"What's the matter?"

"How could you have done this?"

"They say the product will sell so fast, I'll barely be able to keep it in stock. And I should make back the investment and my membership fees in practically no time."

"Mom, I can't believe you fell for this."

"You were at the seminar. You saw how great this opportunity is. And the back-hair remover is available to only an elite group of members."

I looked closely at Mom. She didn't seem crazy or drunk from the magic dreams. She looked perfectly normal, as far as I could tell. Except she had spent thousands of dollars on a scheme that never would have interested her before.

The power of Tom's magic chilled me to the bone, now that I saw a family member so fully under its sway.

"Mom, how on earth are you going to sell this stuff?"

"I'm going to display it in my store, of course. But the members in the tier below me will do most of the selling."

"What members?"

"You, for one, as soon as I sign you up."

"No. Absolutely not. I'm sorry, but I can't get involved in this."

She, of all people, looked at me like I was nuts.

"How could you not see this for the world-changing opportunity it is?"

"I don't know any guys with serious back-hair problems. And I also don't know anyone who would believe spreading a cream on their thighs would make the fat go away."

"You're lacking vision."

"No, Mom. I'm lacking magic. That's why I wasn't influenced by the spell Tom used to enchant all of you."

"You really think it was magic that got me so excited?" Mom said, a glimmer of reasonableness in her face.

"Of course! The same magic that gave you those lust dreams."

She blushed. "After a few of those dreams, I realized they were just fantasy."

"It's the same thing with these pyramid schemes, Mom, can't you see that?"

The glimmer of reasonableness disappeared.

"They're not pyramid schemes. They're multi-level marketing ventures. Totally legit."

"Yeah, I'm sure. Look, I'm only looking out for you. You shouldn't be blowing your savings on products you can't sell."

"I'll sell them to my teams."

"Mom, I'm warning you, don't drag Sophie into this."

She turned away, too late to hide the guilt.

"Please tell me you didn't sign her up. She doesn't have any money, as far as I can tell."

"She's ready to sign up."

"Don't let her. I'm serious. Tom is a con artist and a serious threat to us. Remember, he enslaved my husband."

"You should really learn to forgive, Darla."

"He still has Cory under his influence! He still uses him like a slave. Please stay away from Tom. Don't buy anything else from him. And if you have any crazy dreams, ignore them."

Mom looked like a battle was raging inside her between her common sense and Tom's magic. I gave her a big hug.

"You're a strong woman," I whispered in her ear. "You can resist."

I had come here today to shop for a set of bedside stands to replace a pair in 301 that didn't match the style of the room. But I decided to put off this task for another time. I had too many worries in my head.

On the drive home, I listened to news on the public radio station. Young Melissa was still missing, but the story had grown more complicated. Her parents had dropped her off at what they said was a private school. But the address was a vacant storefront at a retail center. The parents insisted the empty store had signage for the Enterprise Academy, and that they had met the principal. The parents were now considered persons of interest in the case.

I filled in Cory.

"I was afraid of this," he said, shaking his head sadly. "The parents were enchanted by the Fae. They probably saw what they thought was an actual school and met who they thought was the principal. But faeries are expert illusionists. One of their favorite pastimes is to trick humans. Sometimes, just to amuse themselves. Or, in this case, to harm us."

"Did Tom learn from the Fae how to change his appearance?"

"I think he already knew how. They just helped him get really good at it."

"Why?" I asked.

"Why, what?"

"The Fae have helped Tom so much. Was this all in exchange for his help in getting them human children? I mean, faeries have been stealing human kids since forever."

"If he's supposed to pay them back in additional ways, I don't know," he said. "I hope he doesn't get the opportunity."

CHAPTER 21

SCARY FAERIE

I awoke to the yowling of a cat, the squeal of an unidentified creature, and plenty of undecipherable words that sounded like curses. The disturbance was in the cottage living room.

Cory wasn't in the bed or the bathroom. Oh no, had he been dragged back to the ley lines? I had ignored Samson's advice to keep Cory locked up. There was no way I could do that. Perhaps I made a mistake.

A cat's hissing now came from the living room. What had Cervantes cornered? It definitely wasn't a rodent. But it didn't exactly sound like a human, either.

I threw on a robe and peeked from my bedroom door.

Cervantes crouched on the floor, his prey literally backed into the corner of the room.

The creature was humanoid, but tiny—only two feet tall. He had sharp features, a pointy nose and ears. And he had gossamer wings like a dragonfly's, one of which was being held in Cervantes' mouth.

It had to be a faerie. What else could he be?

"Please get your beast to release my wing," the faerie said in a high-pitched nasal voice, rather like how you'd sound after inhaling helium.

"Cervantes, come here. Want a treat?"

Even cats who were witches' familiars liked treats. But not now, apparently.

"I can force his jaws open with magic," the faerie said. "It won't be pretty."

I knelt down, petting Cervantes, and forced my thumb and index finger into the sides of his jaw. He opened his mouth, and I picked him up.

"Thank you, Ms. Chesswick. My name is Eek Jaekeree."

That's my closest English transcription of what his name sounded like.

I blinked my eyes, and now Mr. Jaekeree looked like a full-sized human. No wings, dressed normally. Not entirely displeasing to the eye, if you're into compact-built guys with European features. Younger than me, I should add, though I doubted he appeared to me as his actual age.

"Do you normally enter people's homes uninvited before dawn?" I asked.

"All the time. Especially humans. I love to mess with them. Normally, they don't have paranormal cats, though."

"So, you're here to mess with me?"

"I came here under the orders of my queen, Ookee the Thirtieth, may she reign in glory."

"Okay. And?"

"It has been prophesied that you, Darla Chesswick, will be a nemesis of the Fae or a trusted ally. Either way, you cannot be ignored."

"Me? I'm just an innkeeper."

"You have the paranormal running thick in your veins."

"But I'm not a witch or wizard. I don't know magic."

"You have powers that will only grow stronger. Your destiny is one of greatness."

"For what?"

"I'm not here to be your career counselor. I am a messenger, 'tis all. The priests of the Fae have seen omens that you will grow in power—of what sort, they didn't say. The queen then ordered a parley with you. Which is why I'm here."

"Why are your people helping the wizard Texas Tom?" I asked. "He's causing great harm to the magic community here. If the Fae are his ally, then you are our enemy."

The faerie seemed flustered.

"That is a separate matter with which I am not involved. An oath was made between the wizard and our queen, and it must be honored."

"Can't you guys just stop helping him?"

"The oath must be honored. If you want to stop him, you must do it yourselves."

"And you guys are stealing our children. We can't let you do that. You must return the little girl you took."

"She has already been replaced with a changeling. Her parents are none the wiser."

"But that's—it's not right."

"This has been the way between humans and the Fae since the humans first appeared on the earth like a pestilence."

This little guy was not being helpful.

"So why are you here?" I asked. "To only introduce yourself and refuse to help?"

"I come bearing a gift," he said with a sly smile. He reached into the bulging leather satchel that hung from his shoulder, and withdrew a large, creamy white object.

The giant pearl from Tom's wizard staff. I gasped.

"You're the one who stole it from the museum?" I asked.

"Of course. This pearl is meant to be a gift from us to a worthy recipient. It is to be passed directly from a faerie to the recipient or returned to us. It was not meant to be passed from human to human. And especially not intended to be displayed in a glass case for humans to gawk at."

He reached out, offering it to me.

"Me? Why are you handing it to me?"

"A gesture of friendship from our queen to you. It may be useful in your conflict with the wizard and in future endeavors."

I hesitated. He was probably right that the pearl could help against Tom's magic. But I sensed I would be entering into an obligation if I accepted it.

"Come on now, don't be rude," he said. "One should not refuse a gift."

The pearl shimmered in the faint light of dawn. I sensed its power down to my solar plexus.

I put Cervantes down and reached out to take the pearl, feeling its smooth surface and solid weight. A sensation of humming energy, barely perceptible, came from within and spread through my hand. It was powerful, yet warm and reassuring. Benevolence was in this gem. As Cory had told me, the pearl had healing qualities and could undo harmful magic. I actually felt safer holding the pearl in my hand.

I believed I had to accept the gift. It couldn't hurt to be friendly with the Fae.

Right?

"Thank you," I said. "You are very kind. But I don't know how to use it."

"There will be someone in your magic community who knows. And the pearl will reveal additional secrets to you over time."

"Um, not to sound rude, but do you expect anything in return?"

The faerie smiled with innocence.

"Only your friendship with our race."

"I still can't believe there's anything special about me," I said.

"I am certain you will discover these things, eventually."

I made an awkward little bow. Why, I don't know. It just seemed like it was called for.

"I must go now before the sun crests the horizon," the faerie said.

Suddenly, he transformed from a tiny faerie to a massive monster whose head touched the ceiling. His pointy face was now a bulbous, boil-covered mass with an enormous mouth revealing yellow sharpened teeth. His eyes glowed red. Instead of gossamer dragonfly wings, he now had black, heavy membranes like bat wings.

The room was claustrophobic with his presence, and I stifled the urge to scream. Brave Cervantes shot into the bedroom and dove under the bed.

"Do not cross the Fae and our queen," he said in a deep, phlegmy voice. "You do not want to be on our bad side."

And then, he was gone. Vanished. I breathed easier now that the malevolent mass had vacated the room.

I looked at the pearl sitting sweetly in my hand.

What had I gotten myself into?

I DROVE TO THE PARK WHERE OLD COURAGE STOOD AS THE sun was rising. And, sure enough, a person slept at the base of the tree. At first glance, it was a homeless person, but I knew it was Cory, summoned against his will to have his energy stolen like his blood drained by a vampire. I parked along the water-front and walked over there to get my husband.

My life had changed so much since I first returned to San Marcos and purchased the inn. Back then, I was tortured with self-doubt and low self-esteem. I had assumed Cory walked out on me because he couldn't stand being with me any longer. Then our B&B went down the toilet. Thanks to the crazy real estate market in Key West, I made enough money on its sale to make a down payment on my inn.

All I wanted was to prove I could run a successful business on my own and to spend more time with my daughter and mother. And maybe, just maybe, rebuild my self-esteem.

Somehow, I turned into a trouble magnet. Beginning with the murder of my friend, Danielle, I got mixed up in more and more supernatural activities. And I became obsessed with solving mysteries I didn't have any responsibility to investigate.

Okay, I admit, my guests dropping like flies was part of my incentive to find who was guilty for their deaths. But it seemed like my thriving ability of psychometry, and my telepathy, made me feel obligated to put them to good use.

I've believed for a while now that having the paranormal in you attracts otherworldly things to you, from ghosts to vampires. Even gargoyles.

I think I've become stronger since I returned to San Marcos. A bit of that was the strength being near family in your home-town brings. But much of my strength came from necessity, from running a difficult business to fighting murderers and monsters.

And, yes, it came from finding my husband and helping him return to me.

It breaks my heart to see him lying on the ground in a public park, spent, still not completely free from Texas Tom.

And still not completely returned to me. I was at an awkward transition point between being independent and being one half of a married couple. I have to get used to sharing my home, emotions, and secrets again. While at the same time, Cory wasn't completely there yet. Until he is free of Tom, he will be a shell of a man.

And once he is free of him, then what? When Cory disappeared from my life, he didn't know a thing about magic and had no idea he had it in his blood. Now, he was a witch in training with the ability to harvest immense amounts of energy from ley lines and who knows what other sources.

Will his magic create a gulf between us? I've pitied myself for being the only non-witch of a family with the generation before and after me having magic. Now, my husband did, too.

How ironic the witches were more vulnerable than me. Mom and Sophie were helpless to Tom's magic, as was Cory. Arch Mage Bob, who should be leading the battle against Tom, was nowhere to be seen.

I felt like I was the only one capable of handling this crisis. No, maybe not capable, but willing to handle it. Why did it have to be this way?

To make matters even stranger, I'm visited by a faerie who says I have the potential for greatness. What in the world was he talking about? It was like some weird fantasy I might have had when I was an adolescent.

Then, I accept the pearl from the faerie and suddenly I'm a signatory to a contract I know nothing about?

Listen folks, if you want someone to represent humankind against the Fae, I'm not your number one pick.

Yet, who else is going to do it? Should I hand the pearl to a total stranger and have them figure out how to defeat Tom with it while not selling their soul to the Fae?

I finished the walk from my car to Old Courage. Kneeling, I caressed Cory's cheek.

"Are you okay, dear?"

He moaned in reply.

Okay, so now I had to get him to the car without attracting attention, almost like helping a drunken husband home from the corner bar. That analogy was unfair to Cory, but it nailed the way I felt.

I only wanted to grow to be strong for myself, not for the world. But weakness in others only forces me to summon the strength inside me. Good thing, because I fear I'm going to need it.

I returned to San Marcos to be with my mother and daughter. My husband finally returned to be with me.

So, why do I feel so alone?

CHAPTER 22

THE GOLDEN BELL

After I helped Cory to bed, I sat down to rest before I had to make breakfast for my guests. I sat in my wingback reading chair, while Cory slept in the bedroom and Cervantes perched on the armrest beside me.

"You should be ashamed of your hasty retreat in front of the faerie," I told him

He looked at me in the condescending manner cats excel in. If I could communicate telepathically with him, I'm sure he would point out that he caught the faerie in the first place, and that I was the stupid one for not running away when the creature turned into a goblin.

"Whatever, Cervantes."

My eyes strayed to the kitchen drawer where I had quickly stuffed the pearl. Probably not the smartest idea to store a precious magic gem in there with the cheese grater and garlic press.

The pearl held Cory's memories from when he stole it from

Tom and kept it in the tree. I wondered if it had any faerie memories on it. I hadn't sensed any when I took it from the faerie this morning, but it didn't mean there weren't any. Faerie psychic energy could very well work differently than human energy.

I went into the small kitchen, separated from the dining area by a breakfast bar. Cervantes leaped from the chair to follow me, hoping I would give him treats. Even magicians' familiars think with their stomachs.

When I retrieved the pearl from the drawer, Cervantes headed to his hiding spot under the bed. He knew very well who that large white sphere had come from.

I brought the pearl to the reading chair. No memories nagged at me while I held it. Even those left by Cory seemed buried below the surface. It was as if the faerie or faeries who handled it had wiped it clean.

But no, there was psychic energy on and inside the gem. It was delicate and intricate, not loud and messy like human memory.

I held the pearl in both hands. It warmed beyond the temperature of my body heat. I rolled it between my palms and tried to coax its secrets into revealing themselves.

Faint notes of music appeared in my brain, coming from a lute or similar stringed instrument. A woman's voice sang an ancient-sounding tune in a foreign language.

Though I tried to keep my mind blank, my thoughts intruded.

How can the pearl help me break the spell that held Cory to Tom? How can it heal Cory's broken free will?

Words came to me in a woman's voice, not as a memory I was reading, but as if someone spoke to me through the pearl. I couldn't understand the language, though.

Until, suddenly, I did. The words were still in the foreign tongue, but now, they were easy to comprehend.

When the cords of cruelty bind you,
And you wish that freedom will find you,
You summon forth the golden bell—
Its tinkling ring will break the spell.

Okay, cool. I got my answer about what will free Cory. Too bad it didn't make any sense at all.

Did I have a magic golden bell lying around somewhere? I didn't think so.

Trying to be gentle, I shook Cory's arm to wake him. After I had removed his grass-stained T-shirt and shorts he had originally worn to bed before being summoned to the ley lines, he had crawled back under the covers and fallen asleep immediately. He had no intention of waking up again anytime soon.

"Cory, please wake up. I have a question."

He mumbled and tried to roll over. I wouldn't let him, shaking him by the shoulders.

"Wha—?"

"Do you know anything about a golden bell? I got a message from the Fae that a golden bell can break the spell that binds you to Tom."

He inhaled deeply as he tried to engage his brain.

"I don't know. Never heard of this bell. It might not be a literal bell, though. Maybe it's the name of a spell or song."

Before I could ask him another question, he was snoring like a buzz saw. Harvesting ley lines and then being drained was not good for your health.

I didn't know what else to do other than make the rounds of the other witches I knew. Sophie wouldn't be awake yet, and she was too much of a beginner to likely have my answer. So, I called Mom.

"Have you heard of a magic golden bell?" I asked.

"I think I have one of those in my store, upstairs."

"Really?"

"Or maybe it's a gong. Come to think of it, I think it's brass, not gold. I'll sell it to you really cheap."

"No, thanks."

I explained to her why I was asking. "Do you know of any spell or song involving a golden bell?"

"No, dear. You should ask your cousin, Missy."

Calling Missy was tricky at this time of day, not knowing if she'd still be up after tending to her vampire patients overnight. But I was lucky, and she answered her phone.

"Golden bell? That sounds vaguely familiar, but I can't place it," she said. "Cory's right, it's probably not a literal bell. I know witches who use bells in their magic, but only as enhancements. Let me try to reach Don Mateo and see if he knows. I'll call you back."

Don Mateo was the ghost of an ancient Spanish sorcerer who was Missy's sidekick and familiar. He had written several spells in the grimoire that Missy and Bob had contested.

Twenty minutes later, she called.

"Don Mateo said the golden bell is a magic ritual from thousands of years ago, but he doesn't know it himself. Arch Mage Bob is the only magician I know who might be familiar with it."

I hadn't spoken with Bob since we returned from 1891.

"Did Bob get the block removed from his magic?" I asked.

"Yes. Don Mateo's spell from the grimoire did the trick. Bob should be able to help you now if he knows the spell."

If he knows it. And if he's willing to use it to help.

BOB WAS IN THE WORKROOM IN THE BACK OF HIS SURF SHOP when I showed up. The store had quietly reopened after Bob returned from 1891, and he spent most of his time here after basically abdicating his role as Arch Mage.

"Bob. How are you?" I asked, after an employee led me back here without the suspicious attitude I used to get when wanting to see Bob.

He turned to me, and I was shocked. He'd lost even more weight than when I last saw him, and he looked ten years older. His eyes were haunted and sad. He seemed about to flinch if I made a sudden movement.

"You look great," I lied.

"I've been staying out of the way," he said. "Re-learning things I used to love, like shaping a board. I've hired some excellent craftsmen over the years to make and repair boards while I ran the business, but, dude, I never realized how much I missed doing it myself until now. I guess I've gone back to the basics."

"The magic folk say they've missed you."

He waved a hand dismissively. "Bull crap."

"They need a leader right now," I said.

"Their new leader has already taken command."

"Let me ask you. You say you've missed the craft of board making. What about the craft of magic? You're an expert with a reputation spanning the world."

He waved his hand again.

"I'm serious," I said. "You learned some really rare spells. You invented some from scratch, too. Don't you miss that?"

He stared off into some distant point beyond the walls of the room.

"The truth is, you're a better magician than Tom. You know it, and so do I. Tom knows it, too. The art and beauty and technical excellence you bring to board-making, you brought to spell-making. Tom is a con man and a grifter. He steals energy from others to increase his power. He's just a thug compared to you. You're a maestro."

He shook his head and bowed it as he returned his concentration to the board he sanded by hand.

A tear ran down and through the crags of his weathered face.

"Bob, I need your help and expertise."

He didn't answer. The only sound was the repetitive back and forth of his sandpaper.

"Are you familiar with the magical ritual called the Golden Bell?"

The sanding stopped abruptly. But his eyes remained focused on the board.

"I've been told it can break the spell that binds Cory to Tom," I said.

Finally, he looked up at me with his haunted eyes.

"That is Fae magic," he said.

"Yes. They told me about it. And they gave me this." I pulled the pearl from my purse.

His eyes widened. "Is that the one Cory stole from Tom?"

"Yes," I said. "And a faerie gave it to me to use for this."

"Ah, but you'll be in their debt."

"I guess. But I'll do anything to free Cory. And I'm hoping the pearl can help us break Tom's control over the Magic Guild, too."

Bob had a new light in his eyes. He came to me and bent to look at the pearl.

"May I?" he asked.

I handed it to him. He took it in both hands and delicately rotated it, examining it closely, holding it up to the sunlight coming in the window. He expelled a deep breath.

"So, it's true," he said. "When we were prisoners, Cory told me about it. I wasn't sure I believed him. Now I do."

CHAPTER 23

GAINED AND LOST

We were on the beach at midnight, Cory, Bob, and I, on a stretch where people rarely walked and never swam. Wide coquina rock formations covered the beach from the surf to the dunes. The dark shelves of limestone were covered in barnacles and had round holes and tidal pools. They were the materials used in building much of ancient San Marcos, from my inn's exterior walls to the fort, but they made swimming and surfing hazardous and walking difficult.

We sat atop the highest formation, on a flat, smooth surface. Bob and I faced each other. Cory sat in the center, holding the pearl in his hands atop his lap. The white sand of the beach and the surf foam were bright in the moonlight.

Tom always summoned Cory a couple of hours before dawn, so we had to complete the Golden Bell spell before then. And it had to work.

"I practiced elemental magic before I became a mage," Bob said. "I was a water witch. Like, what else would a surfer be?

This beach has a lot of energy. Nothing like ley lines, though." He looked at Cory. "I envy you, dude."

Cory laughed ruefully. "Thanks to the ley lines, I'm a cow to be milked whenever needed."

"Hopefully, not anymore," I said.

"I haven't conjured the Golden Bell in, like forever," Bob said. "It was taught to me by a wizard who said he learned it from the Fae. I thought he was lying about the Fae, but I guess not. I only used it once, against a big company that stole a logo I designed for my board and T-shirt line. It's a spell that breaks the power of the mighty over the weak, the rich who exploit the poor. The Fae used it against evil kings, the wizard told me." He took a deep breath. "Clear your minds and your souls and, like, no talking."

I sat unmoving and listened to the crashing of the surf, the timeless, never-ending song of the sea. Cory closed his eyes. And Bob began his spell-making process.

It was different from how Missy worked. He didn't sit within a magic circle. He did make a small circle, though, out of shells placed atop the coquina rock. Chanting an invocation in a language I didn't recognize, he swayed back and forth. Then he removed every other shell from the circle, tossing them backwards, alternating between his right and left shoulders. He removed two large osprey feathers from the pockets of his hoodie and placed them inside the shell circle, forming an X. He continued chanting, making undulating motions with his hands. This went on for a long time until something caught my eye.

The pearl in Cory's lap glowed.

"I call upon the Golden Bell of Justice," Bob said in a mighty voice that was much deeper than normal. "Free this man, Cory Slaughter, from the oppressor who binds him. Free him from the injustice and exploitation. Free him to be the agent of his own destiny."

I couldn't believe it: an apparition of an actual golden bell appeared in the air above Cory's head. It was crude and primitive, but it shined brightly in the darkness, as brightly as the pearl did.

"At the toll of the bell, you will be free."

The bell rang once, twice, three times. The sound was a strange, off-key note that seemed to echo down the entire beach and across the ocean.

The light from the bell increased until it was too bright to look at. Then the bell vanished. The glow of the pearl slowly subsided.

Now, there was nothing but moonlight and the soughing of the surf.

"Okay, dude. You're free," Bob said.

"I am? I don't feel any different."

"Freed people don't feel different. They just feel normal."

"Well, I do feel normal. Actually, kind of energetic. Like I could go for a swim."

He leaped to his feet and jogged toward the water, where he stripped off his T-shirt, shorts, and sandals before diving into the ocean.

"Be careful of the rocks," I called after him.

"That felt good," Bob said. "Practicing magic. Being myself again."

"What happens if Tom summons Cory, and he doesn't respond?"

"Tom will probably come after him, so Cory needs to keep the pearl with him at all times. It will protect him from other spells. But this thing is nowhere near being over. We have to drive Tom out of San Marcos. Maybe even kill him."

"Is that the only way to end his control over the magic folk?"

"Without the power he was getting from the ley lines, he won't be able to broadcast his dream spells to everyone. But he'll still be able to control individuals. That's why we need to get rid of him."

The hour when Tom would summon Cory came and went, and Cory was not affected. Later that morning, Cory slept peacefully with no summons.

But I had a foreboding sense that something bad was coming. And I was right.

WHEN WE GOT HOME FROM THE BEACH, I TOLD CORY TO follow me into the cottage and take a seat.

"I have a safety lecture for you," I said.

He smiled. He had told me during the drive that he already felt liberated in his soul and could sense that Tom had lost his magic grip on him.

As for me, I felt anxiety.

"Tom is simply not going to give up and go away," I said. "He needs energy from the ley lines if he's going to control all the magic folk. And he can't harvest it himself. Will you please stop smiling like that? Do you think this is a joke?"

"I'm enjoying my freedom."

"Tom could very well capture you again. And we have to be ready. You're going to stay in the cottage with all doors and windows locked. You will keep the pearl with you at all times. And I have a handgun I want you to keep handy."

"You have a gun? You?"

"Yeah. A guest left it behind. I'll explain later. It's in the bedroom closet on the top shelf. I'm too short to reach it without a stepstool, so it wasn't the smartest hiding place for me. I want you to make sure it's loaded. With regular bullets, not the silver ones."

"*What?* Silver bullets?"

"Yeah. Long story."

"What have you been up to while I was away?"

"You don't want to know. The good news is the bad were-wolves are gone. The only one I know now is a good one."

Cory shook his head in amusement.

"I was literally a captive for a year," he said. "And since I've returned home, I've been under Tom's influence. I want to enjoy my freedom. I don't want to live under siege."

"We have no choice until he is gone. I don't want to lose you again."

Cory nodded and came to me, holding me tight, and kissing the top of my head.

"I won't leave you again, I promise."

The sad fact is no one can make a promise like that. Fate always has ideas of its own.

"I have to make breakfast for the guests. Stay here! I'll bring you any leftovers."

DARLA, YOU MUST COME TO THE FRONT PARLOR AT ONCE, Archibald's words said to me in my mind. I was in the kitchen cooking eggs for twelve guests, and it was really a bad time to leave the stove.

I'll be right there, I said telepathically.

It's quite serious.

Burned scrambled eggs are also quite serious.

I finished the two skillets and shoveled the eggs into a large chafing dish, which I placed in the oven's warming drawer. Only then did I hurry to the parlor.

I was surprised to see Dr. Noordlun in the room, conversing with Archibald, who was in animated form beneath the mantel.

"Sorry I kept you waiting," I said. "My scrambled eggs—"

"Diana is missing," Dr. Noordlun said. "A friend went by her house this morning to find all the lights on, the front door unlocked, and Diana nowhere to be found."

"Texas Tom is obviously the culprit," Archibald said. "He either lured her away with magic or kidnapped her outright."

"Does your husband know where the wizard lives?" Dr. Noordlun asked.

I explained he had been living in 1891, and the particular house didn't exist anymore.

"But I have a better way of finding Diana," I said. "My husband's magical abilities include harvesting energy from ley lines. Tom can't do it himself, and the main reason he kept Cory captive was to force him to take in as much energy from the ley lines as he could, which Tom would drain from him in turn. Diana can work with ley lines, too, although I don't know if she can harvest them as effectively as Cory. I believe that's why she's missing—so Tom can use her now."

"I can manipulate energy from ley lines, too," Dr. Noordlun said, referring to his paranormal ability, rare for a non-witch.

"Don't let Tom know that or you'll be next. Anyway, I bet that tomorrow before dawn, Diana will be at the point where two ley lines converge, harvesting energy under Tom's control."

"You mean the park where the Southern live oak stands?" Dr. Noordlun asked.

"Exactly. And we need to be there, too, to rescue her."

"I should think the police can help us," Dr. Noordlun said.

"My dear professor," Archibald said, "your naivete is so adorable."

"This is entirely a supernatural affair," I said. My detective friend can arrest Tom for murdering Mrs. Ogglethwarp and abducting Diana, but only after we disable his magic. And as far as I'm concerned, arresting him might not be the best solution for getting rid of him."

"Are you suggesting harming him?" Dr. Noordlun asked.

"I'm suggesting making him never, ever want to bother us again."

"Humans can be made to disappear rather easily," Archibald said.

"The Memory Guild does not assassinate people."

"Then, we'll find another way to solve our problem, Dr. Noordlun," I said.

"Fool him in the same way he fools himself," I said to Cory. "Someone brilliant gave that advice."

"It was you."

"I know. So, tell me, how does Tom fool himself?"

Cory chuckled. "In many ways, but most of all, he believes he's smarter than everyone else. That's why he chose the path of a con man. He believes he can spot a mark and trick them into trusting him. And he thinks he's a brilliant strategist. But he's not."

"Okay. If you were Tom, what would be more important to you: recapture and be-spell Cory, your proven ley-line harvester, and get the pearl back? Or use someone new, namely Diana?"

Cory pondered this for a moment, seated in the reading chair of our living room.

"I don't think he cares that much about the pearl. It was a gift from the Fae, but it's mostly a defensive weapon, and Tom is always on offense. As for me, I'm a proven source of high-grade energy. Plus, he's really ticked off at me for showing him up. I don't know Diana, how well she can harvest the energy, and how much she can absorb at any one time."

"In other words, he'd prefer to get you back?" I asked.

"Yeah. And if he couldn't get me back, he'd rather kill me."

That put a dark mood on us. But I wasn't surprised to hear it.

"So, if you were Tom, thinking you were super smart, what would you do?" I asked.

"Trick us into trying to rescue Diana while he comes after me."

"Then, let's make it seem that we're going to rescue her, and lure him to you."

"I'm just supposed to stay here, locked in the cottage with your handgun, and wait for him to come here? Then what?"

"No. That's not what we're going to do at all," I said, sounding confident in my plan before I was even sure what it was.

CHAPTER 24

RUMBLE 'ROUND THE
OAK TREE

Diana was new to the role of being Tom's ley-line harvester. While she could acquire power from the lines, like many witches, she had surely never done so on the grand scale Tom needed. In fact, it could be dangerous for her health to do so.

This meant she would need to be supervised until she learned the routine. She couldn't be sent there on her own, like Tom had done with Cory. Tom would need to transport her there and force her to engage with the electromagnetic energy.

My big gamble was to assume Tom would use Diana as a decoy to attract our attention while he swooped in to find Cory alone or lightly guarded and take my husband from me once again.

He was correct about our plans for Diana, and wrong about Cory.

It was 4:00 a.m., the usual time when Cory would be summoned to the park. At this hour, the electromagnetic energy was at its peak, and the neighborhood was at its most deserted. The couple of hours before dawn was enough time to harvest the energy and transfer it to Tom to be used in whatever powerful spell he had up his sleeve.

I was waiting near the park, in a car parked a block away but close enough to see the park. It was a rental car, in case Tom knew mine. The rest of my crew of amateur commandos were stationed nearby: Summer, hidden high in the branches of Old Courage to protect the tree in case Tom became too destructive; Dr. Noordlun, parked on the other side of the park; Bob, lurking in the shadows nearby.

A Maserati sports car rolled down the empty street toward the park, past my car. As it passed beneath a streetlight, I got a glimpse of Tom at the wheel and a slumped figure in the passenger seat.

No wonder Tom always had money problems, if that was the car he preferred.

He parked on the side of the street ahead of me, got out, and circled around to open the passenger door, his wizard's staff tucked under his arm. He made hand motions, and Diana stepped out and walked stiffly beside him to the park. It was as if he were controlling her like a marionette.

When they arrived at the park, Tom received a surprise.

Cory stepped out from behind the ancient live oak tree.

I slipped out of the car and, sticking to the shadows, made my way closer to the impending battle.

Cory had the pearl with him in a satchel worn over his shoulder. It should prevent any attempt by Tom to enslave him again. Plus, he was armored in a powerful protection spell cast by Bob.

Tom stopped dead in his tracks and brandished his staff. Diana stood at his side in a stupor. I heard raised voices and hurried to get closer to the park.

"No, you must release her now," Cory said.

"Only if you come back to me, my friend. A ley-line harvester like you should be put to good use."

"You're going to all this trouble to enchant the magic folk of San Marcos just to cheat them out of their savings?"

"I've given them a once-in-a-lifetime opportunity."

"And you're tricking them into giving their children to the Fae. It's evil, and you're pathetic. You're just a low-life con man."

"Harsh words to use against your mentor and benefactor. I taught you how to take incredible amounts of energy from the ley lines. Very few witches in the world can do what you do."

"It's only so you can exploit me. And you never taught me the craft you had promised. I was just an object to you."

"I will teach you more if you return to me," Tom said in a suddenly tender voice. "There is so much more you can learn. Secrets that no other magician knows."

"You don't have the best teaching style, Tom. Being enslaved is not a pleasant educational experience. I can personally attest to that."

Cory stepped toward the wizard.

"I insist you break the bonds that subjugate the magic community."

"You insist, do you? It's really none of your business."

"My mother-in-law and step-daughter are among your slaves. To say this pisses me off is an understatement."

"You talk tough, as if you could make me do anything," Tom said. "Even with the pearl you stole, you can't harm me."

"*I* can hurt you, dude," Bob said, appearing out of the shadows.

"Oh, it's you!" Tom said mockingly. "You've come out of your shell. Are you still crying over the money you lost?"

Bob, about thirty feet away from Tom, thrust his arms forward in a pushing motion. Tom went flying backwards and landed on his butt.

I had to get Diana out of harm's reach. I ran to her, knowing I was in danger, too. When I wrapped my arm around her shoulders, she blinked at me, not knowing who I was, or even where she was. I quickly led her away from the wizard and the mage.

Tom leaped to his feet, brandishing his staff. Fireballs shot from its tip, and instead of hitting Bob directly, bounced off an invisible barrier around him.

More fireballs flew to Bob, bouncing off with showers of sparks.

"I sense flaws in your protection spell," Tom said. "It's not going to hold up much longer."

Bob repeated his thrusting motion but did it sideways. Tom left his feet, flew across the small park, and hit the trunk of Old Courage.

"Hey!" I shouted. "Don't hurt the tree."

The three combatants turned and looked at me like I was nuts.

Tom took the opportunity to shoot fireballs at both Cory and Bob. Cory was knocked to the ground but looked unhurt. Bob's protection shield was, indeed, wearing down. A flame popped up on his shirt, and he quickly swatted it out.

Tom was on his feet again, aiming the staff at Bob, when Cory tackled him from behind. When they hit the ground, my husband pummeled the wizard with his fists, the most basic form of human violence without a touch of magic.

Then Cory's next punch bounced off an invisible barrier inches from Tom's face. Cory screamed in pain, holding his fist with his left hand.

"Protection spells can also be offensive," Tom said. "I could have taught you to cast one, instead of you burning your hand. But you've betrayed me."

Cory flew backwards, landing inches from the street.

Tom turned right, before a sprinting Bob slammed into him. Bob screamed as he hit the protection spell.

Bob staggered backward, but he didn't go down. Crouching, he waved his hands in a complex dance, pressed his palms together, and pointed them at Tom.

A lightning bolt arced from his hand, hitting Tom, whose protection shield glowed with sparks. The sparks landed on Tom.

It looked like his shield sizzled out.

Tom then did the most un-wizardly thing. He pulled a pistol from the back of his pants.

"Wait a minute," I shouted. "That's cheating."

As if this were some magic tournament instead of a fight to the death.

Tom fired his gun. Bob twisted like he'd been hit in the shoulder. But I didn't see any wound. Bob's protection spell must have hung on just enough to save him.

Bob shot another lightning bolt at Tom, who convulsed with electrocution, but managed to run to the other side of Old Courage to take cover.

Where was Cory? I'd lost sight of him.

Oh no, he was poised on the junction of the ley lines. He stood rigidly, glowing faintly from the power pulsing into him.

Another shot rang out from the cover of the tree.

Bob dove to the ground but was unhurt. He was also pinned down in a slightly sunken section of grass. If he moved out of it, he'd be exposed.

Meanwhile, Cory stood in the open, an easy target. I motioned for him to get down, but he remained unmoving.

Tom saw him but didn't shoot. He must have realized Cory was handing him a new weapon. If Tom could leech the energy Cory was collecting, Tom would be unstoppable.

So, what the heck was Cory thinking? Did he know how to attack with the energy?

It looked as if he was about to. He glowed as brightly as a lantern, and even seemed larger than life, with all the power inside him. He turned toward Tom and pointed his hands at Tom, much like Bob had, before sending forth his lightning bolts. They landed on the ground on both sides of the tree.

Instead of hiding, Tom crept around the trunk of the tree.

"Get down, Cory!" I screamed.

Too late. Tom fired his gun, and Cory crumpled to the ground.

I rushed to him, not caring what happened to me. Cory lay on his back, bleeding from the bullet wound in his abdomen. I knelt beside him, tore the silk scarf from my neck, and pushed it into the wound, trying to stop the bleeding.

Cory still glowed from the power. I felt it tingling through my hands. And, the odd thing was, his wound appeared to be slowly healing. It must be because of all the ley-line energy in his body, and the healing powers of the pearl in the bag resting against him.

But then Tom showed up. He pushed me out of the way and crouched beside Cory. With one hand still holding the gun aimed at Bob, he placed his other one on Cory's chest.

He was stealing Cory's energy.

"Don't you dare!" I shouted. "He needs it to heal."

I tried to push him away, but already the power was flowing into him, and his strength increased.

And already, Cory seemed weakened.

I went into full hysterical mode, punching and kicking Tom. But petite me was not a match for paunchy Tom, especially as his power grew before my eyes.

And the guy had a gun. I couldn't forget that.

With Samson stationed nearby, I prayed the battle would be over soon. Hearing the gunshots, Samson would have called for backup and, hopefully, an ambulance.

But the battle over would only mean Tom would escape.

A stunning blow hit me as Tom swung his pistol hand at me with his enhanced strength. I landed on my back and tried to regain my senses. Pulling my phone from my pocket, I called 911, just in case. The operator told me paramedics had already been sent on their way.

Before I hung up, movement caught my eye. Someone was running up to the park. Was it Samson?

No. It was Dr. Noordlun. What the heck was he doing?

Tom lifted his hand from Cory and stood up. He beamed with delight. I crept back to my husband and continued to press the scarf against his wound. A knot formed in my stomach as I saw how pale Cory looked.

"Okay, Bob, my protection spell is back," Tom said. "And it's ten times stronger than it was before. Now, it's your time to die."

I honestly didn't care about them anymore. Removing the pearl from Cory's bag, I placed it on his wound, not knowing if this would help, unable to cast a spell to bring out the pearl's healing powers.

"I'm coming for you, Bob," Tom said, cackling with glee. He marched toward Bob lying in the low patch, almost hidden by shadows from Old Courage that blocked the moonlight and the distant streetlights.

Then the oddest thing happened. Dr. Noordlun arrived at my side. He knelt beside me and placed his left hand on the center of Cory's chest. He pointed his other at Tom.

A gigantic bolt of electricity arced from Tom to Dr. Noordlun, and then down his arm into Cory.

"I'm returning the energy the wizard stole from him," Dr.

Noordlun said, as he used his energy-speaking, the ability I had learned he had only recently. "The energy should help him survive."

"It was working before Tom stole it," I said.

"No!" Tom screamed, as he realized the power he had stolen was being stolen back from him.

"Okay, then. I still have my gun, if that's what it will take," Tom said, aiming at Dr. Noordlun.

An explosive *crack* filled my ears.

But it wasn't the gun.

A massive branch fell from Old Courage and landed on Tom.

What just happened?

Tom lay unmoving beneath the branch, and Summer climbed down from the tree.

"Did you do that?" I asked her.

"No," she said, smiling. "Old Courage did it on her own. She's quite perceptive after a lifetime being next to the ley lines. She knew there was a dangerous parasite here, and she took action to remove it, to protect her fellow trees and us. I admit I formed a bond with her."

Saved by a tree. Can you believe it?

Everyone was coming out of hiding. Bob walked over to check on Tom, then came to us.

"He's alive, but out cold," Bob said. "Plus, he's like half-squashed and looks pretty gnarly. He's not going anywhere."

He joined us, kneeling beside Cory. Placing his hand on the pearl, he intoned a brief verse in an unfamiliar tongue, and the pearl glowed.

Cory's wound was healing quickly beneath my scarf.

"How can he be healing so quickly?" Samson asked, standing over us.

"How do you think?" I snarked.

"Yeah, magic. I should have known."

The flashing lights of an ambulance swept over the park. I took the pearl from Cory, knowing it could be lost when he was taken to the hospital. Besides, the pearl had more work to do this morning.

While the paramedics worked on Cory, I watched Bob, out of sight from everyone, conjure the Golden Bell to break the magic that bound Diana to Tom. This time, Bob used a circle scratched in the dirt and acorns from Old Courage, plus the osprey feathers he had with him.

After the three tolls of the bell, Diana snapped to alertness.

"How did I get here?"

"It's a long story, but you're fine now," Bob said.

"Can you use the Golden Bell to break the spell Tom has over the Magic Guild?" I asked.

"It's not a single spell like he used on Diana and Cory. It was, you know, the combo of all the dream spells he attacked the city with. If he stops sending those out, the effect's gonna fade away. And he doesn't look like he's sending any spells any time soon."

Bob was right. Tom was still unconscious. A second paramedic team had arrived to tend to him.

Before I got into the ambulance with Cory, I stopped next to Samson.

"You're going to interrogate Tom as soon as he regains consciousness, right?" I asked.

"Of course. *If* he regains consciousness."

"You need to get him to admit he was behind Mrs. Ogglethwarp's death."

"I'll do my best, ma'am." He gave me a sarcastic salute.

Yeah, this morning couldn't have been easy for Samson. In truth, it wasn't easy for anyone.

CHAPTER 25

ABSOLUTE RUBBISH

Okay, so I survived a climactic magical battle and freed my husband from an evil wizard, all before dawn. So, how could I possibly cap that off?

By dragging my butt into the kitchen to make breakfast for my guests. My life is hardly glamorous, believe me.

Guests trickled in slowly and attendance was sparse. Franny and Jonathon showed up and ate a light breakfast. No other guests were in the room at the time, but they didn't respond when I tried to engage them in conversation. They only whispered to each other as if in the middle of a disagreement.

I recalled reading their empty glasses after wine hour. The paranoia I'd sensed in Franny's memories had bothered me. Something about it had nagged me ever since. These folks were up to something nefarious and fraudulent. It had to be more than a pyramid scheme.

The more I thought about it, the more I wanted to search for her memories in their room. But I have ethical lines I won't cross. I might get dangerously close to those lines, sometimes actually touching them, but I won't cross them.

One such line is that I refuse to use my psychometry to invade the privacy of a guest's room. I only use it if the guest is dead (which happens all too frequently) or is suspected by the police in a crime. Vague suspicion isn't a sufficient cause. I treat my telepathy the same way, though I can't control that ability very well. Sometimes, thoughts just pop into my head without my bidding. I hoped that would be the case with Franny and Jonathon.

One exception to my psychometric snooping is trash. Yes, the rubbish guests leave in their room's bin for the housekeeper to remove. The garbage exits the privacy bubble of the guest room and enters the public domain, eventually ending up in a green plastic bag tossed into the small dumpster behind the inn.

I thought I'd never stoop to rummaging through trash, but I knew it was a common investigative method used by police. So, this morning I asked Bella to save the Davenports' rubbish for me.

She didn't even ask me why. She was well trained in how nutty her employer was.

The plastic bag from the trash can was filled to capacity. Guests who stay for several nights tend to produce more garbage per day. It's probably because they feel more at home and do more in their rooms. I wish I had thought to check their trash earlier in their stay, but I had to work with what I had. I examined the bag on the workbench in the utility room that served as a laundry, workshop, and storage facility. Wearing gloves, I clenched my teeth as I pushed aside used tissues and a banana peel.

What I found surprised me. Empty glass vials like my mother

had in her magic apothecary chest. Scattered dried herbs I couldn't identify. Burned matches. The melted nub of a candle that smelled of incense. Two white bird feathers. A piece of string with equally spaced knots.

Having witches in the family made me certain of one thing: these were ingredients used in a magic potion or spell.

Jonathon had scoffed when I asked him if he believed in magic. He acted insulted, even. But I guess this was a case of the man "doth protest too much." He, or Franny, or the both of them practiced magic. And he was trying to put me off the scent. Very interesting. Too bad I didn't know enough about magic to guess what kind of spell the ingredients were used for.

I came upon an empty juice bottle. Shame on you guys for not recycling! I was wearing latex gloves, so I picked it up and—

—am furious at them! They knew Jonathon is vulnerable to these things, and they conned him into signing up, and now we're out over a hundred grand, if you add in what we lost last time. Over a hundred grand down the toilet! Now I can't retire. I'll have to work until I die at my desk at that sweatshop. I begged both of them to refund some of our money. Sykes just laughed at me. Mabel acted sympathetic, but did she open up her checkbook? No! She frowned with sadness for me, but her eyes showed she didn't care at all. They used us, treated us like suckers. I still can't get over it—

—I dropped the bottle. It was Franny's memory, and it was so angry and intense it got to me through the glove. I should have worn something thicker than latex.

My pulse quickened as I realized I had stumbled upon a trail that was very important.

There was nothing left in the trash but a plastic stick for stirring coffee made by the room's coffee maker. Though it was tiny, it held psychic energy I could feel through the gloves. I removed my right glove and touched the stick. There was only one memory of—

—*stirring in the nasty artificial creamer while I struggle to wake up. Boy, I feel drugged after that dream I had. It seemed to go on all night. He was the sexiest, most desirable man I had ever seen. And he was nibbling at my ear . . . no, I have to put it far from my mind. Mostly because he looked a little like Sykes. But not repulsive like him. This man was like the sexy brother of Sykes. I mean, Sykes doesn't seem so loathsome now after seeing this mysterious man. Maybe the mysterious man really was Sykes. My subconscious could have been telling me that Sykes is actually attractive, that I am actually attracted to him. All that lust I felt in my dream has been buried inside of me this entire time. Why am I thinking this way? It was just a dream. I need my coffee—*

—she tossed the stirrer into the trash.

Well, this memory answered a question. I was certain now that Franny was a witch. That's why she experienced the lust dream broadcast by Texas Tom. Jonathon could be one, too, for all I knew. But at least, I knew Franny was.

My mind churned over possibilities and crazy theories. A thought came to me, a question, really. It involved Mrs. Ogglethwarp and her final night on earth.

I recalled my conversation with her while she ate breakfast that morning. I tried to remember her mood when she invited me to accompany her to visit Old Courage. She was in a decent mood. Her invitation seemed spur of the moment. But she had two folding chairs, as if she had already planned for a guest. No, that didn't mean anything. Lots of people buy them as pairs.

I wish I had more memories of hers to read. I replayed the image of her in my mind, drinking coffee, coiffed hair, heavy mascara on her eyelashes.

It occurred to me I hadn't read every single possession of hers. I hadn't read her makeup kit.

When I quickly searched her room after the accident, I didn't recall seeing it, but I might have simply missed it.

Her suitcases, packed by the Davenports, were in a large storage closet near the inn's foyer. Two large bags on wheels. For me, they would have held enough clothes for a month, but Mrs. Ogglethwarp seemed the type who wore more than one outfit every day to match the setting and activity. I went through each bag, being careful not to muss up her clothing.

There was no makeup kit. Where was it? Her handbag, which I had searched at the police station, didn't hold the kit. I recalled seeing only lipstick and a compact inside the bag.

Her room hadn't been occupied since her stay. I hurried up the stairs, avoiding the elevator I now knew was haunted, and let myself into 303. I headed straight for the bathroom. There was a small drawer in the vanity below the sink that wasn't easily noticeable, and I yanked it open.

There was the bag. That's why it didn't catch my eye when I went through the room before, and why the Davenports didn't find it when they packed her stuff.

I ran my fingers through the various accessories until I found the mascara and pulled out the narrow tube. It held many memories. You're naturally introspective when staring at your face in the mirror, performing the elaborate ritual. Scanning the memories, I tried to find the most recent. There it was. I grabbed the top and—

—*unscrew it, pulling out the brush, forcing my eyelids wide as I apply the mascara to my lashes . . . Jonathon seemed disappointed that I canceled with him tonight. He was so proud he had communicated with Auntie Bessie's spirit in the tree and wanted to be the master of ceremonies tonight. I did the right thing, though. Saying I wanted to be alone when reacquainting myself with Bessie seems reasonable to me. But I can tell he was sulking. He said Franny had plans and would be gone all day and evening, so he would be alone. I'm sure he can find something to occupy his mind. I just think it's time to stay away from those two. They've been so resentful about the marketing network. Franny especially. They know there's nothing I can do, but she keeps asking for their money back. Sykes has most of it, so they can kiss it goodbye.*

I'm surprised Jonathon wanted to go with me tonight, if he was so angry. I'm more surprised Franny let him go. It's his ego, though. He wants to show off Auntie Bessie, basically. What an oaf. Of the two of them, I don't think he's as angry at me as Franny is. He still thinks he's going to get rich. From back-hair remover? Ha! No, he'll only make money if he signs up a lot more salespeople below him, but he and Franny don't know enough gullible people. And it's not as if I'm getting rich, either. I simply have a better network than they do. They're only a small part of it. So, okay, a little more on the left lashes, and I'll go down to breakfast. I just hope Jonathon isn't eating now. There we go, done! —

—she closed the mascara and dropped it into her bag.

I was unsteady on my feet as the implications sank in.

Franny must be the magician who killed Mrs. Ogglethwarp. Her spell made the limb fall, though it fell imperfectly because of her lack of a more competent spell.

I had no proof, of course. But she had a motive: revenge for losing her money. She had the opportunity, knowing Mrs. Ogglethwarp was going to be there. And she knows hypnosis. Now, I wouldn't be surprised if she was the woman at the surf shop Aaron had mentioned when he described feeling "brain dead." She could have hypnotized or be-spelled Aaron and told him to weaken the limb. Although, she could have picked anyone who knew how to operate a chainsaw, she must have seen him at the shop working on a surfboard and decided to use him. Maybe it had been a deliberate ploy to damage Bob.

I remembered the shaman's spirit living in the tree said the magic was intended to kill Mrs. Ogglethwarp and her companion. He never said it was me specifically. Like Cory had suggested, I'd simply assumed it was me after being traumatized by my near miss. And who else might be Mabel's companion?

Jonathon, of course. He told me he had wanted to introduce Bessie to Mabel, but Mabel canceled their plans.

Franny planned to kill her husband, too. The woman she blamed for her money loss, and her husband, who had gotten them into the whole mess. She just didn't know he wouldn't be there as planned, and that I would be instead. I didn't know how her spell worked, but she must not have been able to see it was me sitting there instead of Jonathon.

Or maybe, she didn't care.

I was certain my theory was correct. And I was stunned. I pulled out my phone to call Samson and tell him about it.

"Drop the phone."

Franny stood in the bathroom doorway, pointing a small handgun at me. Her face was almost unrecognizable with fury and hatred.

"Drop it now!"

I placed the phone next to the sink.

"I put a warding spell on Mabel's bags," she said. "It warned me the instant they were opened. Something told me deep in my gut that it was you."

"That," I nodded toward her gun, "would have been a much easier way to kill Mrs. Ogglethwarp. And your husband."

"No kidding. But the tree was the cleverest way to do it. It looked like an accident. And I can sue the city and win a big settlement."

"All anyone thinks about is money these days."

"Because I need it," she barked. "I lost more than a hundred thousand dollars. I was about to retire, and now my dreams are gone."

"It was your husband's money, too."

"It was his fault we lost the money because he got involved in that stupid scheme. Fortunately, his life insurance will cover the loss."

"*Will* cover the loss?"

"You know the saying, 'If at first you don't succeed.' And I will get another opportunity, because you're not going to say anything to anyone."

She held the gun in firing position, inches from my skull.

"If you shoot me," I whispered, "you'll be in jail before your gun cools."

"I'm not going to do it here. I'll do it where they won't find your body for weeks."

This wasn't sounding good.

"You can't move me around at gunpoint in the middle of San Marcos without being seen," I said. More like, I hoped.

"You've forgotten that I'm a hypnotist. And I'm also a witch."

I wanted to make a snarky comment that if she was a decent witch, she wouldn't have to get rid of me now because the tree limb would have already done so.

But I didn't say anything. Because I couldn't. My mouth was frozen shut.

And when Franny beckoned for me to follow her, I did. I didn't intend to do so, but my muscles simply obeyed her. I trudged out of the bathroom, through room 303, and down the hallway to the elevator I didn't want to ride. It was waiting on the third floor and opened immediately. As it clicked and clanked down to the ground floor, I stared straight ahead at the doors, not because I wanted to, but because that's where my head and eyes were pointed, and I couldn't move them.

As I zombie-walked with Franny through the foyer, I hoped

with all my heart that someone would see me and intervene. But no one was around. And I shuffled along beside her to her car parked on the curb nearby. I got inside without being asked.

When she drove away, I feared my brief glimpse at the exterior of my inn would be the last I'd ever see of it.

CHAPTER 26

DARLA THE ZOMBIE

Franny drove while I sat in the passenger seat. We rode in silence, grim and staring straight ahead, like two spinster sisters on their way to church. The car soon left San Marcos and entered the countryside as we headed inland, past pine forests, cow pastures, and small lakes.

I tried to assess my non-material shackles. How much of what turned me zombie-like was caused by hypnosis and how much was from magic? I'd never been hypnotized before. Magic has been used against me in the past, but nothing quite like this.

Obviously, I still had the ability to think for myself. But I had no willpower to disobey Franny and save myself. My muscles moved, but only at her command.

I tried to pick up Franny's thoughts, but it was as if my brain was wrapped in a woolen blanket. My senses were dulled to the point of numbness. I needed to snap out of this somehow.

Franny had turned onto rural roads that I didn't recognize. The farther we went into the boondocks, the easier it would be for her to kill me and dispose of my body with no witnesses. She hadn't taken my cellphone, but I was completely incapable of using it. Even if I weren't a zombie, there was a gun barrel to make me behave.

And I had no weapon to fight back. I wasn't a witch with an arsenal of spells. Nor was I a shifter able to turn into a mighty beast to maul her. My only offensive weapon was biting sarcasm, and last I checked, that didn't trump a loaded weapon.

The car turned onto a dirt road. Dirt roads usually meant you were headed to the end of something. In this case, the end of my life. I had to escape fast. But I couldn't even move freely or think straight.

The car jostled as it went over a bump, knocking me around in my seat. My hand landed on the armrest and stayed there.

And then, despite my zombie state, I felt energy trickling into my hand from the armrest.

The psychic energy of memories.

My mood improved as I realized that even with my brain locked down, my psychometric abilities were strong enough to work.

As memories poured into my mind, I couldn't control them as I usually could. Nor could I remain above them and choose which ones to dive into. Now, I received an unfiltered mish mosh of thoughts at various levels of intensity, as if I were manically zipping through hundreds of TV channels a minute.

I heard clips of sound at different volumes, such as whispers and shouts. But soon, I realized they were mostly the voice of one person.

Jonathon. He must ride shotgun frequently and leave memories on this armrest.

I couldn't make sense of the memories; they were just too random and scattered. There were a lot of thoughts about money and the many multi-level marketing ventures he was involved in. There were angry thoughts about Franny's practicing magic. He didn't want to believe in it, and she was proving him wrong.

And there were romantic feelings and whispers about love. But they didn't involve Franny.

An image of Mrs. Ogglethwarp lying in bed waiting for him, shocked me. The old bird was shacking up with him? The thought of them together made me shudder.

And made me wonder if Franny knew about it.

The memories kept pouring into me until we hit another rough patch of dirt road and my lifeless hand fell off the armrest. I didn't have the strength to lift it.

But a realization hit me. The burst of psychic energy I received from the memories just now seemed to have freed my mind from the drugged feeling that had constrained it.

I could think normally now. Well, normal for me, which probably isn't anywhere near normal for you.

My body was still under Franny's spell, but at least, I had my mind back. I set about trying to figure out what her plan for me was, hoping my telepathic ability would kick in and give me an assist.

In a while, it did turn on, though it didn't give me anything immediately helpful. Franny thought about calling her insurance agent to increase Jonathon's life insurance. Then, a quick thought about a drug she read about that induces heart attacks without being traced. Next, a reminder to herself to schedule a pedicure for Monday.

Like I said, this wasn't helpful.

But then, an image in her mind popped into mine. A small lake, more like a pond, surrounded by tall grass and thick trees. Several gators. And the end of the dirt road.

This was where she was taking me.

I heard a few snippets of thought questioning if she had anything heavy enough to anchor my body on the bottom of the lake. Was the spare tire heavy enough if she let the air out of it?

She wondered if the gators could be relied upon to take care of my body. She seemed satisfied with leaving it to them.

This wasn't helping me. It was just freaking me out.

Now, I tried reaching out with my telepathy. I sent pleas to Cory and Samson to rescue me. The former was more likely to hear me. The latter had lots of weaponry. But I had no sign either had heard.

My mother was one of the few telepaths I knew. She was my best chance of being heard, but the most likely to go into hysterics.

Mom, can you hear me? It's Darla. I'm in danger and need your help.

The thoughts I sent were met with silence. Boy, I hope she's not taking a nap or something.

Mom! Help! It's Darla.

Then, faintly, came the words:

What's wrong? Where are you?

My guest, Franny Davenport, has bound me with a spell, and she's driving me somewhere to shoot me.

A stream of hysteria from Mom rushed into my brain.

Calm down, Mom. I'm not sure where we're going, but this is where we've been.

I mentioned the main roads I had recognized, though we turned off onto an unfamiliar one, and I didn't see a sign until about twenty minutes later. Then, after maybe fifteen minutes, we got on a dirt road that led to a small lake surrounded by trees.

Let me ask Billy. He's right here in the kitchen.

Of course. Eating scones. Flirting.

I waited for a response while the car rocked and rolled as the dirt road got rougher. Up ahead, the trees widened out from the road, and I got a glimpse of sky.

And the glitter of water.

Mom! Are you there?

We seemed to have lost our connection. Did I mention my telepathy wasn't very reliable?

Franny stole a quick glance at me. I remained staring ahead like a good zombie, not wanting her to know my mind had been freed. But that meant I had to stare at the lake getting larger and larger through the windshield.

The lake where I was going to be gator chow.

"We're visiting a lovely little lake," Franny said to me in a sing-song voice like I was a child. "It's very peaceful because no one ever comes here."

The cadence of her voice suggested she was trying to reinforce her hypnotic hold on me. I steeled my mind against it. But the content of what she said made it clear I couldn't expect to be rescued by a random fisherman or birdwatcher.

And I realized if Mom and Billy managed to identify which lake this was, it would take forever for someone to get here. How long had we traveled? Close to an hour, but that was an estimate by a brain encased in fog.

I would have to escape on my own. Or, if I couldn't, I would need to delay, delay, delay until a rescuer showed up. Or, until Franny died of old age, whichever came sooner.

The road dipped, then rose. We left the woods and entered the open space of the lake. It was surrounded by a forest of oak, pine, and palmettos with a narrow belt of meadow around it. There was enough room for one car to park and turn around on the grass. And based on the pristine condition of the tall grass, no car had done so in a long time.

But on the positive side, the fishing must be great here because the fish were never bothered by anglers.

Franny did a Y-turn to position the car facing the way out. Then, she killed the motor.

She got out and walked around the front of the car, opening my door.

"Follow me," she said.

My body obeyed. There was nothing I could do about it. The magic was too strong. The only thing I controlled now was my mind. Maybe my mouth, too.

I stiffly pivoted in my seat and stepped out. She closed the door behind me.

"Come," she said.

She walked to the lakeshore, her zombie in tow. She was taller than me, as most people are, and seemed fit for her age. But the strength of her magic was all that mattered.

Turning right, she began following the circumference of the lake in a counter-clockwise direction. If I hadn't been under her spell, I would have made a break for the trees. I would have run like mad, hoping she wasn't a good marksman. Instead, I plodded through the tall grass, hoping I didn't step on a snake.

A loud splash startled both of us. It was a giant gator diving into the water after seeing us. I hoped it wasn't hungry.

Franny had her gun in her hand, but she wasn't aiming at me, knowing she didn't need to. But soon, she would. The lake wasn't that big, and it wouldn't be much longer before we got to the spot she'd chosen for my execution.

I probed her mind. She was thinking the same thing I had about snakes. And how this was ruining her nice shoes and slacks. The poor dear.

I couldn't put it off any longer. It was time to engage my only weapon: my mean mouth.

"Did you know Jonathon was sleeping with Mabel?" I asked in a snide tone.

Franny stopped short, her mouth open in shock. Was it because of what I said, or because I could speak at all?

I continued, "Is that why you want to kill him, aside from the life insurance?"

"What are you talking about?"

"I'm a psychometrist. I read your husband's memories of doing the nasty with Mrs. Ogglethwarp. It says a lot, him being more attracted to her than you."

"You're lying!"

"I'm not. I read his memories he left on the passenger armrest. You do a lot of the driving?"

"He's a distracted driver. And I prefer to be in control."

She tried to fix me with her eyes. I avoided her stare.

"You're going to stop talking and do as I say," she said in the sing-song voice.

I wasn't having any of it. If my mind was sensitive enough to pick up others' thoughts and read their memories, it was also supple and strong. It resisted her attempts to re-hypnotize it.

"Let's go back to the car, and I can tell you more details from his memories on the armrest. There will be things that would be impossible for me to know. You'll believe me then."

"I don't care."

"There were glimpses of other women, too. Let's find out who they were."

Franny was upset. "I told you I don't care." She didn't say it convincingly.

"And there were thoughts and memories about you. Some of them were quite flattering."

"Really? Like what?"

"About your beauty and your fashion sense. I didn't have time to read them."

"You said he found Mabel more attractive."

"He enjoyed sleeping with her. It didn't mean she's more beautiful than you."

"Stop trying to bamboozle me. I'm tired of you. Let's move along."

"Whether or not you kill Jonathon, you should know the things he thinks of you."

"Maybe I'd rather not have you know them," she said angrily.

Oops. Maybe I pushed too far on this angle.

"Get moving," she said.

"There's something you should know, and it has nothing to do with Jonathon. It could make you very wealthy."

"Oh, please. You'll say anything to delay this."

Darned right.

"When you broke the tree limb, it revealed an object that had been hidden inside a knothole in the tree over a hundred years ago. It's an extremely rare gem, probably the largest of its kind. And I know where it is."

"Why should I believe you?"

"I'm the only one who knows how the gem ended up in the tree. The people who have it now don't know who it belongs to. If no one claims it, the city will keep it. Unless you claim that it's yours and you put it in the tree." I didn't want her to know I had the pearl, because she'd kill me anyway and search my property for it.

She appeared genuinely interested. "What kind of gem?"

"A giant pearl, about the size of a tennis ball."

Franny's eyes went wide.

"I don't know," I said, "how much would something like that go for?"

"A lot. But I don't need you. I'll just claim it now as mine."

"You don't know where it is," I said. "And if you go calling around, asking who has it, you'll look like an imposter."

"You want me to let you live if you help me gain ownership of this pearl?"

"Yes."

"What good would the pearl do me, when I wind up in prison because you ratted me out? Don't you understand that I have to kill you, regardless?"

I was running out of ways to delay my death in the fragile hope I would be rescued. If there was only a way to know more about the spell she used on me, like how long it lasts or if it can be broken. Man, how I wished Missy was here with her negation spell. Even if I reached her telepathically, she couldn't help me from half a state away.

"Why do you assume I can get you in trouble?" I asked. "You can't be prosecuted for using magic to break the limb."

"They would find a way to get me."

"No, really. They have security video of Aaron, the young man from the surf shop, cutting a notch beneath the limb. That, plus the force of gravity, or some heavy winds, would be all it took for the limb to come down. They'll convict him with manslaughter in the second degree, or something similar. Case closed."

"I wish."

"I'm serious. I'm close friends with the police detective investigating this. All they want is for the city to not be held liable for Mabel's death. They want to charge Aaron and be done with it."

"But you and your psychometry know about me."

"I told you, magic has no place in a court of law. Magic

doesn't exist as far as they're concerned. How could they find you guilty of killing her with it?"

Franny frowned as she thought about this. I think she believed me, but still couldn't get past the fact that I knew the truth. She slowed her walking and studied the grassy ground at the edge of the lake.

Looking for my execution spot.

"To be honest," I said, "I don't believe you know magic that could have brought that limb down."

She was angry now. "What do you call your inability to control your own body? I did that to you."

"I call it psychological suggestion."

"Nonsense."

"Then what is it? You didn't pour a potion on me. You weren't inside a magic circle invoking the elemental powers."

"You know nothing about magic."

"I know several witches. I don't believe you're a true witch," I said. It was a lie, since I did believe she was one. Her memories showing she was affected by Tom's dream spell proved it.

"I don't need those hoary old cliches about magic—being in a magic circle—ha! I can put a spell on you just with my concentration."

I stared at her for a second while an idea dawned.

Franny said I couldn't control my own body. She wasn't completely correct. I could control my own breathing. I held my breath long enough to grow dizzy and make my vision turn gray. As my equilibrium left me and I began to collapse, I willed my captive muscles to contract just enough to aim the direction of my fall.

Kind of like directing an oak tree's limb to come down in a certain direction.

I keeled over, and my thick skull smacked her right in the nose.

Franny staggered backwards as I collapsed against her and landed on the ground. Little petite me couldn't knock her out. She didn't even fall down.

But her concentration on her spell was broken. Suddenly, I had control of my own muscles again. Maybe only for a moment before she be-spelled me again. But I wasn't waiting.

I jumped up and took off like a jackrabbit into the nearby trees.

A shot rang out, just as I had predicted.

Another report, and something whizzed past my ear like an angry hornet.

But I kept running, dodging trees, crashing through the underbrush. My pants snagged on a prickly pear cactus, and I wrenched them free, ignoring the pain.

She could hunt me down, corner me, and shoot me in these woods. But I sure as heck would not allow her to cast a spell on me again. And I truly doubted she could do so on a moving target running away from her, half hidden by tree trunks, while she was running, too.

Were there snakes around? I'd almost forgotten about them. I was running too quickly to properly look out for—

My foot hit a fallen log, and I went flying, landing on the ground with a blow that nearly knocked the wind out of me.

Footsteps crunching in the fallen leaves were coming up quickly. I grabbed a broken branch from beside the trunk and scrambled to my feet.

Holy moly, she was right over there. How did she catch up to me so quickly?

Impulsively, desperately, I ran right at her instead of running away.

I screamed as I approached her. She hadn't expected this behavior. Swinging the branch like a bat, I hit her shoulder, and she fell sideways, losing her balance.

Her gun went off. But no bullet struck me.

She landed on her side upon the ground, and I kicked her hand that held the gun. I kicked again, and the gun slid off into the leaves. Then, I booted her in the head.

"Franny Davenport, surrender now," said a voice over a megaphone from somewhere in the woods. "This is the Sheriff's office. Surrender now for your own safety."

Franny, still on the ground, looked at me with a crazed expression and snarled. Suddenly, she scrambled for the gun.

I kicked her in the head again. And in the stomach. Very unsportsmanlike of me, I know. And I felt bad about hurting someone. That's not the kind of person I am. But she could very well kill me before the sheriff found us.

The last kick seemed to do the trick, though. She remained on her back, stunned like an upended turtle. I pushed the gun out of her reach with my battle branch.

"You assaulted me," she said. "I'll sue you for every dime you own."

I laughed. "Listen, sweetie. You're going down for attempted murder after your little stunt today. And, despite what I said, we'll find a way to charge you with the murder of Mabel Ogglethwarp. Magic or no magic, it's all going to land on your head."

"Good luck," she said with a mocking laugh.

So, I kicked her in the side for good measure.

CHAPTER 27

SEE THE FOREST FOR THE TREES

I t was late at night, and Cory was sound asleep. Not because he'd been drained of energy. And not because he was healing from his bullet wound, because the healing was long behind him. In fact, the doctors had called his recovery miraculous. Medical science had no inkling the energy from ley lines, and an ancient pearl infused with faerie magic, could speed up the healing process. Cory was enjoying the sleep of a man free of servitude and magical influences.

Thinking of the pearl, I felt the urge to handle it. It was still kept in a felt sack placed in the back of a kitchen drawer, where you wouldn't be able to see it behind the turkey baster, meat thermometer, and such. As far as the city museum was concerned, it was stolen property. As far as I was concerned, it wasn't anybody's property.

Carrying it over to the reading chair, I removed it from the sack and held it in my hands. Oddly, it held few memories compared to most objects. I'd been able to read Cory's from when he had stolen it, but it held no memories from Tom (who must have only touched the staff and not the pearl on it). Before that were traces of inscrutable memories I could only assume came from faeries.

The faerie who had given the pearl to me said it could help me learn more about the weird promise that I was destined for power or greatness. What the heck did that mean, anyway? Was the faerie blowing smoke up my derriere?

Cervantes casually strolled from the bedroom where he'd been sleeping on the bed with Cory. He was instantly curious about what I was holding and jumped upon the arm of the chair.

He was fascinated and frightened by the pearl simultaneously. His nose touched the pearl and then jerked back as if it had been shocked.

Cervantes' brow furrowed and his ears pointed forward. His tail whipped back and forth. He stepped onto my legs to get closer to the pearl.

The hair on his back stood straight, and he jumped onto the other side of the chair, hissing at the pearl.

"It has benevolent magic in it, Cervantes," I said. "Or it's supposed to be benevolent."

The cat looked at me as if determining if I was telling the truth. Then back at the mysterious sphere in Mommy's lap.

He jumped to the top of the chair back and crouched up there, still staring at the pearl. Though he was scared of it, he simply couldn't let it out of his sight.

I assumed he sensed the faerie magic. Was he afraid of the Fae? The faerie who visited me certainly scared him, but any cat would be freaked out by a stranger who transformed into a monster.

But what did Cervantes feel about the Fae in general? I really wanted to know, because this cat was more attuned to the world of magic than I was.

I craned my neck to look at him, and our eyes locked. Boy, I wish I could speak with him like Cory and Sophie could. Even so, I got a feeling of what Cervantes was thinking.

Be careful, Mommy, was the gist of it.

My friend, you must not know me well enough yet. When am I ever careful?

I returned my attention to the pearl. How was it going to tell me anything about my future? Maybe I needed a witch to cast a spell on it to coax it into revealing its secrets.

Cervantes began purring. Which was odd, since he had been so agitated only moments before.

It had to have been the late hour plus the soothing rumble of the cat's purring, but my eyes grew impossibly heavy. I'm not the type who falls asleep while sitting. But I did.

And I dreamed. At first, my dream resembled the in-flight movies I'm forced to watch when I astral-travel to Memory Guild meetings. I was soaring in the sky, like an eagle, above a giant forest that stretched as far as I could see in every direction. Clearly, this was the earth at an earlier time before clear-cutting and deforestation.

Usually, in the astral-travel picture shows, I pass through an ever-changing landscape or across time periods. But this time, I stayed with the giant forest.

I dropped in altitude and skimmed just above the canopy of deciduous trees I couldn't identify. They were lush with leaves, and the branches of each tree nearly touched each other. It seemed as if I flew above a giant carpet of green.

Suddenly, I dropped through a gap between trees and flew above the middle story, younger trees shorter than those of the overstory and with sparser branches that didn't spread as far.

Here, in the patchy light, I observed birds and squirrels that didn't see me and weren't alarmed.

I dove again, to the lowest story above the forest floor. These were the youngest trees, thin, spindly saplings, starved of light, waiting for their chance to grow higher.

Finally, I passed just inches above the forest floor, among the decay of rotting leaves and dead trees, the moss and fungus and ferns, as well as the shoots of new life just sprouting from acorns and seeds dropped from above.

And the weirdest thing was, I heard voices coming from below ground. No, not scary utterances of ghosts, but gleeful gibberish in a language unlike any I had ever heard.

It was clearly not a human language, or the vocalizations of animals.

Somehow, I knew it was the language of trees.

I snapped awake. The pearl was warm in my hands, almost too hot to touch. And Cervantes watched me with fascinated eyes that seemed admiring.

I put the pearl back in its sack in the rear of the drawer and went to bed.

And in the morning, I called the only person I thought could explain my weird dream: Summer.

AFTER I DESCRIBED IT ALL TO HER OVER THE PHONE, SHE SAID talking was not sufficient. We would need to go on a little outing together. To a nearby forest.

The state park was a short drive from San Marcos. I offered to drive. The thought of a half-elf driving me just seemed a little off, though as far as I knew, elves should be able to drive as well as humans.

"The forest you described from your dream sounds like an old-growth one from up in Canada or Northern Europe. Here in Florida, we don't have clearly delineated understories like that. We have too many varieties of tree species coexisting and creating their own societies."

Societies. A word I never before would have associated with trees.

"A state forest would show you a better example of tree societies in their natural states," she said, "but I suggested this park for convenience."

It was a beautiful park. Part of it was on a river leading to the Intracoastal Waterway, with a dock and a ramp for launching canoes and kayaks. There was a section with majestic Southern live oaks, like Old Courage. And there were several hiking trails winding through thick forests, swampy areas, and higher hammocks. Summer led me down one of these trails, where we saw no other people.

"What am I supposed to do?"

"Oh, I don't know. Just be yourself," she said with a mischievous grin, her pert nose and blue eyes looking particularly Elven today. "Relax and take in the scenery. Keep your mind open to the trees around you—all of them, mature as well as saplings. If the forest wishes to speak to you, it will. Let it happen naturally."

And we walked along the winding trail. Summer was right, this forest was extremely diverse with everything from long-leaf pines to cabbage palms. The underbrush was much denser than the one in my dream, with saw palmetto bushes and black needle rush. I took it all in, not quite sure what I was hoping to happen.

A hiker going the opposite way surprised us, an old man in a wide-brimmed straw hat and a walking stick. He smiled and wished us a good day. The guy was much more of a naturalist than I could pretend to be.

After the sound of his footsteps receded, I tried to clear my mind again, listening to the birdsongs, the buzzing of insects, the slight sifting of a breeze through the branches above. I enjoyed the rich smell of leaves and organic matter spiced by a hint of brackish water from the nearby waterway.

It happened subtly, so much so I didn't notice it until I was fully engaged.

The gibberish. Just like I had heard in my dream. A buzzing, a chatter, a low hum of conversation came from beneath the soil.

I couldn't understand any of it. After a while, though, it became clear that it was coming from nature. More specifically, from the roots of the trees around me.

I sat on the ground. Being a psychometrist, I instinctively wanted to touch something. I felt compelled to choose the earth in front of me, and I placed both palms on the moist, spongy soil.

There were no human memories here, of course. But I was surprised to feel a great deal of psychic energy.

And the gibberish grew louder and more constant in my head.

Goosebumps spread across my skin as I realized the trees were conversing with each other, and that hundreds of conversations were going on at once.

To be clear, it wasn't as if these were the kinds of conversations you would overhear from humans. The "gibberish" wasn't babbling words. It was the slow and simple conveyance of information. I'm not talking about gossip and corny jokes. It was essential signals that told the trees of approaching threats, of pockets of underground water to be tapped, of members of the family who needed extra nutrients to be shared with them.

I didn't comprehend any specifics, but somehow I knew in my heart what was being conveyed via the roots. Summer had already explained to me how certain fungi help transmit these communications. I stood and strode across the forest floor, sensing the thousands of miles of roots winding beneath me, stretching distances that surpassed the heights of the trees by magnitudes.

The earth beneath me was packed with the woven roots of all the trees and plants. Anyone who has ever dug into the ground can attest to that. But these roots were not blindly sucking water for their own tree or plant. No, they were interwoven with the roots of their comrades in this forest, and they were sharing the water as well as the nutrients from their photosynthesis.

They were truly communicating with each other.

I couldn't understand any of it, but emotion overtook me, and I had to sit down on the ground again.

Summer watched me kindly, as tears rolled down my cheeks, and my chest shook with the sobs I tried to stifle.

This forest was so much more than I had ever imagined, and I felt honored to be able to realize this.

I sat there for a long while, oblivious to the bugs buzzing in my ear and the sweat on my back. All I did was listen. There was profundity in these conversations, and I felt it. I just couldn't fathom what it meant.

After the longest time, a thought entered my brain. A message from the trees. It didn't come to me as a human word in English. It came as an understanding and an emotion. If I had to translate it, this message was simple:

Mother.

That's what I heard. Being a mother was important to me, with my human child such a fundamental part of me. But this concept was being communicated by organisms nothing like me. Still, I heard it:

Mother.

"What did this mean?" I asked Summer, after describing it all as I drove us back to town. "Why did it happen to me? You're the wood-speaker."

"As a wood-speaker, I can read all kinds of wood. Living trees, of course, but also wood that's been dead for centuries, and has been sawed and milled and sanded and nailed and painted over. You'll never have that ability, and you don't need to, because you've got me around. But you appear to have the ability to read the fungi that live upon tree roots and allow trees to communicate. Just like you read the human memories left upon objects. This means you'll be able to learn to listen to trees. And maybe even to speak to them in their own language."

"How do I learn?"

"Simply by spending time in the woods listening. Soon, you won't see a forest but will see the individual trees who have created it. Soon, you'll recognize which ones are speaking. And eventually, you'll be able to understand them."

Finally, the emotion faded, and my mind was pulled back into the rapid but shallow collective mind of humankind. In other words, it was back to mundane, normal life. Complete with the vibrating of my phone from an incoming call. It was Samson.

"Hello, Michael. How are you?"

"Man, you sound blissed out. Don't tell me what drug you're on, because I'm an officer of the law in case you've forgotten."

"I'll never forget."

"I wanted to let you know we've got Franny Davenport dead to rights. The most we had hoped to charge her with was the attempted murder of you. We'd never be able to prove she hypnotized or be-spelled Aaron to weaken the tree limb. And we sure as shootin' can't prove her magic brought the limb down on Mrs. Ogglethwarp. But that doesn't matter now."

"What do you mean?"

"Only hours after she bonded out of jail, she shot her husband, Jonathon, to death. She admits she did it and claims he deserved it for cheating on her."

"I told her he was. This is my fault."

"Will you stop it, Darla? You're always so hard on yourself. I'm sure she already knew he was cheating and simply denied it. Now, we can charge her with good old-fashioned homicide by firearm and don't have to explain to a jury about her magic."

"But that means Mrs. Ogglethwarp won't receive justice."

"Oh yes, she will. A bit indirectly, but the end result will be the same."

"Wait a second," I said. "Please tell me Franny didn't shoot Jonathon at my inn. Please tell me I don't have yet another fatality on my property."

"No worries. She did it at the fort. During the ceremonial firing of the cannons for the tourists. No one heard her gun, but it's on surveillance video."

I thanked him and hung up, focusing on my driving. It wasn't such a good idea to be driving while blissed out.

But I thought about the pearl and the dream it gave me. It pointed me toward a possible change in my life. At the very least, the pearl helped me form a rare bond with trees, the organisms we take for granted until they give us fruit or needed shade or are the victims of the tree surgeons we call to remove them.

But ever since that dream, something else has haunted me. It began nagging me a day later.

It was a memory, the oldest one I have. A memory of a

former life. But it was hazy and eluded me just at the edge of my consciousness. It was beyond my reach and comprehension.

And I felt in my heart it was critical that I could see this memory and understand it. Because somehow, I knew this memory of former life in a distant past would determine my future.

CHAPTER 28

FATE AND FAE

"Mom, I don't need any back-hair remover," I said.

"I'm not saying you do, but maybe some of the males in your life do. Cory doesn't seem like the type who would need it, but your friend, Detective Samson, probably does."

"I wouldn't know." I had never seen his unclothed back. And I assumed that when he shifted to wolf form, he didn't mind having thick fur there.

Mom had stopped by the inn this morning unannounced, parking her SUV full to bursting with boxes of product she couldn't unload.

"You can help me sell my products to your guests," she pleaded.

"Nope. I won't try to sell them anything."

"Then you can buy from me and have complimentary products in the bathrooms, along with the soap, shampoo, and moisturizers."

"Mom, Blubber Buster is not the type of premium item

262

people want in their room. And especially not the back-hair remover."

"You're not going to help me at all, are you?"

"I tried to prevent you from buying into this scheme, but you wouldn't listen."

"I was brainwashed by the magic."

"I'm thanking my lucky stars that Sophie didn't get sucked into this fraud."

"Think again. I signed her up to be one of my distributors."

"You didn't!"

"I did. But she hasn't bought any product yet."

"And she won't, if I have anything to say about it. It's time to accept your losses. Write them off on your taxes."

Mom huffed. The door chime rang. We looked up as Samson walked into the foyer.

"Detective, are you troubled by an overabundance of back hair?" Mom asked. "Don't be ashamed if you are. It's a sign of high testosterone."

"I'm sorry, are you talking to me?"

"Just ignore her," I said. "She's trying to sell you stuff."

"Back-hair remover. It's completely painless compared to waxing. Are you interested?"

"I'm not really into that kind of . . . grooming," he said, the only time I'd seen the hard-nosed detective knocked off balance. "I stick to shaving my face and getting my hair cut. The hair on my head."

Mom looked him up and down. "You don't need Blubber Buster, it seems. Though, it looks like you have a taste for beer." She patted her stomach.

"Mom! You're being rude. Will you please stop? I'm so sorry, Mike. What brings you here today?"

"I need your help with a psychic matter."

"Okay, I'll be on my way and let you two talk," Mom said. "I'll leave some product for your gift shop."

"I don't have a gift shop," I said.

"You will."

I shook my head in exasperation after she left.

"Back-hair remover?" Samson asked.

"It's among the stupid products sold by Tom Sykes' multi-level marketing schemes. This is what he be-spelled the magic folk into buying. How's it going with the prosecution?"

"He's been charged with false imprisonment of your husband and attempted murder. The feds are also looking into his marketing schemes. His magic allowed him to pull off those shenanigans. It's also how he fooled some parents into giving their kids to the Fae, correct?"

"Yep."

"That's why I'm here. We have a good lead on finding the missing child."

"I was told by a faerie that they replaced the child with a changeling, like people believed in the Middle Ages."

"This wasn't a convincing replacement for the child. It was a litter of kittens."

"Oh. That's a problem. Adorable, though."

"The good news is, there was an object found at the empty storefront that the parents thought was a school. I want you to read this object. The crime scene techs didn't think it was evidence. They even checked it for prints, and it had none."

"What is it?"

"A stick. A wooden stick found propped up against the door-frame of the store. The techs thought it was merely landscaping debris somebody placed there. But it was worn near one end, as if it had been handled a great deal. To me, it looked like a walking stick. Or a staff."

A staff, like that of a wizard?

"It was odd that there were no prints on it, though. Then I thought of you. Can you read it and see if it holds any memories?"

"Of course," I said.

"It's in my car."

I followed him outside. Mom had unloaded at least a dozen boxes onto the sidewalk.

"Mom! Put those back in your SUV."

Samson's car was halfway down the block. He opened the trunk and unwrapped a small blue tarp. The stick did indeed look like a walking stick, about four feet long. It was hardwood, somewhat curvy like a tree branch, but stripped of its bark, sanded, and stained a dark mahogany. One end, for about six or eight inches, was polished to a shine from repeated handling.

I didn't get the prickly feeling that magical items give me, so maybe it was only a simple walking stick after all.

"You can take it into the inn if you want privacy," Samson said.

I looked back at my mother, who was carrying a box of product into the inn.

"Let me sit in your car," I said.

The front seat was crowded with Samson's laptop on an adjustable stand, so I crawled into the backseat with the long piece of wood. Handcuffed perps sometimes sat back here, so I avoided touching anything they might have touched.

With one end of the stick on the far end of the seat, and the other resting on my lap, the part worn smooth protruded just past my leg. I hovered my hands over it and felt a long history of memories. And by long, I mean at least a hundred years. That was the impression I got.

And they were faerie memories, in a language I didn't under-

265

stand. However, I sensed the urgency of a very recent memory. Somehow, I knew I needed to read it.

With my hand almost touching the wood, I picked up fragments of thoughts in English with a feminine voice. So, I grabbed the wood and—

—*Hello, Darla. We knew this message would eventually reach you. And obviously, we know about your ability to receive it. We know much about you and your fellow paranormals and supernaturals.*

I am an envoy of Her Majesty, the Queen, though my name is unimportant. We have decided to show mercy on the witches whose child we took, since magic is a common ground, we Fae share with them. I will tell you where the child is. But be warned, the promise has been made to give us human children to help us save our race. It is a promise we expect to be honored. We will leave the supernatural people of your city alone, but we will take the children of common humans when we find it necessary. Be warned. Unless a better deal is struck between us and your city.

The address where you will find the child is 1369 Hemlock Drive. That is all—

—the memory shut off.

I felt stunned. Never before had I read a memory that was deliberately placed on an object as a message for me. And the fact they knew so much about me was unsettling.

I got out of the car and told Samson what I'd learned.

"I knew it!" he said, smiling. "When I saw the stick, I knew I should bring it to you to read. Was it just a gut feeling, or am I developing some paranormal senses?"

"Maybe you should just stick to being a shifter for now. So, are we going to the address they gave me? What if it's a trap?"

"I'm sending over uniformed officers, along with the social worker, to meet us there. The Fae wouldn't be stupid enough to attack the police."

"I guess not."

We headed to the address in a not-so-nice part of town near the railroad tracks. I texted Sophie, asking her to look after things while I was gone, and sending the address, just in case.

The brick house was small and rather run-down. A commercial crabbing boat sat on a trailer beside it in a weed-infested yard.

Right after we arrived, a police car and a civilian vehicle parked on the street. Two officers and a young African-American woman joined us as we climbed the rickety porch steps.

There was no doorbell. Samson knocked on the wooden screen door.

"Be right there," a female voice with a Southern accent called from within.

A heavyset woman with stringy brown hair appeared holding a child and smiled at us through the screen. The child was too young to be the one we sought.

"We're looking for Melissa Simpson, age five," Samson said.

"She's inside. We've been expecting you."

"You have?" I asked.

Samson elbowed me to be quiet.

"Yes. I provide daycare for clients," the woman said. "Her mother told me you'd be coming by."

"Her mother told you the police would pick up her kid?" Samson asked. "Did she explain why?"

"No. She dropped off Melissa and said you would pick her up. She acted like it was normal," the woman said. "I thought maybe you were friends with the family."

"Didn't you think this woman could be an abductor?"

"No."

"What did she look like?"

"Nothing special. A blonde about my height in her thirties."

"What name did she give you?"

"Judy Simpson."

Samson was trying to learn about the faerie who brought the child here, but that was the actual name of the child's mother.

"Can we get Melissa now?" he asked.

"Of course. Y'all come right in."

Still holding her own child, she stepped out of the way and pointed to the right as the five of us marched inside.

In a small living room, the adorable girl sat on the couch transfixed by a television. She had a sippy cup of juice in her hands.

She seemed in good condition and in good spirits. The social worker sat beside her and asked her several questions. She nodded at Samson.

"Let's go home to your mommy and daddy now," she said as she led the kid from the room and out of the house.

Samson secured a promise from the day-care woman that she'd come down to the station for an interview, if needed.

The social worker drove away with Melissa, and the police car followed them.

"My gut is telling me something's not right here," Samson said.

We stood on the lawn at the edge of the street and looked back at the house.

"I have the same feeling," I said.

I walked back to the house.

"Wait, what are you doing?"

When I climbed up onto the porch, I found the front door closed. I peeked in a window to the side.

The house appeared to be empty.

Samson had joined me on the porch.

"I don't think there's anybody here," I said.

He pounded on the door. When he tried the handle, it was unlocked. The door swung open, and we stepped inside.

The house was completely empty, heavy with a musty smell. Every surface had a thick coating of dust, including the floor.

The footprints we had left walking into the living room stood out in the dust. Otherwise, there was no sign anyone had been in this house for years.

"Something tells me we're going to be seeing a lot more of the Fae in this town," I said. "How are we going to keep them from taking other children?"

"I don't know," Samson said. "And who knows what other things they have in mind?"

It would be so much easier for me to focus on my inn and family, closing my mind to the supernatural. But I couldn't.

I had a feeling my life would never be the same again.

WHAT'S NEXT

GET A FREE E-BOOK

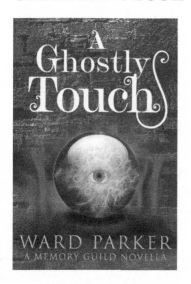

Sign up for my newsletter and get *A Ghostly Touch*, a Magic Guild novella, for free, offered exclusively to my newsletter subscribers. Darla reads the memories of a young woman, murdered in the 1890s, whose ghost begins haunting Darla, looking for justice. As a subscriber, you'll be the first to know about my new releases and lots of free book promotions. The newsletter is delivered only a couple of times a month. No spam at all, and you can unsubscribe at any time. Sign up to get your free book at wardparker.com

ENJOYED THIS BOOK? PLEASE LEAVE A REVIEW

In the Amazon universe, the number of reviews readers leave can make or break a book. I would be very grateful if you could spend just a few minutes and write a fair and honest review. It can be as short or long as you wish. Thank you so much!

NEXT IN THE MEMORY GUILD MIDLIFE PARANORMAL MYSTERIES:

Book 6: A WITCHY TOUCH

Destined for Craziness

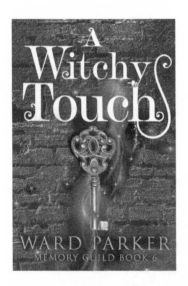

Magic runs in my family. I even married a guy who unknowingly had latent magic. But in the Chesswick family of witches, the magic gene skipped a generation. Namely, mine. So, I can only watch from afar as my daughter learns the ancient craft.

Until a magic tutor I hired ends up dead, and my daughter is falsely accused of his murder.

Now, it's time for me to get involved. I might not have magic, but I have telepathy and a mind-blowing ability of psychometry. I can read the thoughts and memories of the real killer, and, boy, they take me down a twisted path.

On the way, I discover other abilities I haven't harnessed yet. Maybe they have something to do with what a faerie, who showed up at my inn, said:

That I have a destiny of greatness and will either be an ally or enemy of the Fae.

Whatever. I have a daughter to protect, an inn to run, and a clogged toilet in haunted room 303 to fix. Priorities, folks.

Get it at Amazon or at wardparker.com

HAVE YOU READ FREAKY FLORIDA?

Check out this series of humorous paranormal mysteries featuring Darla's cousin, Missy.

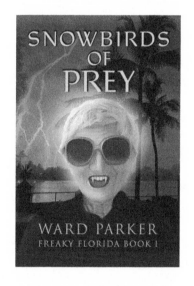

Centuries-old vampires who play pickleball. Aging werewolves who surf naked beneath the full moon. Plus dragons, demons, ghouls, and more. They're all in Florida, land of the weird, where even monsters come to retire. That's how Missy Mindle comes in. She's started over in midlife as a home health nurse for elderly monsters and as a witch with growing powers. She uses her magick to solve mysteries, with a little help from a cute reporter. But dangerous secrets from the parents she never knew keep bubbling up.

Get Book 1, *Snowbirds of Prey*, on Amazon or at wardparker.com

ACKNOWLEDGMENTS

I wish to thank my loyal readers, who give me a reason to write more every day. I'm especially grateful to Sharee Steinberg and Amanda Peters for all your editing and proofreading brilliance. And to my wife, Martha, thank you for your moral support, Beta reading, and awesome graphic design!

ABOUT THE AUTHOR

Ward is a Florida native and author of the Freaky Florida series, a romp through the Sunshine State with witches, vampires, werewolves, dragons, and other bizarre, mythical creatures such as #FloridaMan. His newest series is the Memory Guild midlife paranormal mysteries. He also pens the Zeke Adams Series of Florida-noir mysteries and The Teratologist Series of historical supernatural thrillers. Connect with him on social media: Twitter (@wardparker), Facebook (wardparkerauthor), BookBub, Goodreads, or wardparker.com

ALSO BY WARD PARKER

The Zeke Adams Florida-noir mystery series. You can buy *Pariah* and *Fur* on Amazon or wardparker.com

The Teratologist series of historical paranormal thrillers. Buy the first novel on Amazon or wardparker.com

"Gods and Reptiles," a Lovecraftian short story. Buy it on Amazon or wardparker.com

"The Power Doctor," a historical witchcraft short story. Get it on Amazon or wardparker.com

Made in United States
Orlando, FL
23 January 2024